BEYOND HAZEL BRIDGE

Elizabeth Boyle

Elizabeth Boyle

BEYOND HAZEL BRIDGE

INTRODUCTION BY MARY MARMION

Enjoy Mary Marmion

First published in 2021 by Herstories Publications
Co. Wicklow
Ireland
mpmarmion2020@gmail.com

Paperback	ISBN: 978 1 78846 199 5
eBook – mobi format	ISBN: 978 1 78846 196 2
eBook – ePub format	ISBN: 978 1 78846 197 9
Amazon paperback	ISBN: 978 1 78846 198 6

Produced by Kazoo Independent Publishing Services
222 Beech Park, Lucan, Co. Dublin
www.kazoopublishing.com

Kazoo Independent Publishing Services is not the publisher of this work. All rights and responsibilities pertaining to this work remain with Herstories Publications

Cover design by Andrew Brown

Printed in the EU

Introduction

BY MARY MARMION

Chintz, a Chanel handbag and a King Charles spaniel – my grand-aunt Elizabeth Boyle had class. We called her Lily, although she was also known as Girlie and later Goggie by her grandchildren. During a summer holiday in 1968, she gave me her copy of Walter Macken's *Seek the Fair Land*. This was my introduction to historical fiction. Little did I know that while I read in the sunroom, she was writing her own history. She wrote several books, plays and poems but there was one special work that she was eager to have published. She described it as romantic fiction, but publication eluded her. This was always a topic of conversation when we visited in later years. She was no longer with us when the manuscript came into my possession and I began to understand why she was so passionate about the novel, which describes the experience of a young girl in rural Ireland in the summer of 1921, just as Lily herself was.

Elizabeth Boyle was born in 1905, the third and youngest daughter of Michael and Theresa Cox of Clooncholry, Dromod, in County Leitrim. Michael had just retired from the Royal Irish Constabulary, having served in Mayo at the height of the Land Wars. Theresa was a respected handywoman.[1]

Clooncholry was a place of bog, bulrush and wildness, where Theresa cultivated a garden and a hearth and a pathway to progress for her children. Here Lily's attachment to nature took root. All six children were educated and some boarded with Theresa's clerical brother in Birmingham, when

1. Handywomen provided midwifery services and, though experienced, were often unqualified.

they completed secondary school. "Uncle" Fr Wenceslaus Memnagh was a powerful character in their lives.

A convent education infused in the girls a curriculum devoted to creating a home and securing respectability through marriage. Birmingham, then a thriving centre of the industrial revolution and the economic hub of central England, offered fresh opportunities for the Cox siblings. A photo of Lily in Birmingham shows a shy, genteel girl. She formed a lifelong friendship there with Gaelic scholar Bill Sullivan. Their correspondence over the decades revealed Bill's experiences as an underground worker for "The Cause". Letters detailing visitors to his home suggest that his was a safehouse and that he was pro-Treaty. He also sent Lily a moving letter expressing his condolences after the death of her brother.

It was said that the girls got their airs and graces from their time in Birmingham, where women were participating more publicly in society while their men were at war and the suffrage movement was in full swing. The sisters were now well placed for marriage. Lily returned to Ireland during turbulent and changing times. She was now an articulate and educated young woman, but the nationalist climate in Ireland was moving towards containment of women to the private and domestic sphere.

Lily was just a young girl when her brother walked all the way home from the Fairyhouse races along the train tracks, on Easter Monday in 1916, as news trickled from Dublin about an armed insurrection. At the time there was a the discussion of expanded enfranchisement of women and men and how the success of Sinn Féin in the 1918 election campaign had led to the first Dáil. Charismatic Michael Collins was a regular visitor to Granard in nearby Longford, where the family of his fiancée, Kitty Kiernan, were hoteliers. Lily often spoke of dancing with the charming icon. Fundraising dances offered opportunities for a young, romantic beauty to enjoy a twirl, or even a flirt.

Lily was a dreamer, a romantic at heart, judging by the cache of her writing, generously offered to me by her granddaughter Emer Boyle Cahill. Trawling through the copybooks, photographs, letters and reams of typescript, I came across a manuscript titled The Sword and the Sandal. The typed pages began at Chapter 5. As I set about reconstructing the earlier chapters, I began to wonder if this was, in fact, part memoir. The preamble, which she added later in life, draws on her memories, bravely facing the cruelty of recovery that time can sometimes obscure. A mature woman returns to the place of her childhood. Her reflections on the futility of war are a powerful indictment of the fight for freedom: "the blazing wheel with its fiery red spokes". She, like many others, has become disillusioned with the political evolution of the new state. Bittersweet memories flood in. She does not hold back on what we know to be true:

> A feud of bitterness and jealousy, hatred and revenge, divided friends, divided neighbours, whose reprehensible cruelties against each other are scarcely believable in a world of peace and sanity.

Overcome by memories, she wonders if she, too, has become invisible. Through her writing she is ensuring that she will not be forgotten and that the voice of a young girl will be heard one day, when it is safe. She gives vent to her hatred, but bitterness dissolves into nostalgia. For all she witnessed and experienced, she is now able to look through the other end of the lens on her youth.

In real life there were heavy losses and a high price to pay as lines of loyalty and identity became blurred. However, in fiction she could fashion the identity she preferred. Her female characters lift and open the narrative of male heroism in its myriad forms, from the violence of Crown forces to the authority invested in the patriarchy, and are brave and active in their confrontation. Military service pension claims are testament to how the roles women played were valued during this period – overlooked and unrecognised.

The narrative is set in the summer of 1921. Protagonist Sally Glynn is an eighteen-year-old romantic girl in the rural midlands of Ireland. Sally is in love with childhood neighbour Peter, who fought with her brother in 1916 but joined the British Army in the aftermath. The young men are now at odds. Sally's second brother is also opposed to Peter on political and religious grounds. He is a reluctant Catholic clerical student and passionately Republican. Peter is Irish Protestant. Sectarian aggression and intimidation was commonplace, as Protestants were associated with the British tradition, which many regarded as having no place in the new Catholic state. Lily would have been aware of several rebel priests in the area.[2] Boundaries blurred as the conflict descended into civil war.

Sally is fearless in the face of guerrilla war. A photo of Lily in an armoured car indicated her attachment to an individual in the military. The War of Independence was the first time British government forces used motor vehicles against insurgents, many of these upcycled into armoured cars. Thirteen of these were given to the Free State troops during the Civil War, offering "hencoop" protection.[3]

Women were warned against liaisons with the opposite side. Hair cropping was employed as a gendered war weapon. "Frightfulness" was a definite feature of British policy.[4] Military statements testify to the practice on both sides and it was widely reported in the newspapers of the time. To be shorn was to be shamed and consigned to the secrets of the past. It is this assault in particular that led to Sally's becoming politicised in the book.

In 1920 there were 48,474 raids on private homes. Most attacks took place at night-time when women were alone with their children and their menfolk were on the run. Lily's description of raids by Crown forces convinces me that she witnessed or experienced such an atrocity in her young life. "The brain sometimes receives impressions so deeply that they are seared into our minds and never grow fainter or dimmer with the years."[5]

With men on the run, captured or killed, the tougher work on the farm fell to the women. Women in rural Ireland were no strangers to farm labour, but saving hay and stacking turf during the drought of that year added a physical burden to the psychological impact of the period. Waiting for news. Receiving bad news. The worst news. Protecting elderly parents. Waiting. Wondering who is passing information, who can be trusted.

It is to nature that Sally turns for solace. The lakeside, the meadows, seasons turning offer escape from the incessant intrusions on her dreams. Her touchstones are all in nature. She seeks out those places when she returns years later for comfort and their absence represents the losses she has suffered. Lily had a deep connection with the River Shannon, and she

---

2. Boyle, Ken and Desmond, Tim: *The Murder of Dr Muldoon*, Mercier Press (Cork, 2019).
3. *History Ireland*: Vol 18 (March/April 2010).
4. Macardle, Dorothy: *The Irish Republic*, Corgi (London, 1968).
5. Ward, Margaret: Diary extract by Linda Kearns from *In Their Own Voice*, Attic Press (Cork, 2001).

fashioned gardens wherever she found herself. The rambling rose, the honeysuckled arbour and abundant raspberries, which never made it to the kitchen.

The truce of 1921 brought great celebrations nationwide while unleashing resentments that had built up during the previous desperate months. Sally wants to dance and plan her wedding. After months of curfew and the ever-present threat of Crown forces' intimidation and brutality, the country rejoiced. Lily, too, was a fun loving girl, and during this period she found love. She often told the story of her first fiancé, who was killed in "the War". It is likely she was referring to the War of Independence or Civil War. Extensive research to identify this suitor has been inconclusive, but an incident at Rockmarshall in County Louth in 1922, involving a captain in the Free State Army and a volunteer, bears striking similarity to the fate of Sally's lover, Peter, and her brother Tom. This district was pro-Treaty. Dundalk, which was mainly occupied by Free State troops, found itself in the Republic when the border was established.

Around this time Lily became involved with the Boyles of Knockanarney, just north of the Border, believed to be friends of her brothers. She had a brief dalliance with one brother, Peter. However it was Dinny who found her favour. Dinny was working in the Dromod branch of the Northern Bank, when they were married in Dublin in 1929. It was a fashionable affair, judging by the photos.

Lily always remained close to her sister Theresa, my grandmother. There were regular visits when card games, lubricated with whiskey, would meander into the early hours and Lily would listen to my grandfather relate his stories from the War. My grandfather Seán Kennedy was from a Fenian family from Chaffpoole, outside Tubbercurry. The young married couple were living there when the Black and Tans rampaged through the town in reprisal for the fatal shooting of an RIC man. My grandmother spoke of how they lost most of their wedding gifts when the house was burnt down.

Seán wrote in the centenary edition of the *Roscommon Herald* of his activities in the Sligo and Arigna areas during the revolutionary period. Ambushes at Scramogue, Roscommon, and Selton Abbey, Leitrim, are well documented. Areas of Sligo, Leitrim, Roscommon and Longford were interlinked by the activities of flying columns, and Michael Collins said that these areas were the most treacherous in Ireland.[6]

This was the world in which Lily and my grandmother lived. The psychological effects of violence and the threats on female relatives in their homes often affected women more deeply thant men at whom the violence was aimed.[7] My grandmother was an insomniac and suffered greatly from chronic dermatitis. Long gaps between children suggest miscarriages. She is remembered as a demanding and volatile woman with a dependence on her doctor.

It wasn't long before Dinny was appointed bank manager. Following partition the Northern Bank had branches on both sides of the border, and it was sensitive to its personnel in the border areas. As the wife of a bank manager, Lily enjoyed a splendid social life. She had status. She participated in amateur dramatic societies, preferring the plays of O'Casey and Beckett. She wrote her own plays. Photographs chronicle a lifestyle of picnics, balls and society, from Maghera to Lanesboro. Babycham was her tipple of choice. Holidays were spent in Bangor and Portstewart in Northern Ireland. This circle wore their class well; they were the "in" crowd, with their Model Ford, Dinny's plus fours and Lily's fashionable twin sets and trousers.

This lifestyle appears incongruent with the economic war and the struggles of many families in the fledgling Free State. However, the Northern Bank grew rich from war lending to the British government. On both sides of the border the couple would socialise among the small privileged circle of well-off Catholics. There were few such families north of the border, where Protestants had fled following sectarian antagonism. South of the border, the couple embraced the identity of the evolving middle class in a new state. The new government was determined to create a unique society that was in every way opposite to Britain, even if the Treaty demanded an oath of allegiance to the King.

Meanwhile Church and State collaborated to ensure the strict mores of Catholicism would prevail. Lily was not a religious person. She didn't participate in daily family Rosary, a Catholic tradition. Her disregard for Catholic traditions is evident in a stunning photograph of her in a backless

6. Bands of Republican guerrilla fighters who lived on the run in the countryside and carried out ambushes.

7. Clarke, Gemma: *Everyday Violence in the Irish Civil War*, Cambridge University Press (Cambridge, 2014).

dress. Lily would find herself in the first generation of Irish women whose role was officially confined to the domestic sphere as wife and mother. While this ideology was promoted in Europe and the West, Ireland was the only country to render it constitutional in 1937. Women were to be used as the beacon for the high moral ground of the Free State and were expected to sacrifice their identity, personal freedom and ambitions outside marriage. Legislation was swiftly enacted to secure this ideology. Lily found herself straddling life and identity on both sides of the border as she moved with her husband's postings. Dinny spent several years working in Belfast. The only thing Lily liked about the city was her hairdresser.

War was never far away. Following the Treaty and the Civil War, the IRA persisted with a bombing campaign along the border. In the thirties there was a bombing campaign in Northern Ireland. During the fifties a guerrilla war was waged. The sixties saw the outbreak of the Troubles, with Republican Catholic pitched against Unionist Protestant. The international civil rights movement sprang up in Derry.

Lily abhorred violence and unrest. Family members recall her intolerance and quick temper when the topic came up in conversation. She simply wanted to get on with life, citing the uselessness of war. Her disappointment and impatience is borne out in Sally's preamble when she returns to the place of her youth. She laments the many hideous crimes committed in the name of freedom.

In the sixties Lily wrote a long letter to my mother to explain why she had not been in touch. She had been hospitalised in St Edmundsbury private hospital for "her nerves". She had developed an alcohol dependency and was treated for depression. My mother's diaries chronicle her own mother's persistent unexplained illnesses. Both women were intelligent individuals in a country that did not support women. Their relationships were fraught with difficulty, psychological and physical, and both are remembered as "difficult" and "highly strung".

I believe these reputations can now be viewed through a more informed lens. Today post-traumatic syndrome is recognised as a response to exposure to war, be it through personal experience or through witnessing events that are beyond our control. We understand more how trauma impacts the body and mind, and indeed even the impact of intergenerational trauma.

Contemporary studies have sought to explain how the unbearable is passed to the next generation. They have postulated that memory is organic, grounded in personal experience, and that after three generations memory is codified and ossified.[8] Trauma and its legacy has damaged generations. When trauma shuts down recall, time and disclosure may allow revelation. While memory is concerned with the past, it also has a relationship with the present. When I consider how circumstances beyond their control contributed to their mental health, I begin to appreciate the obstacles my grandmother, my grandaunt and my mother endured and which gave rise to their difficulties in relationships.

Following a short period in a nursing home after Dinny's death, Lily spent the last years of her long life in Galway with her son and his family, until her own death in 1995. Sadly her son also predeceased her. Here the Albertine Rose clambered over a trellis to hide the land beyond, which she would never garden. She remained precious about her hair, always coiffed with the aid of several wigs. She composed the preamble in Galway, but while Sally becomes reconciled with growing older, Lily never did.

During their lives, Lily and her sisters adapted themselves to what society demanded. Sometimes this was to their advantage. In Lily's case it was a high price to pay during a period of social and political restructuring on the whole of this island. The loss of her brother, her first lover, her husband and her son, and the betrayal she witnessed in families and communities scarred her. Nevertheless she sought out the good life and found status as an upwardly middle-class socialite. She has left us her story in the character of Sally Glynn, a young girl who learned what it meant to do your duty, to be brave, and still believe in fun and take comfort in nature. It is a story of ordinary people in extraordinary times, a story of loss, love and betrayal. Lily's fiction belongs on the bookshelves alongside Walter Macken, a valuable contribution to the commemoration of the decade of centenaries, as we dredge the legacy of this painful period of our history. Sally Glynn is the voice of a young woman in the period of 1921–22, after which Ireland would never be the same.

---

8. Beiner, Guy: *Remembering the Year of the French,* University of Wisconsin Press (Madison, WI, 2007).

Prologue

The newspaper came from the greengrocers, wrapped around nursery plants. I crumpled it up and threw it in the bin. I was about to close the lid when a page caught my eye.

> Holiday in Ireland this year. Come to the Sally Glen guesthouse by the Shannon. Enjoy fishing, boating, pony trekking and beautiful scenery. Fresh fruit and vegetables, excellent cuisine, licensed.

I reread the paper and, taking it indoors, I smoothed out the creases with the palm of my hand. I glanced at the various holiday offers over the length and breadth of Ireland but the Sally Glen advertisement drew and held my eyes. I took a chair over to the window and reread the corner of the newspaper. I could be mistaken. But no. Odd little things, maybe coincidence. Pony trekking. I thought of the two fat, friendly cart horses of long ago and the slightly more elegant trap horse we rode in turn, and without a saddle. The word *licensed* sounded almost sacrilegious. And a phone. A bicycle had been the fastest method of getting news around then. And the news was always bad.

On impulse I went to the telephone and rang the number. A far-away voice with a slightly American accent answered. Yes, accommodation was available at present. Later it might not be so, as the mayfly would be up and the fishermen would be coming. Recklessly, I booked one night, so as to be there and gone before the invasion of the fishermen and the mayfly. Monday it would be. A car would meet me at the station. So it was done. There was no changing my mind now. I was going.

The train eased into the station. The diesel-driven engine was quiet compared to the old puffing, whistling, fussy steam engines. How clearly I remembered how the carriage doors would be flung open, almost before the train stopped, and the stream of passengers would flow onto the crowded platform. How eagerly I ran between them in all the noise and bustle, searching for a face. Finding its owner, throwing myself into his willing arms with all the lack of inhibition of a young girl with her first love. Now, only one door opened and one passenger alighted. Uncertain, timid and wondering. Who would be the driver of the car to meet me? Would he think I was young, sophisticated, or just as I was – a wispy faded blonde? Good enough figure, sprightly walk. Years etched on my face, the first furrow placed on my smooth young brow, just here, before I had left my teens.

We had no trouble identifying each other. Just the two of us on the platform. He came forward in a welcoming way with outstretched hand.

"You would be the lady for the Sally Glen," he said, shaking my hand, as his other hand relieved me of my holdall. There was warmth in his greeting. The old warmth that new ways and new governments could not dispel. It gave me a hope and confidence. He escorted me to the car through the same old door in the wall. A shining Ford car awaited me outside.

Fleeting memories. Memories of people walking their horses around and away from the noise of incoming trains, hands firmly on bridles so that the unfamiliar noise would not put them in a runaway panic. Many of them had driven miles to send their dear ones to America, Australia and the far corners of the earth. Perhaps into some religious order or the ever-popular seminary at Maynooth. In each case they were gone for ever. The wild geese.

My driver opened the car door, made sure I was comfortably seated, then ambled around and heaved himself into the driver's seat. He was a clumsy hulk of a man with grey stubble on his chin. His striped shirt and red tie held his collar in a strangled knot, as though it secured his head to his body. He wore a checked tweed hat, decked with tatty bait flies, doubtless a hat forgotten by a fishing guest of some season past. There was something in the way he peered at me from beneath its brim that sent my eyes searching the crown for a stray bullet hole. As he eased himself into the seat, with one hand on the steering wheel, he said, "Are you comfortable, ma'am? Any 'auld seat behind a wheel does Chris. I was brought up to it. Me father, God rest him, had an old Model T for hire when I was only a lad." As I thought. I only hoped no telltale sign from the past clung to me as it did to Chris.

We set out on the few miles' drive to the Sally Glen. Chris attempted to make the journey interesting for me, the visitor. He made no forays into history, except his occasional references to "the Troubles", as though the world around him had begun then. He waved a hand here and there as we passed through the town, to indicate a few new flashy shopfronts. All chromium and Vitrolite. Neon signs, which would glow. Evening dropped into night, casting into the shadows the less up-to-date shopfronts. Some, I recollected, though the town held little interest for me now.

As we left the town behind, what had been a white dusty road in my childhood was now a strip of tarmac. We approached my first dreaded obstacle: Clanratty Castle. I could feel my heart give a sickening thump. The sort of thing I had feared when I put down the phone after my booking. I hoped Chris would pass it quickly without comment. But no. It appeared to be his special item of interest to the tourist. He drew the car onto the roadside and turned off the engine. He explained nothing of the castle's history or origin, only the reason for the state of decay which had overtaken it, and the final curtain which had fallen on it during the Troubles. The stumps of its walls stood up irregular against the skyline. The curving hills were naked of all vegetation apart from a few straggly hedges and good pasture. The great ornamental iron gates were no more. Part of the decorative railings remained, their rusty sturdiness peaked here and there from the tangle of briars and other nameless things they supported. Malevolent bindweed decorated the tumbling lot. A wooden gate was fastened to a post with the loop made from an old bucket handle. Where once the gravelled avenue had been, grass and dandelions grew in profusion. A grazing bullock raised his head and looked at us without interest while he tucked a mouthful of grass into his jaw. Then, indifferent to our existence, he lowered his head and continued his grazing.

I could find little reply to the knowledge Chris was imparting to me with such enthusiasm. I kept repeating, foolishly, "How interesting." I asked no questions. My breath came more easily when he started the engine again and we moved on. Every twist and turn in the road brought its memories. I did not want Chris to elaborate on them. What he had to say were his memories, not mine. I would come again, alone, when no one could intrude upon mine. We passed the Crag, the Little Bridge and the little triangle of grass where the road from Barclays' came down. The road appeared to have narrowed. White, lacy hemlock grew in profusion on either side. In the distance the chimneys of a house poked through the trees, rooks and jackdaws its only tenants. Chris gave a wide sweep of his hand in its direction and said, "Nice family lived there. Left, all gone, the troubled times."

"Indeed," I answered, blankly, putting all the interest I could find into the single word, trying to make it sound like a surprise.

"Aye! All gone," he repeated. "Same as the Glynns. Ah! Same as everyone that was any good," he added somewhat regretfully. "Oh! Them was terrible times, missus, terrible times. You were lucky not to have known them. I was in jail myself. Had to do me bit, like the rest, for freedom."

With a lump in my throat, my nervous hands opening and closing my handbag, I took in the driver. Tied to his wheel, paid a pittance, driving through the empty countryside and talking of the freedom he had played his part in acquiring while almost in the same breath proudly boasting of the good money all his family were earning in England.

The word *freedom* spun before my eyes, a blazing wheel with its fiery red spokes, each with a different significance, a variation of shades in the glow of the whole. Freedom. How many hideous crimes had been committed in its name? How many heroes had it made? How many martyrs? How many traitors? Into which category did Chris and I fit? I heard the echo of his words: "I did me bit." God, how I remember that bit, against his neighbour, and how they talked of it with pride. A feud of bitterness and jealousy, hatred and revenge. Divided friends. Divided neighbours. Divided families whose cruelties against each other are scarcely believable in a world of peace and sanity.

I, too, had my hatred and not without reason. I have none now. The years have turned the telescope of my youth, and I look through the other end. I can see the knaves who made the so-called Civil War pay the Rhett Butlers whose only cause was Rhett Butler. And the petty mind who grudged that little bit more honour to the other fellow. If indeed there could be honour in any of it. A squabble over Sam Browne belts and gabardines. There was not enough to go around. There could be no rank and file. And, fifty years after, the patriot sons of the others are still at it, stopping at nothing in their "fight for Irish freedom". Holy Ireland has been bedevilled and cursed by the sheer bestiality of its natives. Have we moved forward at all? My train of thought was interrupted by our arrival at the entrance to the Sally Glen.

"The sallies grow down there by the Shannon, and there's a little glen there too, through the woods. The house is called after a girl who lived there, Sally Glynn. Oh! A lovely girl. I remember her well myself. Loveliest girl you ever saw."

For the umpteenth time I heard myself saying, "How interesting." Fearful he should pursue the subject, I avidly took up the conversation on fishing. We were through the gates and on the drive. It was no longer the dusty, bumpy, lumpy path. Its gravel surface was now tarmac. A tidy strip of lawn ran along each side. A white-coated, fashionable ranch fence ran its length. The house was visible from the road. The long, white Tudor style that my mother had tried to distinguish it with was gone. Now it was just an old farmhouse dashed in drab grey. It conformed to no particular time or style of architecture. Alas, the clump of rhododendrons was now also gone. Their going brought back to me that awful nameless feeling when I discovered the cherry tree had been cut down. Surely someone could have thought of a way to save the rhododendrons. Several times on my train journey, I had thought of how they would now be in full bloom, offering a welcome like smiling jolly topers. Their absence prompted a fleeting nostalgia for the many secrets they had shared with me and what staunch allies they had been to me. So very dear.

My eyes took in the missing. The jasmine arch leading to the garden path. It too had gone. However, over by the hedge were the lilac saplings I had planted but had not waited to see grow and bloom. Now almost trees, with great trusses of perfumed mauve blossoms, their heady fragrance fillled the evening air.

Chris took my light luggage into the hall, and the owner gushed forward to greet me – "You are welcome. Miss … Mrs?" – apologising for momentarily forgetting my name. I prompted her and she continued, "Of course. I ought to remember. People of that name lived around here. I sometimes hear them spoken of by the locals."

I was almost balancing on the knife-edge of my visit. I nearly said, "Yes,

I know," but managed to pause long enough to find another word: "Indeed!"

She smiled and took the holdall from Chris. She led me to my room. I followed her up a stairway that had never been there in my days. She led me into a room that, I guessed, must be over the one downstairs that had been my original bedroom.

This new room had built-in everything. So many doors I could scarcely find my way out. I wondered how the builder had escaped building himself in. It had twin beds with yellow candlewick bedspreads, their corners dangling to make a trap for careless, unwary feet. A replica of the hundreds of hotel bedrooms with which I was familiar. There was a telephone on the locker between the beds and a table lamp to serve both. What would I give for the floor beneath my feet to vanish and to find myself in the comforting confines of my own little chintz room of long ago? No hot and cold running water, just the washstand with its floral basin and ewer. No bed-head lights, just the brass candlestick with its cone-shaped snuffer. No telephone where a voice could come booming into my solitude at any time. Where the perfume of the wall roses drifted through the open window on each little breeze, not this strange indefinable odour that came from the press of the nozzle of a pressurised container. I must bottle down those thoughts now, I resolved. How often over the long years I had dreamt in my waking and sleeping hours of that room and heard again the voice at the window. I later discovered my old room, together with what had been Michael's room, made the guesthouse dining room.

My hostess enquired as to what I would like to eat. Would I have tea now or dinner later on? I plumped for the tea. I wanted the rest of the evening free to wander at will. She suggested I might like some local trout with my tea. I assured her I would love it, and she left me. I sorted out the scant contents of the holdall. I ran a comb through my wispy hair and turned quickly from the reflection in the mirror, lest I see in it the gay laughing face of a young girl looking over my shoulder, the fresh peach bloom on her cheeks making a mockery of my wrinkles. And a voice saying, "You silly old fool! You don't think you're me, do you?"

The guests were few in the dining room. An American clergyman looking up old classmates from Maynooth, an English spinster writing a book on wildflowers, and a gentleman of uncertain nationality who prowled about at night with a flash lamp studying insects and their habits. I had no interest in any of their pursuits and no wish to become involved in conversation. I wanted my brief stay to be wholly my own arranged programme. I sat at the corner table eating the trout, which had not waited for the mayfly. I wondered how many generations linked them with those that Tom, Michael, old Trooper and I had caught.

After tea, the owner took me out on the gravel drive to show me the nearest way to the Shannon and the jetty. There was a boat at my service, she assured me, should I like a bit of boating. Chris would gladly take me around the many beautiful islands for which the place was famous. I thanked her but assured her of the pleasure I got in solitude, especially in country places. I wandered across to where the rhododendron clump had once stood. Overwhelmed by memories I thought of the sheltered seat they had concealed. My father sat here and smoked his pipe when the years and his rheumatism had immobilised him. Here, too, Tom had retreated to read his breviary, reading into its age-old message a message of his own. Tom interpreted it to suit his own ideals. Here Michael sat, his blue eyes looking far beyond the horizon and the inverted bowl of the sky that imprisoned him. Away in a distant world of his own, his thoughts were perhaps the only tranquil thoughts among us. For what can we guess of other people's thoughts?

I slouched away from the spot and, raising my shoulders, wandered around to the gable of the house where once the jasmine arch had been. There was no evidence of it now. I went searching for the garden with the many seats and bowers my mother had fashioned so that my father's daily walk had pleasant resting places. There was no path now. A lawn tennis court had swallowed it up. Chris was mowing the daisy-spattered surface. I kept to his offside, lest he detect something searching in my stray wanderings. Past the tennis court and through the gate in a hedge. The last path through the arch had led to a seat beneath a chestnut tree. It had been a rustic seat and seemed to have grown from its trunk. The chestnut tree was still there. A giant thing now. A few sheep still in their winter coats grazed around it. No farm animals had ever been allowed on this, almost sacred, ground of our garden. The meandering path led from one seat to another. The ground between had been part orchard, part fruit, vegetable and flower garden. Now it was a large pasture.

I tried to find the next bower but it had completely disappeared. There was no trace of its existence other than in my memory. A close-clipped evergreen, on either side of which were branches of old moss roses. Roses known to us as Corney's roses but never catalogued by nursery men under that name. My mother had received them from someone of that name. I never knew him but his roses afforded us much pleasure and the admiration of our visitors. The roses too had gone

I continued my zigzag tour to what had been the Broom Seat. No witch's cauldron but two great wild broom bushes my mother had connected at the top by their intricate lacing. They formed, in one summer, into a solid arch, laden with yellow blossoms. I found my way to the jetty, now a new, altogether more solid, affair. I found the two boats alongside. Gleaming white, with names painted in black lettering. I wondered how we survived our exploits and adventures in our own battered craft. Perhaps it was because we were familiar with the Shannon's many moods. We could dodge the rocks in the shallows and come through the Cut and the Gobbins in sudden storms when stouter craft but less daring hearts quailed. The western sun went sloping over the bracken-covered shoulder of the Crag as I made my way shoreward towards the old boathouse. Meadowsweet grew rank and high with the long riverside grasses. I beat my way through the wild undergrowth with the cudgel of a stick plucked from the hedge. The old link between the boathouse and the jetty seemed to have been broken. Worse, perhaps the old gabled boathouse no longer existed. I dared not allow myself such a thought. I ploughed on, flogging the stinging nettles and the wild sweep of briar tentacles that seemed to try to reach me so that they might forever hold me to that spot. Great clouds of pollen drifted from meadowsweet in the wake of my clearing stick until, preoccupied with my own advance, I came upon it.

Its gabled and arched doorway was now but a cluster of stones covered by a mass of green trailing things. Ground ivy covered its broken walls. The landside gables were in the same sorry state. I found a hole in its jumbled walls big enough to allow me to pass through. Its roof was an intertwining of hazel bushes. The green translucent light was fast fading into the evening dusk. The water beneath was incapable of holding a boat. It was a dark, sluggish pool into which the reeds had been pushed by the dense masses growing around it far out into the water. I sat on a mossy stone wall with my feet dangling. There was no moonlit path as I had always remembered. For an instant I was submerged in a subconscious, almost intolerable, sea of loneliness. No warm place in my heart.

This had been our trysting place. It was here we said our last farewell. The cry of a curlew overhead added an eerie echo to my misery. I saw the reeds move at the water's edge and heard, in my flight of fancy, the splashing feet of Chess, my dog. I thought if there be a happy hunting ground for dogs this would be his. I left the haunted spot. I had risen again, like Lazarus, from the tomb of my memories. Everything was quiet now. I was back in the present.

Out beyond the reeds a swan lay placid and serene, still as a porcelain ornament. Young water hens sported beneath their now-deserted hammock nest in the reeds. My quiet approach caused no panic in the wildlife around me. I wondered if I, too, had become invisible to them as I felt I had to myself.

I became preoccupied with trying to find my old path back to the house, the path that had been beaten by us in our constant trek between house and boathouse. As children we had tied the long grasses to make traps for our fast-fleeting companions, waiting and watching the pollen fly up from the dusty white yarrow, as someone tripped and fell, victim of our skilled tricks. Like all my old paths, it too had vanished. I cleared a way with my stick as evening darkness pressed closer. I saw the lights go up in the guesthouse. Like a lost ship I was guided by them. I walked up the drive to the house, through the hall and up the stairs to my room. I looked down on the yard below. A full moon was shining on the smooth asphalt car park, the cobblestones gone along with the big tree. Many moons had shone through its bare branches. In winter it brought wavering shadows, like charcoal drawings come to life. I remembered with clarity the night I stood by my bedroom window and watched Michael step through the shadows as he crossed the yard with Flash to bed him down for the night in the trap house. I could hear Michael whistle the melody of a tune, then popular, called "Sliabh na mBan". Its melody haunts me now. Later it became better known as the name of the armoured car in the convoy that escorted Michael Collins to his death in the tragedy of Béal na Bláth, the Valley of Flowers, where indeed one of Ireland's most precious flowers was cut down before it came into full bloom. The blight of civil war raged then like a prairie fire.

Michael, our Michael, whistled that night. A sad song. Yet there was no sadness in his nature. Dear Michael. The years have not changed him. There is tranquillity and peace still in his face, his smile, his company. Michael taught me to control my rebel spirit when, at times, all my youth cried out only for revenge. It saddened him to know that I should rejoice because a man should wear, throughout his life, and take to his grave with him, a red scar on his face that I had put there with a blow from a bicycle pump. Back then it had been the only weapon I held when he pointed his revolver at my dog. Later it was Michael who taught me how to turn my revenge into rejoicing when the same man lined up with his comrades to have medals pinned on their chests. The newspapers said they wore "the scars of their fight for freedom". It was I who pinned his medal there. He wears it proudly. He is a veteran now. Long may he wear it. I bear him no grudge. I only hope that when his earthly parades are over he may come by his halo as readily, but more honourably.

I went downstairs to the lounge for a nightcap. An ex-Maynooth student was there with two of his contemporaries. They seemed full of joy and vigour. The sound of laughter and the clink of glasses came from the bar. A young girl in jodhpurs showed him into the room. Coming towards me, she asked if everything was all right. She was getting the horses ready for trekking for the visitors. She told me she loved living at Sally Glen. She was seventeen, a magic age. Brief and beautiful as the mayfly. What lay before her I dared not think. I hoped life would be kind to her. She stood there beneath the halo of light from the plastic chandeliers as once I did under the swinging oil lamp.

Chris drove me to the station next morning. He hoped I had enjoyed my short visit and that I would come again. He would take me on a boat trip along the Shannon and let me see the magic islands of Lough Ree. Yes, I would come again, I lied. I gave him a generous tip, more than I could afford. He stood on the platform, waving to me.

From my carriage window I caught glimpses of the Shannon glittering through the trees in the morning sunshine. Then I was speeding through the woods, with its floor of wild hyacinths. As we left behind the bluebell carpet of my childhood, I gave a sigh at the many times this carpet had been spread for me.

I closed my eyes and laid my head back. It was a relief, my furtive trip into the past. I felt no loneliness, only a strange, elated, joyous feeling. An almost impossible achievement. Perhaps old age brings its own reward. I bade my last farewell to the place I loved. I was leaving with a lighter heart than I had done on so many years ago. Distance and age would be my companions as I said goodbye to the young Sally Glynn who laughs and cries, who has loved and hated her way through life.

1

The Castle

The music from the military band filled the ballroom of Clanratty Castle, echoing back from the high, arched windows and gilded ceiling. All the brass buttons, gold braid, glittering jewels and sequined trimmings, all the noise and gaiety. The soft laughter and merry giggles of young ladies amid the guffaws of older gentlemen and the shallow bleat of the boyish officers. All a marked contrast to the silent shadowy world of the bleak and desolate countryside outside the castle walls. Apart from officers from neighbouring barracks and their wives, or those home on leave from the regular army, there were few residents of the district at the ball, save those in the service of the British government in some capacity – or those who, by being intimate with friends of the officers, held the doubtful honour of access to the ballroom of Clanratty Castle.

This was no hunt or coming of age ball for the heir of Clanratty as in years gone by. Tonight was the farewell dance for the British regiment moving out to Dublin Castle, making room for another British regiment, fresh from England. Although they faced no fighting front, for many of the more experienced men, the blood and muck of Flanders was preferable to this no-man's-land that ran the length and breadth of Ireland. Here, at any moment, without warning, death could flash from the dark woodland curtain of a heavy hedge or over the top of a lichen-covered wall. Many who had survived the fierce battles of the Somme and the Seine had gone down in a quiet valley by the Shannon, the Lee or the Boyne.

It was Easter of 1921. The British Army in Ireland were frowned upon, scowled at, ambushed when the opportunity arose and boycotted by a majority of the Irish people. The failure of the 1916 Rising had, over the years, changed from just a memory to grim reality for the British Army, who had tried to stamp out the fire. However, the spark from 1916 had kindled the tinder of sad and angry hearts and set a determination to follow in the footsteps of the dead leaders. The sentiments of praise and blame in the aftermath of the Rising had now, in 1921, settled into a fixed ideal.

None of this mattered to Sally Glynn as she whirled around the ballroom in Peter Barclay's arms. It was her first dance and her head swam at the unaccustomed excitement in this place of enchantment. She felt she was dreaming. All the blue and pink and gold of her eighteen years. Her first dance with her first love, framed by the tall gilt mirror. Even her reflection in that mirror could scarcely convince her that this was indeed real. Her pale-blue taffeta brocade dress, with its gossamer lace panels and the pale-blue satin high-heeled shoes, might indeed have been worn by Cinderella. For, like in the fairy tale, Sally's time out was strictly limited. For many nights Sally had burned the midnight oil while the family slept, altering the elaborately trimmed gown into something simple enough to meet the more restrained fashion of the time. She had promised herself that she would alter it so that she could restore its original style. It must be replaced in folds of tissue in the camphoric depths of her mother's big trunk, where it had lain undisturbed for twenty-five years except for an annual shake-out for moths. The result was gratifying, like the model in the fashion book she had kept before her. Now, when she caught her reflection in the mirror, she gave no thought to the restoration of the dress. Her mind was wholly occupied with the triumph of her success and the hope that the frail glory of the old brocade would last the night through.

The music stopped and they stood before the mirror. While Peter applauded, Sally adjusted the blue bow that looped the back of her gold ringlets. They kept escaping its satin smoothness, spilling out across her bare white shoulders. With a deft hitch she imprisoned the curls once more. How she would love to tell her friends of this stolen night of pleasure, those who considered themselves so much smarter than she. Kitty Dalton, who bought expensive clothes from Dublin. Or Gerty Duffy, with all her American clothes hanging in the wardrobe because she had nowhere to wear them. But, of course, she dare not utter a word. And she hoped no one would tell them either. Not even her closest friend, Kitty. Kitty had once been at a dance in the castle. When Kitty's brother Harry was shot by the Tans, the Daltons had abandoned their neutrality and all their sympathy had drifted to the lads on the run. Sally knew that Kitty was partial to a young officer's arm around her. Kitty had been to boarding school in Dublin and had many friends in the city. Her favourite was Linda Gordon, in whose flat she stayed when she visited the capital. As Linda was a Protestant, she was one of the privileged few who could fraternise with British officers. Kitty could openly flirt with them in Dublin. It was a long way from Cloona and its small-town gossip. But when someone from Cloona had met Kitty in Dublin with a young British officer, she introduced him as Captain Long. She said he was Linda's friend and, to oblige Linda, she was showing him around the city.

Fortunately the few at the dance who knew Sally were not among her friends. Mrs Brigson, the fussy little bank manager's wife, was having a night off from her ageing husband. She was not likely to notice Sally, as her escort at the dance was Sally's boss, Mr Pratt, the solicitor. Sally was surprised when she spotted him waltzing around. The worried expression on his face was, she suspected, because he did not like being placed in a position of inferiority. The dashing uniforms of the British officers made him and the few other civilians present look like dusty old magpies against the gorgeous splendour of peacocks. Pratt's buffoonery was more amusing than impressive to the people of Cloona. His vanity was as marked as his snobbery and knavery. He was constantly boasting of his family's history. Pratt talked a lot about his father's career in what he termed "The Royal Navy" and the background of blue seas and flapping white sails and gold braid against which he was reared. He had come to Cloona as Mrs Brigson's guest and she had helped him acquire a rundown solicitor's practice in

Cloona. He employed Sally as his typist, where her pay was as light as her duties. Sally's father had nicknamed him The Admiral. The nature of Mrs Brigson's friendship with Mr Pratt was accepted as doubtful. They would hardly notice Sally.

Mr Pratt did not see her as Sally from the office. He saw a pretty young girl in blue who appeared to be very popular with the young officers. When he saw how popular she was with the officers, he tried to force his attentions on her. He patronised her by asking her to dance. She grudgingly granted his request. She had never been so intimate with him and she felt a blessed relief when the dance ended. When he requested a second time, she refused as tactfully as she could.

"When he sees me tomorrow in my old blue serge dress and the black ribbon in my hair, and the clatter of the typewriter replacing the music we are dancing to right now, I will again be part of the office. I am not afraid he will tell anyone I was here. He will not consider the news to be of sufficient importance. So there is no one to tell only you," she joked to Peter.

"I won't be talking to any of the Glynns because the Glynns won't talk to me," Peter said.

He knew only too well what the Glynn family thought of him. Home on leave in his early days in the British Army, Peter Barclay had been a dashing young officer to be wooed by the young ladies of Cloona and the district. Sally was then only a schoolgirl. Peter was almost indifferent to her existence. She was just Michael Glynn's sister. But a year ago he became disturbingly aware of her young loveliness. Now he spent each leave time falling more and more in love with her and trying to mend the rift with her family, especially the rift with Michael, with whom he had fought side by side in the brief bitter battle in Dublin in 1916. While this seemed to have given Peter an appetite for war, it had left Michael dispirited and mourning his lost leader, Patrick Pearse. Tom Glynn ignored him. Tom had no share in the battle or in the comradeship between his brother and Peter. He considered Peter's actions in joining the British Army disloyal to Michael and to Ireland. His uniform placed a greater barrier between them than his religion. Michael, although friendly and polite, never got far into conversation with him. They certainly would not approve of their sister going to a dance in Clanratty Castle and dancing with men in the uniform of the British Army. Especially

Tom, who was training for the priesthood in Maynooth seminary. Tom did not approve of Sally's friendship with Peter Barclay. Peter was a Protestant, and apart from his religion there was what Tom referred to as "the stigma" of Peter being in the British Army. Tom had said he was embarrassed by remarks and innuendos from the young, less sensitive, students. Sally was of the opinion that it was all Tom's own fanaticism. She would live for tonight. The strained relationship between Peter and the Glynn family would right itself.

All too soon it was over. When the last strains of "God Save the King" were done, Peter and Sally stood on the steps outside the great studded door of Clanratty. Sally held Peter's arm and he drew her closer. The snug safety of the ballroom was deserting her. Her navy schoolgirl coat was thrown lightly over her shoulders. As Peter hauled their bicycles from the shadows, she slipped the coat from her shoulders. She hitched up the brocade dress into a tight elastic band in preparation for the ride home. The cold April moon shone silver on her gleaming hair and highlighted the smooth whiteness of her face and neck and arms.

"You look lovely in the moonlight, Sally. Even Lady Isobel of Clanratty couldn't have been lovelier."

Sally turned her head so that Peter might not see the mischievous smile playing around the corners of her mouth. "Wonder what she would make of having to ride a bicycle with her dress tucked up under her heavy coat," she said as she took the bicycle from Peter and gave him her blue satin slippers to carry in his pocket.

"She wouldn't do it half as well as you."

"She wouldn't have to, but I couldn't imagine myself doing without my bicycle."

Not many could. This was their principal means of transport. With bridges blown up and roads blocked, a bicycle had to be shouldered across such barriers. In the chilly dawn Peter and Sally rattled along the potholed road from the castle, carefully manoeuvring the bicycles, sometimes bumping shoulder to shoulder, sometimes separated by the entire width of the road.

"I think you better not come any further," Sally suggested as they neared the gate of the long, low farmhouse that was her home. "Chess barks at strangers."

"And I am such a stranger here now?"

They stood for a while beneath the cherry tree near the gate.

"Can I come up the avenue with you a bit?" he said eagerly.

"No!" Sally said, aware of the wintered trees. "They'd see us from the windows."

Peter put his arms around her and drew her close. He moved to kiss her lips and then released her abruptly, engaging her eyes. "You will manage to come out another night before I go, won't you? What about it, Sally? What night? Any night suits me when it can't be every night!"

"I don't know. If I'm not found out tonight, I can try the same way out any night."

"What about Friday night, then? The new regiment moves into Clanratty, but don't tell Tom that. There's likely to be a party for them. My cousin Dave Sternitt is a lieutenant with the new regiment and I'll introduce you to him. He can get my letters across to you.

"Will it be evening dress again?" Sally's mind clouded with doubts as to how much there was left in the blue brocade.

"It won't be evening dress. I wish I could see you every evening, visit your house, dance and sing with Michael and Tom as we did back before."

"You joined up," Sally teased.

"Don't go over all that again, please, Sally. They'll never forgive me, I know, especially Tom. He's so bitter against me. I think he hates me. But I can get over his hate and Michael's disappointment in me if you love me, Sally."

"Ah, don't worry about what Tom thinks. He's not the forgiving sort."

"They didn't have a home like mine. I told you the way it was, drifting about all that summer after Easter week, meeting with nothing but condemnation from everyone. 'That's your education finished, me boy,' my mother and father told me when they discovered I was in the melee of Easter week. 'No more school fees or fancy degrees at our expense.' And then when Aunt Mabel came from Belfast, she decided I was turning out to be a second Andrew. They had banished Andrew to Scotland for having disgraced them with his shouts for home rule. Oh, you have no idea, Sally, of the naggin' and narkin', and never a penny in my pocket. That was the real reason my brother Geoffrey joined the British Navy. Nothing to do with loyalty to king and country. And that was the reason I snatched at

Uncle Andrew's offer to pay for the continuation of my studies at university in Glasgow. I joined up to pay him back but I haven't any regrets about anything, Sally. Least of all my part in Easter week. Anyway my mother is quite proud of me now, and so was my father before he died. Yet when I was at home I still remember I hadn't a decent suit to wear; they didn't think I was worth the price of one."

Sally heard the clock chime in the hall as she reached the back door. She hoped the chimes would make a cover for her noisy entry. Placing her thumb in the hollow of the big iron latch, she raised it gently and pushed, but the door held fast. Then, bracing her slim figure, she leaned heavily against it, but its solid resistance convinced her that the door was firmly bolted inside. A wave of panic seized her. She felt like crying, something she seldom did. She couldn't even remember the last time. Composing herself, she turned and shuffled wearily into the trap house and flopped down on the fodder bed beside Chess. The trusted setter gave her a welcoming glance. She tried to think of some means by which she might enter the house, unseen and unheard. There was Michael. She could tap on his window and he would get up and open the door for her. However, the risk of waking Tom and her parents was too great. And anyway, she didn't want to bring Michael into her conspiracy.

After exploring many avenues of thought, she finally settled on slipping in when Tom and Michael were out at early Mass in the morning. That meant sleeping the remaining part of the night in the trap house. Her plans of entry decided upon, her uneasiness gave way to resentment against the too-vigilant member of the family who had discovered the unbolted door and set it to rights. She knew that they had all been in bed when she sneaked out. Who had got up and bolted the door? Exhausted, she lay down heavily on the hay and pulled Chess close to her for warmth. The chill night breeze drifted through the wide doorless opening of the trap house. Slipping off her heavy shoes, she wiggled her toes about in blessed freedom after their torturous night's imprisonment in the satin high heels. She tried to find a comfortable position in which to sleep, twisting one way and then another, to the disturbance of the docile Chess. When she put her head down, the straw poked into her eyes and ears. She sat up and pounded her hay pillow flat with her hands. She stretched out again, but the fodder bed grew colder and harder. Impatiently, she got to her knees and pulled wisp after wisp of hay from the centre of the heap in a frantic effort to make a bed for herself. Suddenly she stopped and withdrew her hand quickly as it came in contact with a different texture. She paused for a moment, and then, slowly, she put her hand back into the hole she had made and drew out a man's gabardine trench coat. Standing up, she shook out the coat and searched the pockets and placed her hands into the sleeves. They were still warm from the contact of the body that had worn it. There was no doubt – it was a Shinner's coat. She wondered how the coat got there. Did Tom or Michael know anything about it? She didn't worry unduly about it except to hope that the owner didn't return while she was there. Slipping back into the nest she had scooped for herself, she drew the dog close to her again and, pulling the hard trench coat over both of them, she dozed off to dream sweet dreams of the wonderful night she had had at the dance, dreams of Peter and their next meeting.

She awoke to the bang of the back door. She sat bolt upright and peeped from her dark corner at the wind-dried pavement in the yard. A breeze whipped up a scrap of paper and pinned it to the lintel of the trap house doorway. She saw Tom come forward, chasing the paper across the yard. As he bent to capture it, she saw that it was a little black-edged mortuary card from his missal. The card he received yesterday. Harry Dalton's card. Killed by the Tans. She drew further back into the shadows. Tom had come dangerously close to spotting her. She could see his thin hand stretched out to grasp the card, the red thatch of his hair between his black hat and upturned collar. Then he hurried away down the avenue. She waited a little longer. Michael did not come. Perhaps he was not going to Mass this morning. She dragged herself to her feet, feeling stiff, with an ache in every limb. Catching a distorted reflection of herself in the glass of the trap lamp, she was horrified. She couldn't be as bad as that, she thought as she surveyed herself disconsolately. Pieces of the precious blue brocade dress had come adrift under her heavy coat. The ribbon was missing from her hair, replaced by bits of hay and bracken. She rummaged about for her ribbon and found Chess lying on it. Hastily, she tidied herself arranging her coat to hide her disheveled dress. After replacing the trench coat deeply and firmly in the hay, she sneaked out of the trap house towards the back door. Never before had she felt such a need to reach her bedroom in the shortest possible time. But when she reached the kitchen, her mother was already up and lighting the fire.

"Sally – I didn't know you were up. Are you going to Mass?" she asked, turning quickly as Sally entered.

"I was," Sally lied, "but I had to come back. I don't feel too well."

"Have you fallen off your bike?"

"Oh no, just a headache I think."

"Where's your cap?

"It blew away. I … I have it in my pocket," Sally stammered.

"Well, you look like you have the 'flu or something."

"The 'flu? Do I look as bad as that?" Sally remembered the awful scourge of three years ago when Michael and she were among the few spared to help the entire neighbourhood. The 'flu: the words still had the power to chill Sally. Recollections of closed doors, darkened windows, smokeless chimneys, big coffins. And little coffins.

"Oh no, it's not the 'flu, just a bit of a cold, maybe," she reassured her mother.

"Back to bed, then, and stay there all day. I'll take you up some breakfast."

With a sigh of relief Sally closed her bedroom door behind her. She rejoiced she had not to go to the office. She had not to meet Mr Pratt after his embarrassing attentions of last night. But what would Tom say when he didn't see her at Mass? He would raise some hare, no doubt. But let him. She had all day in bed to consider crooked answers to crooked questions.

2

The Glynn Family and Friends

Behind John Glynn's long farmhouse, the fertile upland fields sloped gently to meet the farms of his neighbours. Past the entrance gates to the avenue, the narrow road ran down into Cloona. Across the road lay the swampy fields. Flaggers' Fields, the Long Meadow and the Crescent Acre. Lough Allen bit deeply into the marsh in the rainy seasons to steal the crops or spoil the grazing. Beyond the lake the land ascended fold upon easy fold of green pasture and purple bog, climbing to hang from the rocky summit of Glenbrae, formidable enough to be known as the mountain. Away to the right, the grey mist marked the town of Cloona. Silhouetted against the leaded backdrop were the great trees of Clanratty Wood and the turreted top of the castle, by way of which John Glynn's wife had come to Dooleagh. The northern nurse of the Lady Isobel met and married the easy-going bachelor, John, bringing little in the nature of a dowry to her farmer husband apart from the lovely clothes of her deceased mistress, which the bereaved young earl had presented to her. Among these was the blue brocade dress, which Sally had altered and worn at the dance at Clanratty. Fine but impractical gifts for a young woman intending life as a farmer's wife. She had, however, readily adapted herself to her new life, her new religion and her new nationality. She proved a good wife and an exceptional housekeeper, with pride in her home and a pardonable ambition for their three children.

Michael, their tall, handsome elder son, she had hoped would become a doctor. She had worked and saved and sent him to Dublin University, only for him to get caught up with his fellow students, including their neighbour, Peter Barclay, in the 1916 Rising in Dublin. Following this he returned to Dooleagh in the hope of somehow finding a way into the life of his own choosing, namely becoming a Franciscan missionary. Tom, their second child, was unlike his brother. He was small, thin and garrulous. As a consequence of a childhood illness he had become his mother's favourite and she spoiled him. Mrs Glynn had manipulated Tom into Maynooth seminary to make a priest of him. Sally, their only daughter, was unlike either of her brothers. A mixed bag, John called his family. Against Michael's fine physique and dark handsomeness and Tom's weedy frame and pale, freckled face, with its crown of flaming hair, Sally was blonde and blue-eyed, with a willowy grace from which her father took her nickname. "Growing like a sally rod, she is," he would often comment. Her mother found her the secretarial position in Mr Pratt's office in Cloona. Sally's protests against her mother's plans met with resistance. Her mother thought there were good matches for a pretty girl like Sally in Cloona. Hugh Dalton with his big shop and his brother Jack, in Maynooth, who was to be ordained with Tom. She did not approve of Sally's friendship with Peter Barclay. He might spoil her chances of making a better match. Her disapproval was obvious. Whenever Barclay's name was mentioned she would give a hem and a haw and say, "They were just adventurers and that is the reason Geoffrey got killed in the war in France."

And there was Mr Pratt himself. It had been known for men of wealth and good family to marry their secretaries. He looked so well trotting around on his horse.

"Pratt!" John laughed at her. "He's just a knave and a humbug. Sure what do we know of his wealth and his family? He arrived in Cloona from the divil knows where, aping the gentry and runnin' around with that … that … woman," he said, referring to Mrs Brigson.

As usual his wife shushed him into silence. His feeble attempts to save his children from his wife's ambition were defeated. Each in turn had opposed their mother's decisions and appealed to their father to be allowed to follow their own choices.

"Sure if he wants to be a Franciscan, let him," John said when Michael first raised the issue.

"Michael! A Franciscan! Michael, the delight of any tailor, traipsing around in a shapeless horse blanket and sandals with his toes sticking out? Unthinkable. Different if he became a priest in a local parish."

She would send Tom to Maynooth. He had never given any indication of a preference for any career in particular and so his uncertainty raised no problems for his mother. But John had misgivings. Tom, he thought, was a lot like his Uncle Bart, with his red hair. Both were hot into politics. John had recollections of his brother Bartley that were not as dignified as the photograph of the Fenian warrior in the frame hanging over the mantelpiece in the parlour. John accepted his wife's decisions in the matter of their children with good grace and suffered defeat gladly. It released him from any responsibility concerning them. In most decision making he deferred to her. "Just ask herself," he would say to Trooper McDermott, his workman. And Trooper, chuckling into his beard, would go off in search of "herself" to resolve the question of the day or the hour. To Trooper, Mrs Glynn's manner was preferable to that of his previous employer, Mrs Barclay of Storm Hill. Mrs Glynn listened tactfully, with interest and amusement, to his tall tales of adventure. His exploits in the Boer War were in a cavalry of such doubtful origin that Trooper himself forgot its name. He regularly transferred from the Queen's Bays to the Queen's Greys, with others in between.

Mrs Glynn thought Trooper a merry old rascal. His quick remedies for all ailments of human or beast were tolerable. But she considered his stories a source of distraction to the other workmen, after she had made a few forays into the yard and spied them standing around leaning on their spades and shovels, enthralled with Trooper's yarns. Her solid, practical

Ulster temperament had clashed with Trooper's highly imaginative one, and so he found more genial surroundings in the company of John Glynn. However, John frequently drew attention to his difficulty in handling the two horses, Raverty and Scarva, particularly the latter, whom he had bought from George Barclay before his death.

"Couldn't be any good," Trooper decided. "Mrs Barclay kept everything about the house on a tight rein, and what would Corney Thornton, an old Connaught Ranger, know about training a horse? Sure he was never a horse soldier. A mule maybe, but never a horse."

The days between Tuesday and Friday seemed, to Sally, to be made up of more than the allotted twenty-four hours each. Now she laid her frock on the bed, the one she would wear tonight for Peter. She sat on the bed while she waited for the call for the Rosary in the kitchen. She wished they would start it and get it over with quickly. She was growing impatient. She hoped that Tom would not insist on prolonging it with his customary Hail Marys and appeals to God's mercy, forgiveness and assistance for so many living and dead. He would be sure to include a litany of the victims of the Easter week rebellion and the lads on the run. Sally could hear the sound of voices in the kitchen. The mixed footfalls of her mother and father as they trailed off down the corridor to their room; her father's stick's clicking muffled by the linoleum. She heard Michael open the back door and through her window watched him cross the yard to the trap house with Chess. She watched him pat the dog on the head, and then he and the dog were lost in the shadows of the open doorway. Michael emerged again into the moonlight and stood for a while looking through the trees towards the mountain lights. He seemed very alone out there in the night. He glanced towards Sally's window before entering the house. She heard him shoot the heavy bolt on the back door. She waited for him to pass her door.

"Have you no light or have you gone to bed already, Sally?" he called.

"I have," she answered as she hurriedly jumped into bed in case he came into her room to offer his lighted candle and found her fully dressed. She breathed relief as she heard him move down the corridor to his own room. His soft humming of the strains of "Slievenamon" evoked a sadness in her. Sadness that she had to sneak out like this on Michael, her brother. Sadness at the differences between him and Peter. But what did that matter now? Peter was heading back to England and it might be a long time before he was home again. All sadness was swept away by her love for Peter and the urgency to be at the Hazel Bridge as soon as she could. She crept silently out of bed and put on her best dress of blue silk, with the neat white collar. By the light of the flash lamp she gave her ringlets a final twitch, looping them back into their stiff taffeta bow. Then, shoes in hand, she slipped like a shadow from her room, tiptoed in her stocking feet across the kitchen floor and, gingerly drawing the heavy bolt, stealthily crept into the moonlight. A few long strides and springbok leaps brought her across the yard into the shadow of the trap house. She spoke quietly to Chess as she perched on the fodder bed beside him to put on her black patent shoes. Her bicycle was propped against the side of the trap, where she had placed it in readiness. Wheeling it out, she kept close to the shadow of the house. She bent her head as she passed under Michael's window.

Grateful for the dark cover of the rhododendrons, she reached the drive and paused for a minute to regain her quiet composure. She was aware of the risk after curfew. She could be neutral in her political outlook, but any one of the warring parties could make her a victim. In and around the grounds of her own home, she was, to the Shinners, the sister of Michael Glynn and so had their protection. Through the gateway of Clanratty she was a friend of Captain Peter Barclay and was equally sure of sanctuary. But on the road between there and the Hazel Bridge, the Black and Tans might catch her and accuse her of carrying dispatches. They might even shoot her on sight as a suspect. She didn't dwell too long on the risks her tryst with Peter might involve. She was in love with him and she tossed her cares to the night winds. Mounting her bicycle, she swept out of the avenue and down the hill to Hazel Bridge. She found Peter waiting. Before long they were climbing the steep hill and sweeping down the straight avenue past the sentries, into Clanratty. Peter introduced Sally to Lieutenant Dave Sternitt, his cousin, and other officers he had met in the few days since his arrival.

"By Jove," one of them exclaimed, "if this is a sample of the Irish girls then we are going to have a right high old time. Ireland isn't a bit as I had imagined it. I thought it a wilderness of hills and streams with furze and heather and shawled women and men in funny hats."

"Called 'clawbeens'," interrupted one of the party, who seemed to be better informed. "No doubt you will have many surprises."

Peter introduced her to some of the young officers' wives who were staying in the hotel in Cloona and were now enthralled by the Irish castle. They danced to the music of the old piano, played by those who could hammer out the new ragtime on its yellow, warped keys.

The night passed all too quickly. It was after midnight when Sally and Peter stood again beneath the cherry tree by the gate. Their brief few hours had sped by and now they dared not linger lest any trunk hid a rebel or a shooting star was the wavering headlamp of a Crossley Tender sweeping the lonely country roads in search of those who by bomb or gun would dare to block the king's highway.

"Take care of yourself, Sally. You'll be in my thoughts ... always," Peter whispered, holding her as close as he dared.

"You will write, won't you?"

"Of course I will. I'll post them to Dave as we agreed."

Each reassured the other how much they would mean and how Sally would receive them. Anxious that Peter would not see the tears in her eyes, she slipped from his arms. She got on her bicycle and pedalled slowly away. Before she came to the turn in the avenue, she looked back over her shoulder and saw Peter standing there in the moonlight where they had parted. He was waving to her. She would carry that in her memory.

Back home Sally went confidently to the trap house, and with a whisper and a pat on the head to Chess, she pushed her bicycle behind the trap. As she turned to leave, the doorway darkened as though a cloud had drifted across the moon. She looked up and her heart gave a sickening thud. A man was standing in the doorway, silhouetted in its frame. She could see the trench coat and the slouch hat – the uniform of a man on the run. This was it, the price of her indiscretion, the price of her disregard of Tom's warning about being out at night with Peter. A torch light flashed in her face. She could see nothing only the beam and the dark terror behind it, then from behind the light came a surprised whisper.

"Sally! What are you doing here? You've been out with Barclay! You must have been, and on a Tuesday night too. If you had been another few minutes I would have bolted the door. How was I to know you were out?"

Sally heaved a sigh of relief. It was Tom. The torch clicked off. He came inside the door and began to unfasten the belt of the trench coat.

"Yes, Tom, I was out with *Barclay*, as you call him. But what are you doing here? Whose coat is that and where's your coat and hat? And your collar?" She caught her breath as a thought struck her. "Surely you're not in that gang too! Surely you are not cracked enough to get yourself tangled up with them! Wait till Mother finds out. Wait till Fr O'Rourke finds out. Wait till—"

Tom raised his hand to stop her. "No one is going to find out if you don't tell them, Sally. Have you no love or loyalty to your country, no love of Ireland at all? What sort of girl are you? Look at all the other girls – the Daltons and the Duffys and the Fallons and all of them. They can't forget Harry Dalton and the others shot by the Tans. And the fellows on the run and in jail. Look at the way Gerty Duffy works while Rory and Terry are on the run, risking their lives day and night. But you are out with one of the enemy. My father is indifferent. Only Uncle Batt links me to Ireland."

"Surely you are not taking his antics seriously with his Fenians and his White Boys and his tight boys and the divil-knows-what. If he's the only ancestor we have whose history gives us a position of trust with the Shinners, then you won't be asked to do much."

"Listen, Sally, stop using that word." Tom was serious. "Whatever task is allotted to me, no matter what risk is involved, I'll carry it out to the best of my ability. I'll ..." His voice trailed off. "What was that?"

Sally noticed his body stiffen as a noise came from behind the trap. She laughed.

"There is nothing to laugh at."

"Yes there is. There's you declaring on the whole wide world and the noise of my old bike slipping down makes you jump out of your skin. I'm going in." She attempted to pass him.

"Wait, we must go in together." He pulled off the slouch hat and took a revolver from his breast pocket. He secured both in the pocket of the trench coat.

"Oh," Sally gasped, drawing back, "you haven't a gun, not one of those things!"

"Of course I have. Do you think I was out picking mushrooms, do ya?"

"I'll tell ... I'll tell Mother. I'll tell Michael, I'll tell Fr O'Rourke."

"If you tell about me, you'll have to tell about yourself, slinking about at night with Barclay, and you won't do that."

He rolled the coat tightly and buried it in the hay. They crept silently through the back door. Sally's heart was heavy and the pleasure of the night almost forgotten. Her concern for Tom was overcome by her love for Peter. Now that had lost a little rosiness in her overwhelming fear for Tom and the almost murderous bitterness in his voice. Like a shadow creeping through her memory was the warm trench coat in the hay the night she was locked out.

3

Cherry Tree

The day after the encounter in the trap house, Tom was due to return to the seminary in Maynooth. It was also the eve of Gerty Duffy's wedding. Sally was going to Pratt's office to do some work and give him no excuse to ask her to come in later in the evening, a habit he had recently acquired. She detested the way he stood behind her, breathing down her neck and covering her hand on the desk with his pudgy paw. Before going, she would go down to the boat and get some of the fishing tackle she had promised Matt Heaney. Maybe Dave had given him a letter from Peter to slip into the saddlebag on her bicycle. She ran down the avenue to cross the Flagger Fields to the boathouse. As she emerged from the shade of the rhododendrons flanking the avenue, the daylight seemed to rush at her. The whole place became brighter and it seemed that she had come to a strange, unfamiliar place. She stood and stared at the all too evident reason for the change.

The big cherry tree by the gate lay felled across the road. Her cherry tree. Distressed, she turned and ran back to the house to tell the others. Her mother, Michael and Trooper hurried down immediately, her father plodding along to join them. All stood gazing at the fallen tree. She ran into the house to tell Tom. Not waiting for his reaction, she hurried to the others at the tree. There was silence except for the little willow wrens hopping through the bud-laden boughs, apparently undaunted by the change. A soft wind moved gently with them. All stood perturbed and shocked. Each had a precious personal memory of the tree. To Sally it recalled her last parting with Peter. There would be no more fond farewells beneath the cherry tree. Tom did not come out with the others to see the commotion. He must have thought she was joking. She ran back again to see why he hadn't come. He told her he was too busy packing for his return to Maynooth.

"There is no hurry in packing now. You can't go on the early train, not until the road is cleared up for the trap!"

He kept on packing and seemed to be preoccupied with it.

Sally returned to the tree. Trooper was the first to break the silence. "The cherry tree down and not a bloody Tan killed."

Trooper knew, as they all did, that it had been intended for an ambush. She forgot about the fishing tackle for Matt Heaney. She would not go to Pratt's office now. She would make her excuse that she couldn't get her bike over the fallen tree. It was a good excuse. She arose from the tree trunk where she had been sitting when she saw Michael and Trooper coming with implements to clear the road. She had no programme for the day now. She decided that she would go to Duffys' to help Gerty and her mother prepare for the wedding tomorrow. When Sally arrived at Duffys', Gerty took her out to show her the barn, now decorated for the dancing tomorrow night. The cobwebby barn was transformed. Its rough rafters were garlanded with sprays of whitethorn and cherry blossoms. Posies of dandelion and furze gilded its beams. She gazed in amazement.

"Who did it?" she asked Gerty, pointing at the floral ceiling.

"The lads," Gerty explained, meaning her brothers and Frank Fallon.

Sally marvelled at the rare beauty of the flower-draped banners of green, white and gold. She had never suspected anything artistic about the Duffys or the Fallons. She supposed patriotism could achieve and inspire almost any art. She helped Gerty and her mother with the table, laying places for the guests and a few extra tables in case of unexpected arrivals. Some of the lads on the run, perhaps. When all was finished she offered to go into Cloona with last-minute messages for Gerty. There was the blue ribbon for Gerty, who clung tenaciously to the old superstition of something old, something new, something borrowed, something blue for the bride. Then she would drop a note into Pratt's letterbox and she would make an excuse to go into Matt Heaney's, leaving her bicycle in hopes that he might have a letter from Peter to place in her saddlebag. She was growing anxious as he had been gone almost a week now. Leaving Duffys' on her bicycle, Sally streaked down the hill, calling in at her home to check if her mother might need anything in the town. As she was passing Clanratty, the tin-hatted sentries called "Tommie" after her. She ignored them and pedalled quickly on. Suddenly her feet were spinning round and round. She braked and jumped, guessing that the chain had come off as it did when she rode too fast. But to her dismay she saw that the chain was broken, trailing like an oily serpent in the dust.

She wheeled the bicycle over to the wall, where she surveyed it anxiously. There was so much she had to do in Cloona. If she left the bicycle at some roadside cottage and walked, she would be late for most of the shops. While she sought frantically for a solution, a grey Leyland swung out through the castle gates. Seeing her predicament, the driver stopped. It was Lieutenant Sternitt, driven by an orderly. She explained what had happened and he offered her a seat to Cloona, which she gladly accepted. The orderly got out and put the bicycle in the back of the car. He appeared more interested in the bicycle than in the disappointment it caused or indeed in Sally's plight.

"Good old bikes they was – Rudge-Whitworth, 'ad one meself at 'ome." He wrapped the greasy chain in a bit of moss from the base of the wall and handed it to Sally.

In the car Lieutenant Sternitt quickly pulled an envelope from a pocket of his tunic. It was not addressed and carried no stamp but Sally knew it was destined for Matt Heaney's. Now she had it in her pocket and she wanted to be alone so she could read it. The car stopped outside Matt Heaney's. The orderly wheeled the bicycle in and she accompanied him, hoping that no one would notice her in a military car. Matt's son, Christy, the bank porter, sat smoking behind the wheel of the old hackney Ford parked in the street outside. Christy's eyes narrowed through the smoke, peering under the rim of his old felt hat with the hole in its crown. He claimed the hole was made by a Black and Tan bullet but Matt said it was a cigarette burn. Dave came in with Sally to see how long the repair might take and Matt reassured him he would have new links in the chain in less than half an hour. Sally was pleased. That would give her time to complete her shopping and there would be no need for Dave to take her home in the car. She gathered Gerty's blue ribbon and the other items. Then she sought the quiet of the nearby chapel where she eagerly opened Peter's letter. It contained no news of any importance. It was a long love letter and it made her very happy. She knelt and offered a quick prayer of thanksgiving.

Matt had the bicycle ready when she returned, the new links shining in the dark, oily chain. While he held the bicycle to help her tie her parcels, he whispered, "I wouldn't get too friendly with them officer fellows if I was you, Miss Glynn. You know the way things are now."

Sally understood Matt's warning was no reflection on the officers' character or morals. It was a warning against incurring the displeasure of the Shinners. She wondered why Matt had warned her now. She began to suspect Christy. As Matt spoke, Christy came up behind them. Matt turned and hurriedly dived into his shop like a water hen to its nest in the reeds. He was a little bird-like man with his oily waistcoat buttoned lightly over his little round stomach.

"What's my father warning you about now, Miss Glynn?"

"He's telling me to" – she hesitated for a moment – "he's telling me to keep my chain well oiled."

She somehow knew that he didn't believe her and that all was not well between Christy and his father. She would have to be careful now about Peter's letters and find some other way for Dave to pass them on. She began to doubt the wisdom of receiving them through Matt. The one she had in her pocket had been destined for that but for the happy coincidence of her broken chain and the military car. Sally rode home slowly and drew up alongside the Hazel Bridge. She wanted to read the letter again. She laid her hand on the stone parapet of the bridge and remained seated on her bicycle. Taking the letter from her pocket she read every word again. She wished he was here now to share the loveliness around her. On the sheltered side of the bridge, young beech leaves, like little green butterflies, basked in the gold shaft of the low-setting April sun and the silver leaves of tansy held the drooping red ringlets of stonecrop. She felt the letter again in her pocket and then, pushing a foot against the low stone wall, she urged herself forward down the hill for home.

Her heart was warm.

4

Easter Recollection

Easter week could be a dreary time. A slow procession of mourning and remembering the lost leaders of 1916. Michael and Geoffrey Barclay had not returned from the Fairyhouse races on Easter Monday 1916. A group of them had gone to Dublin on Saturday. Easter and the races were over but Michael, the two Barclays and Trooper had not returned. Then, the disquieting news that there was a rebellion in Dublin trickled through to Cloona. There were no trains and no newspapers, only the rumours of a rebellion and the city going up in flames. So many were dead and wounded, the hospitals full and the streets of Dublin red with blood. The rumours grew in horror. Tom and Sally were frightened and helpless to console their parents' anxiety over Michael.

Geoffrey, weary and footsore, arrived home after a week. The elation at his arrival was overshadowed by the confusion over the absence of Michael and Peter. Geoffrey had no idea where they were. He had parted with them in Dublin when he went to look after Trooper and the horse, since they required a separate wagon going direct to Fairyhouse. Geoffrey, home on leave from the war in France, had a horse running at Fairyhouse. He had taken Trooper, then a workman at the Barclay house, to look after the horse.

He did not see Michael or Peter at the races. It had never occurred to him that they had not returned home. Geoffrey returned to France and the family relapsed into the state of anxiety his temporary return had alleviated. He was due to marry a French girl in London. He said that her family had been kind to him in France. When Sally was still a schoolgirl she thought she was in love with Geoffrey. She thought he was in love with her as he put her in front of him on the horse's saddle with his arm around her waist and her hair brushing against his cheek. She knew later that it was not love but a storybook romance – the "prince riding away with her to his castle" sort of thing, she decided.

Her love for Peter, Geoffrey's younger brother, was real love. She had no feeling of jealousy for the French girl whom Geoffrey intended to marry. She never met her and she never saw Geoffrey again. He was killed at the front in France shortly after his return. She sometimes saw pictures in the papers of troop trains leaving London for Dover on their way back to the war, the soldiers' wives and sweethearts clinging to them. For many it would be their last embrace. Were Geoffrey and his new wife there, somewhere in the crowd? How would she herself feel if Peter was now going into the battlefields?

The war in France was over now. It was at last quiet there. Only a warm breeze stirred the poppies on Geoffrey's grave. There is war here now, everywhere around, she thought sadly. No going over the top, but there were ambushes and prisons. Executions and firing squads. A different sort of war having the same pitiful ending. Peter was in the British Army now. His regiment in Clanratty was moving out on Monday, returning to England. She hoped events might be safer there. It was this hope that made parting a little less difficult.

A few days after Geoffrey's departure, Michael returned – his arm bandaged, his coat thrown loosely over his shoulders. He said that Peter had been arrested, but Peter arrived the following day with no battle scars. The only thing different about him were the shabby ill-fitting clothes, which he had not worn going away. Both Michael and he had taken part in the rebellion and in the battle in the GPO and the College of Surgeons. They had arranged it with the other medical students before they came home for holidays amid speculation that there would be a call to arms. They never intended to go to Fairyhouse with Geoffrey.

Trooper, with the horse, arrived home some days later and gave a detailed account of his adventure and the hazards he had overcome. The horse, Pegasus, had won and Trooper declared it the happiest day of his life. He was anticipating the welcome that would await him on his homecoming. The train they were returning on was halted some distance from Dublin. No one knew why. The train driver had received instructions not to proceed but had been given no reason. The train with the wagons and their horses drew up behind the passenger train. Trooper went along to find Geoffrey and to investigate how long they would have to wait. He was quite indignant that the train carrying Pegasus should be stopped for any reason. They could hear the din coming from Dublin. They concluded that there was something very wrong in the city.

"They were all drunk. Sure everyone got drunk on Easter Monday after the seven dry weeks of Lent, but they must have been very drunk to stop the train," Trooper said.

The first news came with the arrival of the refugees. Weary and bewildered, they gave different accounts of what it was all about. One woman was convinced it was the Germans. A man, addressing Geoffrey, advised, "If I was you, sir, I wouldn't venture into the city in that uniform. There's dead soldiers and dead horses all around the streets."

The noise grew louder as the number of refugees grew in number. Daylight was fading and anxiety was growing. A few were optimistic enough to think the night would bring quiet and they could go home to their beds. Geoffrey became worried as he had to rejoin his regiment the following day. He suggested that Trooper and he bypass the city and find a road somewhere to follow. They were on the west side of the city and perhaps they could get onto the railway line, but there was the problem of the horse. The jockey who rode him to victory lived nearby and he offered to look after the horse until the trains began to run again. Trooper would not be separated from the horse, but he accepted the jockey's hospitality for a night. Then he rode the horse homeward each day and stayed at a farmhouse each night, where the horse and himself were well looked after. Some of his hosts knew of Pegasus' win and felt privileged to accommodate him. Trooper's return to Cloona was not what he had anticipated: just a tired old man and a tired old horse glad to get back to their home and stable.

Geoffrey travelled alone over the fields and got onto the railway line, joining others in the same predicament as himself. Some lay exhausted, sleeping on the grassy verges along the railway. Others burdened themselves with things not likely to be of use to them in their self-imposed exile. One man carried an empty birdcage. An old man carried his dog, aptly named Flithers, responsible for the empty birdcage. When Geoffrey finally arrived home, he was disappointed to learn that Michael and Peter had not returned. He had not seen them since he parted from them at the station. Since he did not see them at the races he concluded they had gone home before him.

Sally, restless, arose from where she was sitting on the bed. She went to the window. The evening was slipping into twilight but she could still catch glimpses of the lake through the trees and it brought back happier memories of Easters past. The first outdoor holiday of the year, when the boat was taken out from its winter mooring and the men carried it down and slipped it into the jetty. She thought nostalgically of Easters when she had played with Tom and Michael, the Duffys, the Daltons, the Fallons and the other children down by Lough Allen or over at the Crag or on the Sheep Slopes. On the Hazel Bridge spanning the road to Cloona, they fished for minnows in the river below. The little things she would always remember. Like wading out into the ice-cold water to see the hammock of the water hens' nest in the reeds. The time Tom pushed the boat out quickly as she balanced in the prow. She had unbalanced and fallen into the water and had to wade out, drenched. Tom was sorry about it and lit a fire of furze and bracken to dry her shoes and stockings and warm her feet. Once, Tom had caught a newt. When she stood staring at it in terror he told her it was a "mankeeper" and that if she screamed it would jump down her throat. But Michael said, "Don't be afraid Sally – it is more frightened than you are." He took the pulsing body of the little beady-eyed reptile from Tom's hand and placed it back among the stones at the water's edge. Turning to Tom, he chastised him, but Tom only laughed and shouted, "I'll teach you courage, Sally. I'll make a soldier of you."

But pacifist Michael said, "Girls don't need to be soldiers. They only need to be kind and gentle."

As she waited in the silence of her room, she heard the sad cries of the whooper swans flying over from the Shannon. She recalled the story Michael had told her. They were, legend had it, the Children of Lir. He told her the story, and in her expansive childish fancy, she had dreamt of making nests of plaited reeds for them. When they came there, she would put her arms around them and she would take them into the house to warm themselves.

Tom's welcome knock on the door broke the chain of her memories.

"Rosary, Sally."

She knelt with the family and hurried impatiently through the Rosary. With the final Amen she arose from her knees and, bidding a hasty goodnight, quietly slipped away to her bedroom, hoping she might inspire the others to do likewise. She closed the door and stood with her hand on the knob; her ear strained to catch every sound from the kitchen. She knew the routine and was surprised when she heard Tom's light footsteps. He had finished his prayers quickly tonight. She recalled that he had appeared almost as impatient as she and hurried his prayer. This was most unusual. With relief she heard his bedroom door close behind him. That was one counted off. She heard the others disperse and she moved towards the window to look out, before lighting her candle and drawing the curtains. The moon was high in the clear April sky and the night air was clean and cool as crystal. Across the dry white paving stones of the yard, the reflection of the still-bare branches appeared as charcoal drawings. Through the leafless boughs she could see the glimmering of the lights in the cottage windows on the mountain. Only the steady red glow distinguished them from the white gold and silver of the starry night.

Tom returned to Maynooth. Jack Dalton had called for him in the car as he, too, was returning. That solved Tom's transport problem. How was Hugh going to get the car back? Sally wondered.

"Kitty!" her mother answered.

Kitty and Tom together! Then she realised that Jack was with them. Now that Tom had gone, the house had that peaceful, quiet, almost lonesome atmosphere it always had when Tom returned after holidays. Sally would miss his preaching, provocative as it was at times. In Maynooth he would be safe from a Black and Tan bullet or from landing in an English jail. She was uneasy about the trench coat and revolver in the hay. What had he done with it? He must have arranged for someone to collect it. Last night she had heard light footfall on the gravel outside her window. Had someone come for the coat? Or was Tom out there when the cherry tree was cut down? Was that the reason he had not rushed out with the others to see it? Was it sorrow or was it guilt? Now Kitty had gone with them to Maynooth. Sally tried to sort out the relationship that appeared to be growing between them. There could be no question of a romance. Sally thought that Tom would not be altogether Kitty's choice in any case. If it had been tall handsome Michael she could understand. But Sally didn't like the way Kitty flopped so close to Tom on the sofa, almost sitting on his knees. Or the way she pulled him around when they were out together in the meadows. All the advances were made by Kitty. Tom's reaction was one of indifference and, at times, embarrassment. But no one could ever be sure of Tom's reaction to any situation. He was going to be a priest. What would Kitty think if she, Sally, behaved like that with her brother Jack?

Kitty had not yet returned, and as curfew time came, they were all concerned. None more so that Gerty Duffy, who had invited Kitty to be her bridesmaid. Kitty was all rigged out and had her dress, hat and shoes. But Kitty herself was missing. Kitty worked in the post office. The postmistress had sent a message to the Daltons to ask if she was ill when she didn't turn in for work as usual. Hugh, her brother, did not know anything about Kitty, only that she had travelled to Maynooth with Jack and Tom Glynn. Hugh sent a messenger to Glynns'. He thought they perhaps would know something, but it was the same reply. She had not returned from Maynooth. She had taken so much time off from the post office, it was imperative she soon return. She had already sought and gained permission to be off for Gerty's wedding.

It was midday when Kitty sauntered in wearing a jaunty new hat. She gave a not-so-convincing account of her delay. The car had run out of petrol about ten miles from Maynooth. Two students heading for Maynooth in a two-seater car took Jack with them, leaving Tom and herself to await help from whatever source it might come. After a long wait, a car with five passengers came along. The driver gave them a spare half tin of petrol but it was then too late to go to Maynooth.

"Dublin was much nearer. We went and stayed in Linda's flat. Captain

Long, Linda's officer friend, was there. He was not in uniform," Kitty said.

"I hope not," Sally exclaimed. "Tom would not enjoy that company. And the sleeping arrangements? You told me once there were only two beds in Linda's room. I hope Tom didn't have to share with Linda's officer!"

"Oh no!" Kitty said. "Captain Long had to leave before curfew. I had the spare bed in Linda's room and Tom slept on the old sofa in the sitting room."

"I hope he is none the worst for it," Tom's mother said. "Where is he now?"

"He is in Maynooth, of course," Kitty said, as if his mother doubted her and was not quite satisfied with Kitty's explanation. Then Kitty pulled off her hat and whirled around the room to provide an all-round view of her newly bobbed hair.

"Like it?"

Sally thought at first she was referring to the new hat but immediately saw it was the hair.

"I do like it," she said slowly, hesitantly, but truthfully. She liked the way the dark curls framed Kitty's elfin face.

Her mother remained silent, her face a frozen stare as if she had witnessed something hard to believe. To her it was a reckless thing to do. Her eyes widened and shifted from Kitty to Sally, doubtless thinking what a disaster it would be if Sally decided to have her golden tresses off and become a slave to such a barbarous fashion.

Sally told Kitty of the post office messenger and Gerty's worry about her not coming back last night.

"You should go to Gerty's now," Sally said.

"I have been to Gerty's. I'm coming from her now. I showed her my hat and my hair. I got the hat for the wedding. The one I had is too big now with my hair cut."

Sally knew how Kitty would always try to give the impression that anything she did was to oblige someone. Now it was in Gerty's interest that she had bought the new hat.

"What did Gerty say to that?"

"She was delighted."

"I bet she was more delighted to see yourself than the hat or the hair."

Sally returned again to the matter of Linda's flat and asked if Tom had waited all morning in Dublin while she had her hair bobbed and bought a new hat.

Kitty avoided answering by dashing through the door with the excuse: "I must bring the car back. Hugh may be wanting it."

5

The Wedding

The violins playing in the barn drew the dancers from the house. Gerty and Frank were heading off on their honeymoon, blessed with goodbyes from their guests. As they left, they were pelted with rice. Chris Heaney was driving them to the station. A few old shoes and cans tied to the back of the car added to the noisy send-off. Only those too old to dance or those too interested in the barrel of porter under the stairs remained in the house to console Mick Duffy and his wife over the loss of their daughter and to reassure them of the splendid match she had made. Kitty was there enjoying the sensation her bobbed hair had created and aware of having stolen the admiration from the bride. Sally and Michael were among the dancers. Through the noise of the tapping feet came the buzz of a car or lorry creeping through the din.

The rasping violins came to a halt. The hoarse whisper of "Tans" soon froze all to a standstill, palpitating from a mixture of fear and exertion. However, it soon became evident that the noise was not a lorry or the terrifying Crossley armoured car. The revelation came as a relief. Around the bend came Chris Heaney's old Ford, returning with the bride and groom.

A bridge had been blown up along the railway line. There were no trains, so Gerty and Frank joined the dancers in the barn.

Michael left before curfew time but Sally remained and was delighted with the prospect of a whole night of dancing. She was a good dancer and had more partners than she could cope with. But since Gerty and Frank's return there were no requests for her to dance. Bow-legged hoydens were finding partners despite the fact that men were scarce with so many on the run. Sally sat alone. As the dancers passed they didn't notice her; they just whispered to each other. She realised that she was a wallflower. She could sit there no longer. She must find out why. She went in search of Gerty. "What's the matter with me, Gerty? I feel like a leper. Everyone's keeping away from me."

"You were out driving in a car with soldiers from Clanratty yesterday evening, weren't you?" Gerty's answer came fast, as though she had been expecting the question.

"I was not. My bicycle chain broke and I got a lift in an army car. I was in a hurry more about your business than my own."

Gerty didn't accept Sally's explanation. Indeed, she scarcely wanted to listen to it as she rapped out a further accusation. "You were also at a dance in Clanratty with Peter Barclay at Easter and," Gerty continued firmly, "Peter Barclay is not one of us, because he wears the uniform of the British Army."

"He didn't always wear that uniform. He fought alongside Michael and the rest of them in 1916."

"More shame on him for deserting them! If it hadn't been for Michael's fight for freedom and Tom's sympathy for it, you would have had your hair docked long ago."

Sally's temper was rising; she was about to give Gerty a piece of her mind. Docked! It sounded so crude; the word referred only to horse tails. Sally was losing composure. Her temper was balanced on a knife-edge. Just then Frank came along in search of his wife. He, like all the others, knew of Sally's position, and seeing her in conversation with Gerty, guessed by their raised voices just what it was all about. He moved closer and out of hearing of the guests to extricate Gerty from the argument.

"We mustn't let any further incident spoil our evening. This is Gerty's and my wedding day."

"Incident! The only thing I am sorry for is coming to your wedding. You could have told me last night what you told me now. You could have told me before Michael left. I could have gone home with him before curfew."

"We didn't know," Gerty blurted. "We only heard it on the way to the station."

"Christy Heaney told you? You certainly weren't long in spreading the news when you got back." That Gerty should act so readily upon gossip filled Sally with anger and disgust. "I'm going home." She turned quickly to get her coat.

Frank held out a restraining hand. "You can't, Sally. It's curfew."

"Curfew or no curfew, I'm going."

She found her coat bunched with others. She pulled it out and put it on as she hurried through the hall. Outside on the doorstep she fastened the coat and attempted to put her hands in the pockets, but the flap of one was buttoned down. She seldom buttoned her pockets unless she had letters or something needing extra protection. She could not recall buttoning it. She put her hands in the pocket and drew out a letter. By the dim light of the hall she read the address. It was to Lieutenant Sternitt. How did that get into her pocket? Then it dawned on her. It was Kitty Dalton's coat. Their coats were similar. She hurried back with it and, finding her own, she put the letter safely into her own pocket and buttoned down the flap on Kitty's empty pocket and returned the coat to where she had found it. As she left the house and walked down the avenue, she could hear the voices of the revellers raised in song. It was a popular lament dedicated to the lads on the run. She knew it well. Unconsciously she walked to the rhythm of the tune until distance broke her link with it.

As she left the avenue, she realised how very alone she was. The long stretch of sandy road was visible in the moonlight, but where it dipped into the hollow, it was lost in the shadows. At any time the headlamps of a Crossley might pierce the darkness or the crack of a rifle shot might echo through the trees, shattering the silence of the night. The only sound was her own feet, now slowing from the rapid pace of her flight from the house. Slower and slower they moved until she stood still. A bleating goat-like call of a snipe streaked through the air above her. It seemed to mock her, to laugh at her foolish bravado. It seemed to tremble on the air and vanish, leaving the silence to be broken again by the redshank's lonely call, lonely as the moor below and the long shadow of road that lay before her. Uncertain, in a rare mood of panic, she wavered. Ought she to go back? Should she pocket her pride, accept further humiliation by trying to explain the innocence of her seemingly nefarious car ride with Lieutenant Sternitt, apologise for it and promise to ignore him and all other men in British Army uniform, including Peter Barclay? This last thought decided her course. She would not give up Peter. Even if he was a Protestant, he was just as Irish as the Duffys and the Fallons and all the rest of them. He had fought in 1916, which was more than a lot of them had done. It wasn't his fault that the rebellion was a failure.

"To hear Gerty talking, everyone would think Peter had betrayed the whole movement," she thought out loud.

No, she would not give him up. He was Michael's friend in 1916 and friendship is not broken by a change of uniform. Holding her head high and bracing her shoulders, she strode along near the grass verge so that the sandy margin muffled her footsteps, her eyes and ears alert for the hum of an engine or a flash of light in the night sky. Then, in the hollow beyond the Kesh, a shadow flitted across her line of vision. Heart pounding, she stood and stared into the half-light, trying to pierce the darkness and the shadows. Then she saw it again as it flitted past a silver screen of blackthorn blossom. It was followed by another shadow. Two men.

Sally moved slowly over to the clay fence, keeping her eyes on the dark corner of the wood. As her feet stumbled over the rough roadside grass, she lost sight of the two figures. They emerged again for an instant, silhouetted against the blossom of the hedge that ran parallel to the road. She followed the shadows until they emerged, slinking silently like two hunted animals. She saw them crouch low and cross the road before striking into the pasture field. They disappeared from her sight but she knew they crept along the mud bank that would take them into the avenue leading to Duffys'. Curiosity overcame her fear as she hurried back along the road and stood at the gateway, watching the spot where the two men would enter the avenue. She saw them come into view and then stand silent and still like the tree trunks behind which they sheltered. Then, as they proceeded slowly and cautiously towards the house, she recognised them. Terry Duffy and Jim Fallon. They were on the run and were taking a chance because of Frank and Gerty's wedding. Sally was glad she had left before their arrival. The patriotic anti-British mood would intensify and she would feel like a traitor and alien among them.

She hurriedly retraced her steps along the verge. The light was now getting brighter, as though the clouds that had screened the two fugitives were drawn apart. The silver face of the moon lit up the sandy road. Then, slowly the moonlight lost its glow when the unmistakable lights of motor headlamps lit up the sky beyond the wood. Sally heard the far-away drone of an engine. The engine grew louder as the distance shortened. Then suddenly all was peaceful and quiet. Sally stopped. The noise was either a Tan or military car. It could not be anything else after curfew. But why had it stopped? It couldn't be an ambush; otherwise she would have heard shots. Perhaps Terry Duffy and Jim Fallon had felled a tree across the road. This would guarantee their safety from approaching lorries. If that was so then the lorry would start up and return to Cloona or Clanratty. She would hear the noise and see the sky light up again. Not until then would it be safe for her to move on.

She watched and waited. The staring hurt her eyes. She closed them for an instant and trained them again on the distant darkness and then let them run over the thin line of the roadside edge. Her heart leapt. The hedge seemed to move. She wanted to scream but her throat wouldn't respond. Parched. She wanted to turn and run but her feet were fixed firmly to the ground beneath her. Her knees buckled and she sank to the shallow ditch under the hedge. The shape moved again and seemed to glide like a snake towards her. Then, to her amazement she saw what seemed like an illusion become very real. For streaming out on to the roadway was a dark, forbidding company of Black and Tans, sweeping along in the shadow of the fence, heading for Duffys'.

6

Surprise Guests

The Black and Tans came in crocodile formation towards Sally. Gradually they broke into small staggering groups like the wagons of a train that had derailed. They advanced at irregular intervals. Sally lowered her head so that her face would not be seen. She could hear the muffled tread of their approaching footfall. Sally's heart pounded as her thoughts raced. She forgot her own safety as she realised, in a flash, the ultimate destination of the crawling black serpent. There would be a raid on Duffys' in the presence of the lads on the run. If they swooped and the shooting started, God knows what would happen. There was such a lot of drink about as well, and the lads would be in a fighting and provocative mood. Surely they have scouts out, she thought hopefully. The memory of the porter barrels under Duffy's stairs, the frothing beer jugs and the bumpers of wine came back to her. Even scouts might fail in their duty on the night of a wedding.

I must go back. I must go quickly and tell them, she told herself, forgetting the humiliation she had suffered and the circumstances under which she had left.

Pushing herself upright, she stepped further back into the shadows of the hedge. Then, bending her body to the shelter of the high clay bank, she ran with bent knees to where a lone holly bush straddled the bank. Taking advantage of the cover, she slipped into a field. Following a path across the field, she would cut off a good triangle of road. It would be safer. If, by any chance, the tenders she suspected were parked in the shadows at the Kesh, they were certain to overtake her if she continued on the road. The grass was still short in the pasture fields but the bleached tufts of winter rye grass caught and tripped her feet. The cloying earth sods on the headlands stuck to the shoes she had danced in a few hours previously. A hare leapt from a furrow and startled her. His long hind legs kicked the loose clay from beneath him in his flight up the incline while she descended. At the end of the ploughed field, a high scrubby hedge of whitethorn barred her way. She ran its length, scanning for a gap through which she might crawl. It looked hopeless. Just then the low-hanging branches of a sycamore offered her the chance she was looking for. Grabbing an outstretched branch, she swung herself into the fork of the tree trunk. The field beneath dropped sharply, and the bank sloping towards it was steep and dense with young sycamore and ash saplings. Gently, she dropped down and, bending the saplings back, she crept carefully through. As she lowered her head to loosen her dress from jutting spurs of briar and undergrowth, the flexible young ash slipped from her hands and slapped her in the cheek with its clubbed black buds.

Fleet as the frightened hare, she skipped from stone to stone in the slimy cattle pond at the bottom of the field. Now, only a high clay ditch lay between her and Duffys' avenue. She hurried towards it. Leaping onto a narrow foothold, she grabbed the tuft of stonecrop on its loose stone top. The shallow rootlets came away in her hand and she fell back onto the grass. Hastily discarding the cheating handgrip, she climbed over. Steadily and purposefully. Breathless and dishevelled, her hands scratched and bleeding, she stood trying to place the approaching Black and Tans. She spotted them by the hedge. She was well ahead of them. They still had a long stretch of road and the length of the avenue to travel. She had only the corner of a level pasture field to go. Slowing her pace to recover her breathing, she moved along the cart track towards the back of the house.

The barn was deserted. She ran through the back door into the kitchen. There, guests were noisily engaged in shaking the hands and slapping the backs of Terry and Jim. She could scarcely see the faces of the two men as the crowd surged around them. She shouted "Tans!" many times before her voice penetrated the din. When the crowd drew back she saw the lean hungry jaws and the hunted look on the two faces. It hurt her to think that it was she who had to spoil the glory that was theirs. Their brief welcome had become a farewell.

"The Tans – they're coming! I saw them. Hurry! Hurry! The lorry is at the Kesh. Go! Oh, go! Now!"

"Don't believe Sally Glynn," Gerty said. "She wants to spoil the night for everyone 'cause she spoiled it for herself."

Sally ignored Gerty's allegations. Going over to Terry, she laid her hands upon his arm. "I saw them," she said. "I tell you! I crossed the fields. Look at my hands!" She displayed her torn and bleeding palms.

"You wouldn't make a fool of us, Sally. You wouldn't be Michael Glynn's sister if you did," Terry said slowly, and he put his arms around her. "Oh, Sally, your hands – they're bleeding."

"Don't mind them. Just go! Go!" Sally began to shake him.

"Fancy Sally Glynn coming to save us all," sneered Gerty.

"Whisht, Gerty! Sally's right. Come on, Jim," Terry said.

Their departure was slowed by people stuffing cigarettes and some of the wedding cake into their pockets. They shook off the generous hands and darted through the back door as swift as a trout across a stream. They zig-zagged across the yard keeping to the shadows.

"Back to the barn, lads. Back now, everyone, and on with the dancing. As ye were," Frank called out.

They trooped back and the fiddles started up again. They now recognised that Sally's warning was genuine. The idea was to divert the Tans from the house. Thus trying to prevent the usual savage orgy of wanton destruction: smashed china, ripped-open pillows and cushions and the hundred and one devilish acts the sight of a comfortable interior of an Irish farmhouse appeared to provoke in them. They would have no respect for a newly married couple's wedding presents.

"Something lively," Frank instructed the musicians. There followed a wild high-spirited pretence of enjoyment and they swung and bounded to the music of a reel.

Sally sat in the corner. In a quiet way she seemed to have stolen the adulation withdrawn so hastily from the departed warriors.

"It was great of you to come back, Sally. C'mon, we'll have a dance," Frank Fallon said, taking her hand in an attempt to pull her onto the dance floor.

"No, thanks. I don't want to dance," Sally said coldly, withdrawing her hand. "I appreciate your gratitude, Frank, but I still haven't promised to give up Peter Barclay, and I might even take a lift in Lieutenant Sternitt's car if the chain on my bike came off again."

"You're an awful divil, Sally, but I like a girl with spirit," Frank said in an effort to ease the awkward atmosphere. "Come and have a dance," he insisted.

"I don't want to dance, and even if I did I couldn't with these." She looked down at her torn stockings and muddied shoes.

"They're coming!"

Frank whirled Sally into the middle of the dancers.

A sharp command in the all too familiar Cockney rapped out as the Tans pushed through the door.

"'Ands up, every mother's son of you!"

The men raised their hands almost with indifference.

"'Igher, 'igher! Come on! Put 'em up 'igher!" the voice bellowed.

Reluctantly, hands crept slightly higher. The gimlet eyes of the Tan sergeant followed them until his lids seemed to be drawn to the floral green, white and gold of the low ceiling.

"'Oo's put up them colours?" he asked "'Oo owns this 'ouse? 'Oo put up dem colours?" He waited for the answer that didn't seem to be coming from the dancers.

"You!" He pounced, punching the ribs of Jock Hanley, who happened to be next to him. Jock, half-drunk, was preoccupied with keeping his balance, with his hands in such an unhelpful position.

"'Oo put up dem colours?" He pointed to the ceiling.

Jock's hazy eyes followed the revolver-pointing, black-cuffed hand.

"Oh, the flowers, is it?" he asked, with almost sober interest. "Sure they grew there."

"You bloody Irish think the English fools, don't you?" the Tan sergeant snarled.

"We do, sir," Jock answered, drunkenly polite and relaxing his upstretched hands so that they fell heavily to his sides.

"Keep yer 'ands up, you blasted thug!" the Tan roared.

Jock's drunken indifference vanished. "Who you calling a thug?" he said, squaring his shoulders and putting up his fists.

It was frighteningly evident to everyone that Jock intended to hit the Tan. Frank Fallon, sober enough to realise the danger, stepped forward.

"We decorated the roof with what flowers were available. They were the only colours."

"'Oo are you?" the Tan inquired.

"I'm the bridegroom," Frank answered.

"Where's the bride?"

"She is inside helping her mother with the supper."

"Inside where?"

"Inside in the house."

"So this is outside?" the Tan noted sarcastically. "If it is, you're breaking the curfew and I'll arrest the lot of you."

"We got permission off the sergeant in Cloona to have a dance in the barn."

The Tan swung around, walked across the yard, opened the back door and went in, followed by his minions with their revolvers and rifles. They soon discovered the barrels under the stairs, together with the wine and whiskey. They lost no time in having their fill. The consequences of their orgy soon became apparent. Some, in a dazed and drunken stupor, lay in corners. Others became more aggressive and arrogant. They reached up with rakes, spades and any other implement they could lay hands on and hauled down the flower arrangement from the barn ceiling. After this, those with a little more sobriety rounded up the squad and left in drunken disorder.

Terry and Jim were given the signal to return when the Tans were safely away, and they all tried to take up where they had left off. But the riotous departure of the Tans had left the wedding party eerily quiet. Like a calm after the storm.

Those who had anticipated a night of glorious revelry looked forlornly at the empty barrels and bottles. Jock Hanley, swaggering around on unsteady legs, rejoiced at the amount of liquor he had deprived the Tans of by freely indulging himself earlier in the night. The dancing continued in the barn but because of the long night stretching away to curfew's end the next morning, the pleasure of dancing became a toil. The weight of enjoyment lay heavily on the guests. The seats around the walls filled up with exhausted, sleepy bodies. Even the endless chain of cups of tea could not stimulate the ladies. The entertainment was flogged along by patriotic songs and recitations drawn by voices as tired of singing as their feet were of dancing.

Mr O'Dea, the school teacher from Clare, stood up to recite "Who Is Ireland's Enemy?" Many had heard this from O'Dea so often that they knew it off by heart and chanted the lines with him as though they were in the classroom. He raised his hands to command silence, licked his lips, and with a few extravagant arm gestures, started off again in his infamous fiery rhyming oratory.

"Oh, who is Ireland's enemy? / Not Germany, nor Spain. Not Russia, France nor Austria / They forged for her no chains." To make his recitation more convincing and patriotic he roared two words – "BUT ENGLAND!" – springing his dozing audience into wakefulness. Then, lowering his voice to a whisper to make it sound more dramatic as though he was about to divulge a secret, he continued, "'Twas England scourged our motherland / 'Twas England laid her low!"

The uninterested listeners were about to nod off to sleep again when Mr O'Dea's mouth opened and then closed again, like a fish gasping on a riverbank. His eyes became as fishy as his mouth as they goggled, unblinking, towards the door. The sleepy eyes around the wall followed his gaze and then all eyes goggled as froggily as his own at the sight before them.

There, in the open barn door, a sombre, silent figure with a gun in his holster, stood a lone Black and Tan. He was like a jackdaw that had fallen down a chimney and was dazed by his new surroundings. No one spoke for a while. Then, Jock Hanley, the hunger of the fight he had been deprived of still gnawing at him, grabbed the handle of the gramophone and, pointing it pistol-like at the Tan, roared, "Put 'em up! I'll plug ya, I'll plug ya!"

Breathless and inwardly cursing Jock's half-drunken bravado, all waited tensely for the drawn revolver and the volley of shots that might come from hidden men outside. To their amazement, the Tan raised his arms slowly above his head, as though he had forgotten about his revolver. There was fear in his small glittering eyes and his heavy jaw gave him the appearance of an erring cocker spaniel awaiting chastisement. Sally felt sorry for him. His head seemed too big for his body and his bandy legs and long upraised arms gave him a height that was deceptive. His command so promptly obeyed, Jock was at a loss for what action to take. The few seconds before Frank Fallon stepped forward and removed the Tan's revolver seemed like an eternity. Still suspecting a decoy or a hidden gun, the revellers remained at a distance until Frank and Mr O'Dea had tapped the Tan's pockets.

"What did you come back here for? What do you want?" Frank asked.

"I jus' wan' a drink – another drink," the Tan hiccupped, "an' then I'll go 'ome, go back to Blighty an stay there. Hi-depidle-e-ighty. Hurry me back to Blighty!"

It was evident he had lain in the open somewhere, as bits of moss and crisp dead leaves clung to his damp crumpled tunic. His company had lost him and left him behind, so he had strayed back to the lights in the windows of Duffys'. All fear left the guests. Convinced that no rearguard would follow him, they gathered around him as though he were some rare wild creature they had captured. They surveyed him at close quarters: a tame Black and Tan! Someone gave him a push and he staggered against the wall and stood there swaying. He leaned closer to the wall but both his feet slipped away and he slid slowly into a sitting position on the floor. The little black forage cap fell from his head but he groped it back with his long arms and clapped it on his close-cropped skull. The action seemed to be automatic. Two of the men tried to raise him to his feet in order to throw him through the door. They seized his tunic roughly, but he fumblingly undid the buttons and, letting them pull off the tunic, remained unruffled against the wall, his tattooed arms folded across his chest. The tunic was kicked about the floor until Jim Fallon rescued it.

"Wait, lads. This might come in useful sometime."

He picked up the tunic, shook the dust and debris from it, and took the forage cap from the blissfully indifferent Tan's head and stuck it into the sleeve of the tunic. He rolled the tunic into a ball and tossed it into a corner to await a safe hiding place. The Tan kept asking for his hat, which he seemed to miss more than the tunic. As his request became more persistent, some of the girls went out to where a scarecrow stood dressed, ready for taking to the cornfield. They removed its frock coat and bowler hat and pulled them onto the half-dressed Tan. The girls giggled as they decorated the faded green band of the hat with the trampled, wilted dandelions from the ceiling. Then they lifted the Tan and pushed him roughly through the open barn door.

The tipsy Tan sprawled on all fours across the stones. The bowler hat rolled off but he picked it up and replaced it on his head. Then he stood up, straightened himself, buttoned the frock coat, opened it and rebuttoned it, seemingly unaware of the change of garb. His feet seemed to be planted in the ground. They did not move as his body swayed backwards and forwards like a scarecrow in the wind as he tried to find within himself the necessary balance to walk. He kept muttering to himself, "Steady, the Buffs! Steady, the Buffs! Steady, the Buffs!" and, "Let the Lancers pass." He raised his voice, and with his last command he launched forward on a zig-zag course down the avenue. The laughing crowd followed him a little way and watched him disappear through the trees on his way back to Cloona barracks or the hazy destination of which he was as uncertain.

Sally did not join in the general merriment, although she was amused at the ludicrous figure. She feared the Tans would come back to look for their missing comrade.

7

Letters

A cold, grey dawn crept in from the east. With the approaching relief from curfew, Frank and Gerty prepared again for their departure. Their destination was Frank's home, two miles up the road. There was little ceremony about their going away as no one felt in the mood to confer the honour of throwing old shoes and heaping good wishes on them for a second time. They huddled tiredly into Chris Heaney's car and disappeared down the avenue once more. The exhausted guests began to disperse, with handshakes for Terry and Jim, whose future was so uncertain. Coats and hats and bicycles were being sorted when Mick Duffy, Gerty's father, came hurrying from the barn with the Tan's tunic and cap.

"Who's taking this?" he asked, as though a dead body was being left for him to dispose of.

No one appeared anxious to claim the souvenir.

"Throw it away or hide it," suggested Mick irritably.

"Someone had better take it away from this house. If there is any shindig kicked up when this fellow gets back to the barracks, this is the first place they'll search. You take it," he said, handing it to Jock Hanley.

Jock took it and handed it to the next man. The tunic was passed around until Jock took a box of matches from his pocket. "Here! Burn the damn thing and have it done with!"

But Jim Fallon rescued it again. "Wait, lads. It might come in useful. You can never tell." His eyes fell to Sally. "You, Sally," he said, "you take it home and tell Michael to hide it somewhere. There's no one on the run in your house and they won't be searching for it."

Sally didn't like the way Jim said that. It was as though the Glynn family had failed in their duty to their country. She hesitated, and Jim repeated, "Tell Michael. He'll hide it."

Without waiting for her consent, he placed the rolled-up tunic in her hands. Embarrassed, Sally stood there, uncertain what to do next. Why should she help them after the way they had treated her? She felt she had already helped them enough as it was. She was about to throw the tunic back among them when Terry Duffy, prompted by her previous embarrassment and hesitancy, and to relieve his own family from dangerous custody of the tunic, took it from her.

"Come on, Sally, I'll carry it for you as far as your own gate."

Placing a hand under her elbow, he escorted her and the tunic away from the little group and the vicinity of his own house. Where Duffys' Avenue came out of the trees onto the road, Sally witnessed again, in the dawn light, the hunted look come back into Terry's face. She reached out and took the tunic.

"I'll take it, Terry," she said. "You go back. There is no need to run the risk of walking the open road in near daylight."

"God bless you, Sally!"

There was relief in his voice and urgency in his retreating footsteps. Sally marched onwards, the Black and Tan's tunic under her arm. The dawn's smooth and fiery sea of light had surged across the eastern sky, leaving the yellow glow of the morning sun to pierce the low-lying mists by the river and over the bogs. It was as cold as an early May morning can be. Cold and crisp and stimulating. As she walked, Sally tried to shake off the fatigue, boredom and general disappointment of the night of which she had anticipated such enjoyment. Her last attempt at going home seemed like weeks ago, not mere hours. She wondered what would have happened if she had not decided to go back. It was good to realise that her actions may perhaps have saved Terry and Jim from arrest. They knew and appreciated that. However, Gerty appeared unable to forgive her having any truck with British Army officers. She came to the Kesh where the lorries had stopped. She saw the tyre tracks where they had pulled in on the grass verge. Little pimpernels had been crushed and the green spears of the wild arum lilies by the hedge lay flat to the ground. Spent matches and empty cigarette packets were strewn around. The place felt like the lair of a prowling beast. Sally walked quickly away from it to the opposite side of the road, where the rushy meadow sloped upwards from the pool of amber bog water. Her broken shoe strap was slipping off and she sat on the roadside to attempt to fix it.

As she sat quietly on the bank, she saw a little mallard with her ducklings, waddling in slow procession through the tall grasses towards the shrinking pond pools and the shelter of the rushes. Sometimes the little ducklings broke their ranks to get closer to the mother. The wavering moon was withdrawing now and it was bright enough now for Sally to read the letter in her pocket. She looked over her shoulder to make sure no one was around, unlikely as it was. As she lifted the loose flap of the envelope a letter fell from its folds. She caught it in its flight and saved it from falling on the dewy grass at her feet. She saw, to her amazement, the only word on a small inner envelope was "Sally", written in Peter's familiar hand. She stared blankly.

How did Kitty Dalton come by this? Why did Kitty have this? Had Kitty read the words that were written for her eyes alone? Peter said he would be going to Africa later in the year but he would have a month's leave before going. The prospect of the leave raised her spirits a little. He said he would write again when he knew a definite date. She looked at the letter again and read: "Later, later." She thought, How long is later? She wished he was here now. Her mind was a whirl of mixed thinking: the wedding, Gerty's accusations, the Tans and Peter's letter in Kitty Dalton's pocket.

Why was she sitting there? A sedge warbler's erratic song pierced the silence. It startled her, making her jump. She stood up to go then realised she was there because she had sat down to fasten the loose strap of her shoe. She put it right and felt again Peter's letter in her pocket. But the why and how of the letter having been in Kitty's pocket kept nagging at her. There was Tom, but Tom could only receive it through Kitty. The post office? She could not accuse Kitty of anything as nefarious as interfering with the letters in the office. Then she remembered Kitty had been one of the swimmers in the tide against her at the wedding. Sally was walking away when she saw the Tan's tunic in the grass. Her mind was so preoccupied with the letter, she had nearly forgotten the tunic. As she neared the house, the disposal of the tunic loomed larger in her thoughts. Fear assailed her. Suppose, she thought, the Tan did not return to the barracks and was discovered dead somewhere. And suppose they found his tunic in her possession. Suppose they thought that she … She conjured up all sorts of supposes. Perspiration beaded her forehead. She wiped it away with her hanky, along with the thoughts that had provoked it. She trailed through the wooden gate into the yard. Chess pawed her coat and sniffed the tunic. As she reached the back door, she considered the doubtful wisdom of bringing the tunic into the house. It wasn't the sort of parcel you left on the table and said, "Jim Fallon told me to give you this, Michael." No. There was a lot of explaining to be done to Michael, out of earshot of her mother.

She decided to hide the tunic herself and tell Michael when the time was opportune. She thought of the fodder bed in the trap house, where Tom had hidden the trench coat. While she looked for a fork to lift the hay she put the tunic down. Chess sniffed and pawed it with curiosity. This made her decide to find another hiding place. Chess would only rummage it out again from here. She went into the stable. She climbed onto the highway of the horses' manger and, balancing like an acrobat by one hand from a rafter above it, carefully pushed the tunic into a hole in the gable wall. No one ever went in there except the swallows darting in and out to their nests in the rafters, and only her own slim body could access its cobweb-festooned darkness. Only then did she breathe easier.

She jumped down again. "Come on, Chess," she called, and with Chess at her heels she entered the kitchen.

Sally had only a few hours' sleep. Later that morning she struggled out of bed, yawned and stretched, as though she had awakened from a dreadful dream of Black and Tans, the tunic and a very angry Gerty Duffy. But alas it was not a dream; it was all too real. She got dressed slowly. She had to go into Pratt's office to make up for her time off. She was sure he had letters for her to type and post. She wished she didn't have to go in today. Now, passing Clanratty gates would be something of an ordeal since the rebuff she got from Gerty for speaking to and fraternising with Lieutenant Sternitt. Suppose she met him again? Was she to speak to him? It seemed to her wrong to ignore his polite greeting. No doubt she could avoid him but she would have to sacrifice the pleasure of Peter's letters. She had no intention of doing that. Why should she? Surely she wasn't afraid of Gerty? She recalled Gerty's tirade with rising indignation and decided she wasn't going to be put out by her. Why should she be intimidated? She wrote a short letter to Peter telling him she had received his letter with the news of going to Africa. Cautious of Kitty, she suggested that Peter register the letters to Dave, without offering a reason. She gave no reason for it. She wanted to post it on Kitty's day off from the post office.

Her mother wanted to hear all about the wedding so that she could write and tell Tom. Sally said it would take too long now and she would give her all the details when she returned. She dawdled through the gap in the road and stood again by the pasture gate to watch the slow gracious flight of a dragonfly: the beauty of its opaque greeny-blue enamel body and gauzy, lacy wings, skimming slowly above the fairy speedwell and wild strawberry blossom. There was, for Sally, always time to admire beauty.

Then she pedalled fast past Clanratty gates, glancing at the entrance where two sentries were walking backwards and forwards behind the barbed wire fence. She hurried on, secure in the knowledge that it was Kitty's day off, and she had no hesitation in posting her letter to Peter. When she entered the post office, she was surprised to see Kitty there in her usual place behind the counter. As she came forward to speak to Sally, she explained why she was there on her day off. It was, of course, because of the days she took off to go to Maynooth and the wedding. Since she found the letter in Kitty's pocket, Sally came to the conclusion she would have to maintain a more cautious friendship with Kitty. It was Kitty who brought up the obvious topic of the wedding.

"How did you enjoy the wedding, Sally?"

"Wonderful!" Sally lied.

"I was sorry about all the fuss Gerty made of Chris Heaney's story, but you know Chris."

"Do I?" Sally said in an amused sort of way, remembering who Kitty had allied herself with at the wedding.

"I had to side with them, being Gerty's bridesmaid and all. You know how it is."

"I don't know how it is. How is it?" Sally laughed. "Sure it was all great fun."

She wanted to give Kitty the impression that she was more amused than annoyed at the whole affair. She knew Kitty was trying to excuse her own attitude at the wedding.

"Of course you were Gerty's bridesmaid. There is no need to apologise, Kitty."

"You were great to take the tunic, Sally," Kitty continued. "What did you do with it?"

"I burnt it," Sally said. "A can of paraffin and a match disposed of that. I tied all the buttons together and tossed them into the Shannon. They must be near Limerick by now."

She was amazed at her ability to answer all Kitty's questions without having to think. She would not post Peter's letter when Kitty was there. She would go to the railway station and give it to the guard on the train. She had often done this when she was late for the mail out from the post office. Sally got the stamps and went to the letterbox outside to post Pratt's letters. She saw the Leyland car parked a short distance away. Dave got out and came towards the letterbox. He stood beside Sally. Sally dropped one of the letters. Dave picked it up and gave it to her with the one he had for her from Peter.

8

Rory Duffy

Clouds raced across the wind tracks in the long grass of the meadows, becoming one with the shadows in the hills. On the grassy sun-washed tracks, dandelions bobbed like water lilies in a pond of greens. Sally hurried along the springy turf paths to the Crescent Acre, where Michael, with Scarva pulling the heavy iron, rolled the sparse beard of the new corn. She had been to Cloona in the morning and now it was afternoon. She still felt the weariness of last night's rest but also she had to tell Michael about the previous night. She would talk to him when he drank the little can of tea and ate the hot buttered potato cake that she carried in the white enamel dish. Then she had to hurry back in time to post her mother's letter to Tom. She had sorted the things she would tell Michael and the things she would leave untold. She would not mention the trip to Cloona in Lieutenant Sternitt's car, nor the displeasure her continued friendship with Peter Barclay had caused. A frown furrowed her smooth white forehead when she recalled Gerty's accusation: "He's not one of us, and if Michael and Tom knew ..." Why should Gerty should concern herself with what Michael and Tom knew? She shouldn't bother with Michael and Tom, least of all with Tom, about whom she appeared to know more than his own family. And Tom was only home for about three months in the twelve, anyway. It was possible that Gerty was making a cat's paw out of him and was responsible for the trench coat in the hay. But now that she was going to live at Fallons', she would have more to do, and have less time for Shinners' activities.

Sally decided she would tell Michael things he would like to hear: the triumph of Terry Duffy and Jim Fallon's escape while the Black and Tans prowled about, and their return afterwards to enjoy the wedding; and about the stray Black and Tan being stripped of his tunic and revolver and sent home in the scarecrow's rig out with dandelions in his hat. But she would not tell him about her hiding the tunic, so that if, at any time, the Black and Tans questioned him about it or asked if he knew where it was, he could truthfully say he didn't. Neither would she tell him what Jim Fallon had said about giving the tunic to him to hide.

When she reached the headland by the cornfield, she put down the can and waved to Michael at the opposite end of the field. He turned the roller, with its hollow empty rattle, back towards her. He tied Scarva's rope reins about a tall excavated boulder and then sat on the red wooden tail shaft of the roller, his feet swinging at the back. Sally jumped up alongside him and gave him the dish of hot buttered cakes.

"You missed it, Michael. You missed all the fun. It was worth losing half a dozen nights' sleep."

"Bet there was nothing as good as this to eat," he said, picking up a neat triangle of his mother's potato bread and dangling a warm buttery corner into his mouth. As he ate, he listened with enjoyment to Sally's description of the things she wanted him to know.

"The Tan was such a daddy long legs of a thing – just a parcel of contradictions, all heads and hands and feet. He was like Loper, the way his face used to drop when you took a bone from him, only Loper looked more intelligent. You remember Loper, don't you, Michael?" She carefully avoided referring to her own part in the story.

When she finished, Michael asked, "What became of the tunic?"

Sally hesitated. "They kept it."

And before she could hurry away from her own answer, Michael demanded, "Who kept it? It's a dangerous sort of souvenir."

Sally jumped down off the roller shaft. Picking up the empty can and pie dish she said, "I must go."

"What's the hurry?"

"Mother is writing to Tom all about the wedding and I have to post the letter."

"Did you tell her all about the Black and Tans?"

"Yes."

"Tell Mother when you get back not to write until we hear what became of the boyo, or see if they come looking for the tunic at Duffys'. Tell her to leave the letter for a few more days. Are you going over to Duffys' tonight, Sally?"

"I hadn't thought about it. Why?"

"Perhaps we ought to go over for a while before curfew. They'll be feeling a bit lonely now, with Gerty married and Rory and Terry on the run. We'll both go over after tea," he said as he loosened Scarva's reins from the stone.

Sally hurried up the grassy path to the Poplar Gap and across the hill towards the house. As she went, she thought of Michael's concern for the loneliness of Gerty's mother and father, and of his willingness, after a hard day's work, to tramp all that distance to see them. Yet yesterday, when the wedding and the fun was on, he had only stayed a short while. But then it was so like Michael: he always did the right thing, the vital thing that others didn't even see or think of. As she climbed the hill, she felt the sun warm on her back, and a glow came to her cheeks with her exertion. The fatigue of the previous night still clung to her and slowed her steps. Before she entered the Long Meadow she paused to look at the orderly arrangement of a fairy ring of red fungi. She picked up the pale-blue eggshells tossed from the pigeons' nest. She looked at them and imagined the tiny silver doves they had released. The doves would grow up with Michael's field of corn and would be ready to plunder it. Michael would have to put a scarecrow out for them. The thought of the scarecrow reminded her of the letter her mother was writing to Tom. If she loitered deliberately, she would be too late for the post, and her mother would have to agree with Michael. Sally didn't really want to go off to Cloona with the letter now. She dawdled towards the gates onto the road, as she turned away, she saw her father approaching, but not with the customary hobble his lumbago only permitted. The rapid thrust of his stick on the road told Sally there was some pressure behind his labours. She quickened her pace to a trot. Oh, Tom, and his mother's letter, she thought. As if one day mattered. But it was impossible to convince her mother how needless her haste was regarding the letter. When she came within hailing distance of her father she shouted, "Will I be killed?"

But he did not answer with his customary little jokes he shared with his lively daughter. As the stretch of the road narrowed, Sally sensed that there was something really wrong; something more than an unposted letter. It's Tom, she thought. Always in moments like this her thoughts flew to Tom. He's home, or coming home. "He's leaving Maynooth," she muttered to herself. Already she was preparing herself for the news and the searching words of consolation to say to her mother.

"What's wrong, Daddy? There's something wrong. What is it?"

"It's Rory." He leaned heavily on his stick. "Rory Duffy was killed in the ambush at Red Bridge last night. Go back and tell Michael. He'd better come up and head over to Duffys'. Your mother has gone already."

"Rory Duffy?" Sally echoed slowly, handing the can and pie dish to her father, stunned. He took them from her and fumbled with them and the stick, letting the enamel dish fall. It bounced on the road. Stooping, Sally picked it up and handed it to him once more.

"Rory Duffy. Maybe he isn't dead. Maybe he is only wounded."

"I'm afraid he's dead, Sally. He's dead in Cloona barracks."

"Lord have mercy on him. Rory Duffy, Rory Duffy," she whispered as she turned back to tell Michael.

She skirted the red-tasselled alders, striding through the grey-green spears of the flaggers and tramping over the amber meadowsweet, shortening even the shortcut to the Crescent Acre. She called to Michael from the grassy headlands and then hurried home. When she went into the house, her father was sitting in his old armchair, fanning his warm red face with his hat. The pen and ink and the unfinished letter to Tom lay on the kitchen table. After a moment her father put his hat on the table and leaned forward, his hand on the crook of his stick, his eyes fastened on the smouldering turf fire.

"Where's Trooper?" she asked

"Gone to Duffys'."

"Michael and I are going as soon as he arrives."

"Your mother said you were to go immediately. Don't bother waiting for Michael. He has to put up the horse. Go now, they might be needing you."

Sally knew they couldn't be needing her any more than any other neighbour, but it was her father's idea that she was indispensable. She would only join the army of tea-makers and dishwashers who took over the running of a house when tragedy stunned the occupants and rendered them out of action. But she had better go. She threw turf on the fire and filled the kettle, leaving it near the open hearth in case her father would have to make his own tea in their absence. As she went into the trap house for the bicycle, she could hear Michael in the stable tying up Scarva. Her thoughts flew for an instant to the black tunic and forage cap behind the rafter. But she immediately dismissed the disturbing thought.

When she reached Duffys', Trooper came forward to meet her.

"I say, Miss Sally," he whispered, "Gerty has a black dress on her. Make her take it off. A mournin' bride is a mournin' wife. 'Tis an ould sayin' but a true sayin'. Make her take it off."

She scarcely heeded Trooper's superstitions as she answered. "All right" and went into the kitchen. She found the room full of people, mainly women, who were in turn consoling Mrs Duffy and praying aloud for Rory. And above the prayers came the muttered curses of Jock Hanley and Dan Hegarty, now sober, swearing vengeance on England.

9

Cuckoo

Michael Glynn stood on the brow of the hill, holding Raverty by the bridle. He had heard the first cuckoo call and he stood to listen to it. The sweet notes filled the warm, humid air of this May morning. The rain of the past week had given the trees a dripping naevus of leaf and blossom. Below in the big meadow, the sedge swamp, with its drooping masts of broken reeds, was covered by a new lush green. The rains had kept the flowers on Rory's grave fresh. The cross of purple polyanthus that Sally planted there had taken root already. The trampled grass had begun to creep towards it to start the healing work upon the scarred earth.

The cornfield had now become a shelter for corncrakes. The abandoned roller stood out like the brazen face of a trespasser. Michael was bringing Raverty down for the roller when he heard the cuckoo's call. To him it was the bugle call of remembrance, back to that May morning when Patrick Pearse, with his head held high, had walked out to face the firing squad at Kilmainham. There had been no bitterness in his face. Michael believed that Pearse was a visionary whose love of God and Ireland outshone any hatred that might have been. Michael had stood there then, listening to the cuckoo, just as now. Then he had pledged his life to God, as he had wanted to from the first time he had served Mass for the Franciscan missionaries who came to Kilalisheen. He would have gone then had he been old enough. But with the passing years, circumstances forced the course of his life into other channels. It had not altered his longing, which still remained. Not finally abandoned until Tom had gone to Maynooth. There was no choice left him save the duty to his parents. Michael sighed as he thought how this duty, pressing as it was at times, took second place to the almost overwhelming desire for the cloister of the Franciscan monastery. At odd intervals he had timidly brought up the matter for discussion, but always it had been met with the same resistance. Now that his father was almost an invalid with his lumbago, it put the final seal on the hopes of fulfilment of his deepest wish. His pleading and gentle persuasion had ceased, yet in his heart and in his soul the tumult of pent-up longing went on unabated.

The prospect of escape if Sally married some farmer – one of the Duffys or the Fallons, or even Hugh Dalton – who might have been interested in running the farm in Dooleagh from behind the counter of his shop in Cloona, gradually diminished. Sally would marry her own choice regardless of her mother's and Tom's plans, and it was becoming more evident that choice would be Peter Barclay. Michael wished it that way, despite the unpopularity Peter's position in the British Army had placed on him. Peter and he had played together as children and there would always be that link of their student days in Dublin. They had shared comradeship in the dangerous days of the 1916 rebellion. Now Peter was an Irish doctor in the British Army and could be sent to the most remote outposts of the Empire, and Sally would, of course, go with him. Suddenly the cuckoo's call sounded in his ear, startling him from his dreaming. Michael descended the hill with his hand on the horse's bridle, bringing back the roller that had been abandoned at the news of Rory's death. The corn was now green. He could see his father plodding along the grassy headland of the Upland Walk.

This grassy strip was John's favourite promenade. It was a sheltered, sunny spot where, slightly below him, he could see the farmhouse and its ring of outhouses, the flowering orchard and the rhododendron-flanked avenue. Beyond it he could see the fields, sloping away from the winding road down through the First Gap, the Long Meadow to the Crescent Acre and to Lough Allen beyond. Across the lake on the mountain, the sandy ribbons of road linked up the white cottages like pearls on a silver string. To his left was the Rock Road and the spire of Kilalisheen church. To his right the Hazel Bridge and the Crag, like a bit of lost mountain with the rocky bowl, known as the Witches' Cauldron, at its base. From there down to the lake was the part they called Folly Lane. And there was the Bracken Rise and the Sheep Slopes, where he had played as a child with his brother and sisters, and where his own children had played too.

It made him lonely to look at this old playground, and his eyes hurried away from it to the dark woods of Clanratty, and the grey patch in the sky that was the smoke of Cloona. Then he turned to look behind at the hedges that screened him from the east wind and the Elsin, which separated his land from his neighbour's. Sheltering whin hedge was the barrier between his well-husbanded field and his neighbour's jungle of briar, gorse and bracken, and the more prolific type of vegetation that sought and found this happy breeding ground – hazel saplings, mountain ash and the wild broom all pushed and jostled each other. John knew them all, for this hill of trim potato ridges had been wrested from the tangle many years previously by his father, and he had kept at bay the long line of gorse at his back, now in orderly retreat, but always ready to begin again the forward march on their territory.

The May sunshine brought the warm spicy odour of the whins to John's nostrils. The little black wild bees filled his ears with their sharp staccato hum. It was pleasant to sit here on the bleaching roots of an excavated tree and enjoy the sun and the sounds of the fields. At his feet he watched a bumblebee sharing the edge of a dandelion. He could hear its low hum like a bass voice in the chorus of the wild bees. All over came the cuckoo's call from the cornfield below in the valley. John's eyes followed its echo from tree to tree, from the silver armoured birches to the dark woods of Clanratty, until his eyes came to rest on Michael, as he was taking the roller from the Crescent Acre.

No cuckoo oats, John thought with satisfaction, as he noted the velvet greenness. Growth got off to a good start in the race with the rising lake, and the oats were sure to be harvested on time. If the summer was anything like middling they would have it reaped and stooked before Tom went back in September. He thought happily of the pleasure it would give Tom, who was such a devil for conquest. But his thoughts slipped back with a jolt. How would Tom feel about Rory? If Tom had been at home, like Michael, he might have been with Rory. He had always been with them, and perhaps he would have been killed too. John hoped Rory's death would not arouse in Tom a deeper hatred of the English. Sometimes he thought Tom's patriotism ran away with him and blotted out his reasoning and common sense. Tom had been so annoyed about Michael quitting the IRA and about Sally's friendship with Peter Barclay. His red hair would stand on end and the freckles stand out on his livid face whenever he contemplated these things. Tom seemed so often torn between love and duty and was always undecided whether to fight it or to pray it out. To fight it out seemed easier for Tom, but Michael would have preferred to pray it out. They appeared to be cast in the wrong moulds. Their mother was trying to shape them to her way. Maybe it would work out all right. But John doubted it. He thought there was an uneasiness about Tom at Easter. John didn't speak about it to anyone. He thought of mentioning it to his wife but then decided that it was perhaps only his fancy. Perhaps it would annoy her. And God knows she had made a good fist of things as it was. So there was no sense in bothering her with his old notions. She and Sally appeared to shoulder all the family burdens, and to have the most common sense. His lumbago was keeping him from working, giving him too much time to think.

That's what it is, too much time to think and worry about Tom, he thought.

He pulled himself up with the groan and leaned heavily on his stick, preparing to make the slow descent down to the house. What was Michael going to turn his hand to when he came in with the roller? For he must keep his mind more on the work of the farm and less on Tom. He spotted his wife out in the garden at the back of the house.

She was pulling sprays of golden-chain blossom from the laburnum tree to take indoors for the vases. She twisted the tough stems, and where a branch was small enough she pulled it off with the heel from the bark. She carried them around to the front of the house. There she stooped to pick a few blue irises and pink peonies from the herbaceous border. It was then she heard the cuckoo. The very one that had alerted John and Michael. She stood with the flowers in her hand and looked through the blank place in the hedge where the cherry tree had fallen. It was this tree from where the cuckoo seemed to call the first summer she came to Dooleagh, and where the children had played, and where Rory Fallon had so often shinned up and down with Tom, like two squirrels.

10

Mayfly

Sally had just gone to post the letter she had written to Tom about Rory's death. She had intended to make it a continuation of the letter her mother had written about the wedding but she decided otherwise. She threw that one into the fire. What would be the use of telling him about the Black and Tan and the tunic? Tom wouldn't see it as a joke now. He would only be filled with regret over a lost opportunity for revenge. He would have wanted to know why they couldn't have shot him.

When the cuckoo called, Sally was approaching the Hazel Bridge by the Crag. She thought the call came from the whitethorn hedge of Flaggers Field. It echoed again in the thick scrub that trailed along the edge of the wood past the bridge. Sally felt she would like to leave her bike there and go hunting the tricky bird. The cuckoo peeped from its leafy fortress at her puzzled expression, as it did at all the puzzled expressions in its line of flight, searching for its elusive call. It would be good to go off down the woods, down along the stream where she and Peter often rendezvoused. Now, after the rain, the mayfly would be up and the trout rising. Maybe she and Michael would go off to the lake this evening and try for a trout or two. Michael was good at casting, far better than Tom, but never as good as Rory Duffy. Poor Rory. She must hurry and post this letter to Tom. She had almost forgotten about it. What would Tom think of it all? She knew her mother had not written much about Gerty's wedding. It was just as well her mother didn't know everything about the wedding. She didn't know about Gertie's accusation regarding her friendship with Peter and her supposed jaunt with Lieutenant Sternitt. The memory of the Tan and his uniform haunted her at times, driving her to a point where she felt she must tell Michael, but then she'd draw back, undecided. Maybe now it would be best if he knew. She would tell him this evening when they went fishing. She pedalled on past the Clanratty gates, averting her eyes from the entrance lest she see Lieutenant Sternitt, on account of their new and uncertain relationship. On reaching the post office, she bought two stamps, one for Tom's letter and one for her letter to Peter. Then, just about to post the letters in the box, she bumped into Lieutenant Sternitt. Deliberately, she let the letters fall to the floor, offering the opportunity for him to pass any letter he had for her. This he did, deftly, handing her the letter he carried inside his newspaper with the other two.

"Good afternoon, Miss Glynn," he said as she took the letters.

"Good afternoon and thank you," Sally responded with formality.

Slipping the letter Lieutenant Sternitt had given her into her pocket, she posted the other two. Then, picking up her bicycle, she walked back along the street. She had a few messages to do and was eager to read Peter's letter.

Outside the town she passed Ella Rogan on her way to Daltons' land to bring in the cows. Ella was accompanied by Chris Heaney. Ella gave Sally a sheepish grin as she passed. Chris, without taking the cigarette butt from his mouth, growled some sort of salutation and shook his head. Ella and Chris were having quite a romance. Ella's mother boasted that Ella had travelled as often in a motor car as any of the gentry. Sally got well away from them before opening the letter. Its contents were brief, as letters whose destination is uncertain have, of necessity, to be. The news of importance was confirmation of Peter's departure to Africa in August and the prospect of a month's leave before then. The stab of the impending departure was soothed by the leave. Her mixed feelings gradually leaned towards joyous anticipation of their brief reunion. Surely this was a heaven-sent opportunity to decide their future together, or would it be the final cleavage between them? She thought of Africa, remote and cruel with its oppressive heat, tropical diseases and desolation. She had heard it called "the white man's grave". Sally alternated between hope and despair. Already the thought sickened her. She stood for a long time on the quiet road. It was difficult to go home and conceal the awful loneliness that would gnaw at her day and night until Peter arrived to alleviate it.

She heard the roar of an engine approaching and tucked the letter away. She got on her bicycle and started homewards. A lorry-load of soldiers passed her. Sitting back to back on a form in the centre of the lorry, they were wearing tin hats and carrying rifles. As they passed, they waved their hands and some shouted, "I'm forever blowing bubbles." Another lorry passed like the first singing, "Red is the rose / Soft falls the dew / Onward for ever / The red white and blue." The songs clashed against each other in an inharmonious jingle. Behind them came two officers and an orderly in the old Leyland car Sally knew so well. Sally recognised Lieutenant Sternitt, who saluted her as they passed. Following the car and bringing up the rear of the convoy was another lorry similar to the first two except that its occupants were grim, silent and wooden-faced. The procession swung through the gates of Clanratty and Sally was engulfed in a cloud of white dust from the churned-up limestone road. The dust clung to Sally's hair, gritted in her teeth and hurt her eyes. But that annoyance merely served as a way to mask her deeper feelings.

When Sally entered the house, her mother was making griddle scones. Trooper was in from the fields and taking his tea at his customary place at the end of the table. He was feeding Chess with bits of hot buttered scone.

"The Lord save us and bless us, Miss Sally, you're as white as a miller. You're covered in dust!"

"It was the lorries. They passed me on the road."

"Tans. Bad luck to them. Sure many's a one they have covered in dust, and a heavier dust than the dust of the road."

"Wasn't the Tans. It was the military."

"It's all the same. A bullet from any of their guns is the same. They all take their orders from the same boss, be damned to them! And John Bull! When I think of me sweatin' the skin off meself fightin' for that dirty plunderin' gang out under the boilin' sun of Africa! I was a damn fool! I was a damn—"

"Was it very hot in Africa?" Sally interrupted.

"Hot?" Trooper snorted. "Hot?" he screeched again as though the very words burned his tongue. "It was as hot as hell, Miss Sally. That's what it was. 'Twas so hot—"

His African sortie was his favourite hobby horse, but Sally could not bear to listen to Trooper's description of its tortures at this moment. "Would this be a good evening for fishing, Trooper?" she asked, hoping to divert.

"Oh, the best. The best!" he answered with the same enthusiasm he had been about to apply to his African story. "We'll go. We'll go, Miss Sally, as soon as I get this job done. Here!" he finished, throwing the bit of scone he was eating to Chess. He grabbed his cap from the back of the chair and clapped it onto his head, peak to the back. His hob-nailed boots clattered out through the back door as he went to hurry through his tasks and to get away fishing.

Sally stood staring after him. She had blundered by mentioning the fishing to Trooper. She did not want his company, but now she had committed herself to it and would not offend or disappoint him by forbidding him to come. Her hope had been to go with Michael so that she could talk to him about Tom. But now, with Peter's letter, things had changed a bit. She was not sure she wanted to talk about Tom. Indeed, she did not quite know what she wanted to talk about.

Michael came in for his tea.

"Trooper tells me we're going fishing. Good idea. Trout for supper would be a change. The scones look good," he added, sitting down opposite the nest of brown boiled eggs in a little blue dish and a plate of hot buttered scones.

"If ye are bringing home trout to fry, don't stay out half the night. There's a curfew on the lake as well as the road, remember," their mother reminded them.

John limped into the kitchen.

"Trooper says we're goin' fishin'," he announced.

"Heavens!" his wife said. "Everyone who comes through that door says, 'we're goin' fishin'."

She was glad that John had thought of going fishing; it didn't often appeal to him. He had difficulty getting in and out of the boat and it was very damp around the lake. Sally thought it was she who had started this party going. Now, far from the quiet evening she had planned with Michael, she found herself committed to be one of four in the boat. She would be indifferent to the mayflies' brief and glorious dance, except to compare it with the too-short month of stolen happiness she might have with Peter before his departure.

11

June

The prospect of Peter's going to Africa intensified the correspondence between Sally and him. Their letters became very frequent. Almost dangerously so. It meant more secret meetings between Sally and Lieutenant Sternitt and she was getting reckless, throwing caution to the wind. Sometimes the lieutenant himself had to warn her with a nod or a wink or a shrewd chastising glance. As the days lengthened into June there was no twilight in the streets of Cloona. They would slip past the shrubs at the cathedral gate, passing a letter from hand to hand. The ten o'clock curfew fell in daylight, and giving the letters to Matt Heaney to put in the saddlebag of her bicycle had to cease. And Chris was always slinking about. Never was there conversation between them except the usual good morning, good afternoon, or good evening.

It was the second week in June when Tom came home. He looked thin and pale. He was even more querulous than when he went away at Easter. Rory's death had affected him deeply. He went to Duffys' the first evening of his return. He came home before curfew and went straight to his bedroom to unpack his suitcase. His mother called for the Rosary, and after prayers

John went to bed. Mrs Glynn took her husband a glass of hot milk. After their mother had gone, Sally remained with Michael and Tom. Their talk was general. Michael asked a lot of questions about Maynooth and after other boys from the district who were students there and whose ordinations had taken place. Tom's answers were uninterested, sometimes evasive. He was more interested in the lads on the run and the ambushes.

Sally decided she would wait until Michael had gone to bed and then ask Tom, fair and square, if he was unhappy in Maynooth. Or did he find the effort in living up to its high standards unbearably demanding? He might tell her. If he did, she would offer to open the way to negotiations between him and his mother to set his course for another career. She knew he would hesitate to tell his mother for fear of disappointing her. He would not tell Michael in case he took advantage of the news to go off himself to the seminary and leave him at home to do the farm. Sally knew he had no taste for it, and that he would do everything for Ireland save till its soil. While Tom and Michael chatted, Sally sat assuming an interest in her book until Tom swung the conversation around to herself.

"Do you hear from Barclay at all, Sally?"

She pretended not to hear while she thought out her reply. He repeated the question and she raised her head in mock surprise.

"Talking to me?"

"Yes, for the third time, did you hear from Barclay at all? Where is he?"

"Oh, I don't know," she said slowly and hesitantly. She was going to tell him that she heard from him only yesterday and that he was coming home in July before going to Africa, but the bald and truthful statement would confound Michael. She had not told him about Peter, for she would not involve him in the affair if she could help it, nor make him a party to a conspiracy.

"Just as well you don't know where he is. Doesn't know himself, most likely. Got a smart uniform on, that's all that matters with Barclay!"

"No hard words, Tom," Michael said. "Let bygones be bygones."

"It's not bygones," Tom said, turning to Sally and peering closely, yet amusingly, at her hands as they lay on the book in her lap. "I thought I'd see the fireworks! The dazzler! Where is it?" he asked.

"What do you mean?" Sally said, knowing full well he meant Hugh

Dalton's engagement ring, for Tom had always been anxious she should marry him.

"You know, Hugh Dalton's ring."

"I'm glad to see you have acquired one priestly quality – matchmaking," Sally answered. "But you'll have a bit of a job making that match! I don't want Hugh Dalton's ring, and even if I did, it wouldn't be a dazzler, as you call it. That miserable old scarecrow wouldn't buy a curtain ring for a girl!"

"That's why he has the money," Tom pointed out. "That's why he can afford to put up the biggest tombstone in the parish over his father."

"He can keep his money, and his big tombstones," Sally said. "And his bald head! And his buck teeth, which are nearly as big as the tombstone!"

Tom's suggestion that she marry Hugh Dalton annoyed her as much as her mother's wish of Mr Pratt.

"That's a sin," Tom said.

"What's a sin?" Sally snapped. "To despise a man for his looks?"

"She doesn't despise him," Michael put in, in an effort to pour oil on the troubled waters of the argument, which arose all too frequently between his brother and sister. "She just doesn't like his particular style of beauty."

"You shouldn't encourage her to reject Hugh Dalton," Tom said.

"I'm not encouraging her to reject or accept any particular suitor. Sally is only eighteen. She has time enough to think of getting married, and when she does it must be her choice, not ours."

"I declare, Michael, you're getting romantic," Tom said sarcastically. "Not thinking of you yourself maybe bringing Mother home the dreaded daughter-in-law, I hope."

Their mother made no secret of the fact that she considered this a catastrophe to be avoided, for she said that mothers-in-law and daughters-in-law were notorious the world over, and that the Irish variety seemed to be particularly vicious.

"We are all waiting for you to be ordained," Sally said.

Tom's lips curled mockingly.

"'The ceremony was performed by Fr Glynn, brother of the bride' looks well in the newspaper. Can't you see us pointing you out to our children?" Sally said. "'That's your uncle, the priest.' Better hurry up, Tom, if you want to get the marrying going."

"My name won't be in the papers alongside Peter Barclay's name, that's for sure," Tom said firmly. He pushed back his chair and got up. "I'm going to bed. I'm tired."

"Your name wasn't alongside Peter Barclay's in Easter week, either," Sally called after him as he left the kitchen and went down the hall on the way to his bedroom.

"He would have made a better soldier than I did," Michael said.

"No, he wouldn't," Sally told him. "Peter always said you were a great soldier and that you had no fear of death at all."

"Takes more than that to make a soldier, Sally. I think I'll rake the fire," he added, embarrassed by her remark and feeling lonely at the memories they stirred. He arranged the last smouldering coals with the tongs and covered them with a shovel of ashes. After he had done this, Sally began to sweep up the hearth.

"Are you going to cut turf tomorrow?" she asked, as she swept the sandy ashes with the little brush. "If you do, bring back an armful of heather to make a few hearth besoms. These things," she said, shaking the brush, "just go up in a flash."

"So do the besoms," Michael replied.

"Yes, but the besoms don't cost anything and this does," she said, hanging the bald little brush back on its hook.

"I think you would make an ideal wife for Hugh Dalton. You'd mind the ha'pence and help to swell the bank balance." He lit a candle and handed it to Sally. "You'd best go to bed, Sally, and I'll turn the lamp out."

"Save the daddy long legs," Sally said, as she stood with a candle watching him turn low the flaming wick of the hanging lamp. The daddy long legs floundered about inside the scorched globe. She turned to go to her bedroom.

"Good night, Sally," Michael called as he twiddled with the screw of the lamp extinguisher.

"Good night," she called back from her bedroom door. As she closed it, she heard him go down the passage to his room.

The house was quiet, too quiet, Sally thought, for Tom's first night home. Yet she doubted if his presence was reassuring or comforting to them. The quietness did not mean that things were peaceful. He was there in his room, with his black clothes, his gilt-edged breviary missal beside him or sticking out of his pocket, its little jingling marker-medals on the ends of their coloured ribbons rattling like part of a sacred harness. To know this was not to feel safe and secure. Sally wondered what he had talked about at Duffys'. She hoped Gerty had not told him of her friendship with Lieutenant Sternitt and the incident on the evening of her wedding. Perhaps Gerty had forgotten. Perhaps the tragedy of Rory's death had swept aside lesser affairs like the petty gossip Chris Heaney specialised in. But if by any chance Gerty had told Tom, then he would watch her like a hawk. When Peter came in July he would dog them continuously, unless the prospect of Peter's departure left him less antagonistic.

As she undressed she thought again of the trench coat and revolver in the hay. She hoped the grief of Rory's death would not intensify Tom's activities with the Shinners and spur him to new and enthusiastic participation.

12

The Bog

The following afternoon Sally was preparing a tea to take to the turf-cutters. Tom offered his assistance. He would carry the can with the tea, or the basket with the bread or the cups, anything to facilitate the speed of the trip to the bog. It was something he had never done. From time to time he glanced at the clock on the mantelpiece. He appeared overanxious and his concern for the turf-cutters puzzled Sally. They went down the path in the Long Meadow. The day was warm and a heat haze shimmered on the meadow grass. The broad white faces of the moon daisies were turned to the sun and basked in its near scorching rays. On the low bank, where the turf was spread, a warm breeze filled the air with the sweet smell of heather and bog myrtle.

Here Trooper and Michael worked, Trooper catching with precision the slithering oblongs of wet peat that Michael tossed up to him with his slean from the cool depths of the bog hole. Trooper plied backwards and forwards in his ant-like way, emptying his barrow-loads in well-spaced rows. When Tom and Sally appeared, the turf-cutters washed their hands in the amber stream. Sally poured their tea while Tom placed bread and cake in the browned outstretched palms of the workers. With slavering jaws, Chess watched and waited for the discarded bits and the hope of a drink of sweet leafy tea from the can lid.

Here was a blessed peace and tranquillity. Here, Sally thought, were no problems; Tom in the Shinners, Tom unhappy in Maynooth, Tom at enmity with Peter. Here even Tom seemed at peace with the world. He lay in the mossy grass, chewing a straw. The four of them laughed and chatted as if no world lay outside this little piece of brown earth. The incense of heather and bog myrtle, the hum of the bees, the curlew's call, the plaintive cry of a young land gull, and the rising crescendo of a soaring lark whose afternoon song was even sweeter than its much-loved melody in the clear air of a morning. Tea on the bog had something about it, an enchantment Sally could not define. As children they had brought the tea to Trooper and their father, and listened spellbound to Trooper's stories. Now it was Trooper and Michael, but still they listened to Trooper's stories. As his voice droned on, Sally's thoughts wandered.

She thought there was no work on the farm like turf-cutting. It swung her back again to the realms of fantasy and make-believe stuff. The bog did not seem part of the land or part of the farm; it was an island, detached from the mundane things of life. To her, turf-cutters were like explorers, or ship-wrecked sailors. There was a unity about them and among them, a comradeship that could only be broken by the return to the humdrum life of the household. Tea on the bog became a ritual, a sort of feast, a part of the work in which they were engaged, Sally decided, its spell broken only by the workaday sounds that greeted them on their return. The lowing of hungry calves; the rattle of milk pails; the whinnying of a horse at a field gate; the hissing of a big kettle as it boiled over on the embers of the peat fire; and a voice saying, "Here come the men from the bog. They must be starved." They are back; the spell is broken. Sally thought the dreams of an Irish exile must be of the bog. He must dream he is on the bog, that kingdom of the royal purple of heather and magic mists. Her eyes narrowed as, away along the notched-out edge of the turf's bank, a figure moved slowly. It looked a small figure, for distance and the blue smoke from the smouldering scutch fires from the cutaway potato fields dwarfed it. As usual, it was Trooper's keen old hawk eye that was first to recognise it.

"It's Mrs Barclay bringing tea to the men. She has no one at home to help her now, except that old ranger, Thornton, and two ex-soldiers from Cloona." Trooper considered the Connaught Rangers much inferior to his own cavalry regiment. "That's all she has now to keep the roof on Storm Hill, because her sons couldn't live with her, the slave driver! Wonder she didn't marry again, would be cheaper than paying men."

"You weren't so good at marrying yourself, Trooper, and you did your share of gallivantin'." Sally wanted to deflect the conversation from the Barclays.

"Divil a lie on it, Miss Sally! You can always make a fella sorry for what he said with the quick one on your tongue. Sure there wasn't any lasses like yourself when I was courtin'. If there had been you wouldn't be saying that to me now. The only one I cared about was the girl I left behind when I went away, and another fella had her when I came back. The rest of them was auld gaums in my day."

"They weren't such auld gaums that they didn't keep falling in love with your merry blue eyes," Sally replied. "You must have been a powerful dandy, Trooper, mounted on your charger."

"If you had seen me, Miss Sally, with me buckles and me spurs shinin', and me horse like a chestnut fresh from the burr, you would have thought so."

"Sally would surely have fallen in love with the uniform," Tom bit in. "But it would have to be an officer's uniform, of course."

"An officer is supposed to be a gentleman and it's the gentleman Sally would be interested in," Michael said. "It's the character that counts with Sally, so she would have been in love with Trooper because she is a good judge of character."

"I don't think I am. I'm afraid I can never tell a saint from a sinner."

"There is neither would be any good marrying," Trooper said knowingly.

"Suppose you had to marry one of them, Trooper, which would it be?"

Trooper thought for a while before replying. "Sure I don't know. If I married young I think I'd have married a sinner, but if I married now I think I'd have the saint."

"Remember," Michael said, "the answer Rory Duffy – God rest him – gave the bishop at Confirmation when he asked him what a martyr was.

Rory said a martyr was a person married to a saint."

"Right enough," Trooper said, "he mightn't be far wrong at that. A fella wouldn't have much of a time married to a saint."

Tom gave Trooper a scowling look.

"We are all sinners this evening idling away the time," Sally said, jumping up from where she was sitting, in preparation for going home. She gave Chess a can lid of leftover tea and rinsed the plate where the stream trickled from the heather on the high uncut bank. She put the empty cups into the can.

"You can take the can, Tom," Sally said as he also rose from where he was lying in the heather.

"I'm not going home yet. I'm going along the face of the bank to where the Fallons are cutting," Tom said.

"You can bring home a bunch of long-stemmed heather for besoms when you come," Sally said.

"I hate breaking heather, it hurts my hands," he said.

"I'll bring it," Michael offered.

"Yes," Trooper said, "I'll bring home an armful of heather," he said with a hint of sarcasm. "It doesn't hurt my hands."

He stood up and shaded his eyes from the sun with his hand. He looked across the turf banks and said, as though to reassure himself of the identity of the figure in the distance, "There she goes home. She won't lose much time, and she was seated with the men who won't lose much time either."

"Who?" Tom said.

"Mrs Barclay, of course," Trooper said. "And when Thornton comes in from a hard day's work, she'll send him off to pick berries from the boor tree bush, to make what she calls elderberry wine."

"That's the elder bush," Sally corrected him.

"That's no elder."

"No!" Sally said. "There is a difference. The elder grows in swampy places. They grow near the boathouse. They're not nice bushes. The branches are crooked."

"They're no crookeder than the boor tree!"

"Did Mrs Barclay ever ask you to pick the berries, Trooper?"

"She did," he replied, "but I wouldn't go next or near them. Sure only a pagan would have anything to do with that bush. Wasn't it the boor tree bush Judas hanged himself from? But Corney Thornton wouldn't know that. And she says if the flowers from it was boiled, the juice of them would take freckles from a girl's face."

"I must try them on Tom's freckles," Sally said as she smiled and glanced at Tom.

"A girl's face," Tom pointed out.

"Do not, Miss Sally. It's an evil bush."

"I have no more belief in Mrs Barclay's beauty hints than I have in Trooper's cures," Tom said, smirking.

Sally knew how sensitive Trooper was regarding his cures. He retorted to Tom's remark with a definite assurance.

"There is many a man alive today would be dead only for my cures."

"Of course, Trooper, everyone knows that."

"May your load always be as light as your heart, Miss Sally," Trooper said, putting his hat on his tonsured head as he and Michael returned to the turf-cutting.

Sally headed home along the meadow path. Chess trotted happily at her heels. Looking back from the high Poplar Gap, she could see Tom, a lone dark figure on his way to Fallons' turf bank. Farther away was a small figure in pink. Sally knew it was Kitty in her eternal pink. Sally waited and watched until the two met. Together, they disappeared into the little spinney of birches near Fallons' bank. Sally knew it was possible to wander through it and come out the opposite end near Fallons' and Duffys'. Sally guessed Tom had a tryst with Kitty and that Gerty had arranged it. That explained his display of anxiety and haste about going with the tea to Michael and Trooper. Before turning to continue her journey home, Sally looked back to see Michael and Trooper continue their turf-cutting. They were like insects nibbling at the fringe of a great purple carpet of heather.

13

Curfew

Trooper came in early next morning. As usual he had all the news, and he rolled it off like a wheezy old engine letting off steam. He reported that Matt Heaney had been driven away in a car last night by masked men, taken to an unknown destination and tried for giving information to the enemy. In the end he was let off with a caution.

"You got your news very early this morning," Sally said.

"I got it last night, curfew and all," he said with a shake to his head and a knowing wink. "Matt came to my old cottage and stayed until this morning. He was afraid to go into Cloona after they released him on the mountain road."

"And what did he tell you?" Sally asked.

"Nothing, only what I've told you."

"Hope it teaches him to talk less in future," Tom huffed. "He'd do better to stick to his bicycle-fixing and not bother minding other people's business."

"It would be better if they gave his brat of a son a shaking up," Sally added. "That slippery Chris, I mean! It's he who is minding other people's business."

"Whose business is he minding?" Tom asked.

"Everyone's except his own," Sally answered sharply.

"He wouldn't be the porter in the bank if he didn't concern himself with other people's business," Tom pointed out.

"Wouldn't he? He only concerns himself with the people Mrs Brigson wants him to be concerned with—"

"That's his job," Tom interrupted. "Chris Heaney is a decent and patriotic young fellow."

"What do you know about him and his patriotism?" Sally asked.

"Nothing. But I'm a good judge of character, like we talked about on the bog yesterday."

"Well, as I said then, I'm no judge, and maybe I'm wrong in thinking Chris Heaney a tool for Mrs Brigson or anyone else who gives him an odd shilling. But I still think he'd sell his father for the price of a packet of Woodbine."

"Eat up your breakfast, Tom," his mother said. "It's spoiling while you and Sally argue about the Heaneys. You can warm up the argument again but you can't warm up bacon and eggs!"

"They shouldn't have hauled poor old Matt out," Michael joined in. "I don't see what harm he could do. No one listens to his old blatherin' anyway. I'm against that sort of thing."

"What sort of thing?" Tom asked.

"Taking old men out at night to warn them and cutting young girls' hair. Petty things done by what you call brave men, who risk their lives for whatever they believe in."

"Old men and young girls can do a lot of harm. Duty to their country is for them as well as those on the run or in jails. If they behaved themselves, they wouldn't be taken away or have their hair cut," Tom said.

"Behave themselves?" Sally said. "What rules or codes of behaviour are they supposed to keep?"

"You know, or ought to know, the rules," Tom said.

"Tom, please, Tom!" his mother called. "Does this sort of sparring go on at the refectory table in Maynooth? I thought it was confined to political meetings and organised debating. Eat up your breakfast, both of you."

Trooper had finished eating his breakfast at the table near the back door.

He took his cap from his knee and pulled it down on his head, securing it tightly so that the peak stuck out over one ear. "There's too much to be done to be wasting time talking about an old fool like Matt Heaney," he said as he clumped through the back door.

"You shouldn't have brought the news," Mrs Glynn called after him. "Keep news for the evening in future!"

"'Twouldn't be news then," Trooper growled back over his shoulder. "I'm goin' for the slean and barrow."

He returned in a few minutes with the creaking turf barrow, which he put down outside the door. He hoisted the slean across the shoulder, so that the wing of it sloped in the same direction as the peak of his cap. This made him appear lopsided, as though a strong wind was blowing against him. Michael came out and picked up the barrow. They went off down the First Gap across the Kesh onto the bog road.

Tom said he wanted to go into Cloona for the newspaper. Sally had offered to bring it home in the evening on her way home from the office but he considered it would be too late and that he would go now himself.

"I'm taking your bike, Sally," he said, "all right?"

"The chain has new links. It still clicks a lot and it's weak in places. Better walk the hill or it might snap again – and now that Matt Heaney is being pestered by the Shinners he might clear off and we would just have to mend our own bikes."

"I'm anxious to hear all about Matt," Tom said. "I expect there is bound to be a variety of rumours. You know Cloona. I'll call on Jack Dalton to get the latest one."

"You shouldn't listen to gossip – it's an occasion of sin." Sally smiled.

"I must listen to gossip in order to chasten the culprit or sympathise with the victim. We'll talk about it when I come back."

He took his black hat from the deer-antler rack and headed towards the trap house to get Sally's bike.

"Are you going with the tea to the bog this evening?" he asked.

"No, I have to go into the office, as I promised. Maybe you could go with the tea."

"Me!" He sounded rather surprised. "I'm not going hawking a can of tea to the bog and perhaps meeting some of the Cloona people – Hugh Dalton or Kitty or heaven knows who! I might even see some of my classmates who would have it all over college when I got back. Have you no respect for the cloth?" Tom smiled, making one of his rare jokes as he left the trap house.

Sally took little comfort from his reference to when he went back to college. As he pushed the bike out, she stood at the door, and with good-humoured chastisement over his refusal to go with the tea, called out, "Such pride! Go, before I pin all the deadly sins upon you!"

John Glynn limped around the corner of the house.

"Are you going to Cloona, Sally?" he asked, jingling coins in his pocket.

"No, but Tom is." She called out to Tom's retreating figure. "Tobacco for Father!" She had immediately guessed what her father's order would be, and passed it on without waiting for confirmation. Tom waved in acknowledgement. They all knew their father's choice. Walnut Plug – the little brown cube with the red label of a realistic-looking walnut. They teased him about the amount of time he spent cutting off small bits of it with his penknife and rubbing it between his palms, while he held his empty pipe in his teeth.

It was late afternoon when Tom came back. His mother had just returned from taking the tea to Michael and Trooper. She had a bunch of heather. She would make a little branch of scrub with it to wash the churn and the wooden butter pats.

"And they say there is nothing in Irish bogs, only turf. Yesterday a besom, today a scrub," remarked Tom.

"And 'twas the sphagnum moss we sent to France during the war to clean wounds and the green algae and the bog myrtle and the wild garlic flowers Trooper says to put in wardrobes to keep moths away," his mother added.

"The smell of wild garlic would keep anything away. I must go to the bog later, to see how the turf-cutting is getting on."

"I'd rather you didn't. You might go off to Fallons' or Duffys' and stay away half the night and worry the hearts and souls out of us again."

Tom didn't come home from the bog for his supper. It was presumed he had gone to the Fallons'. He did not come home for the Rosary either. Curfew still found him abroad. His mother grew anxious but John reassured her.

"Playing cards, they are. Nothing as good for pushing the hands of the clock around. And now with the long evenings 'tis hard for young people to break up the fun."

"That's just it," Mrs Glynn said. "The long evenings are not the time for playing cards – it's sort of out of season. It's not like at Easter when Tom was home last. And besides, they must be tired. The Fallons are out working on the bog all day."

"But Tom wasn't working," Sally said. "And Tom wants to play cards no matter who doesn't."

"Don't fret about him, Mother," Michael said. "He'll be in any minute now. Remember, if he's a bit late he isn't likely to get caught, and even if he did get caught, the Black and Tans don't just shoot everyone they meet after curfew. They're bad enough but they're not that bad. They'd merely call on him to halt, give him the chance to explain."

"They wouldn't shoot Tom, anyway – he's too thin!" Sally said. "They're not good enough marksmen. And if we could make them waste all their ammunition, then the war would soon be over."

"Don't be so flippant about such a serious matter," her mother scolded.

"It isn't a serious matter, Mother. You're just making it so by needless worrying. If Tom thinks there's any danger, he'll stay at Fallons' all night – same as we did at the wedding."

But her mother wasn't reassured. "Suppose the Black and Tans raid Fallons'. How can they account for the presence of Tom, a stranger out of his own house?"

"Ah, Mother, don't go on thinking of unlikely things," Michael pleaded.

"Tom is a nuisance!" Sally was impatient. "Why can't he come home in good time? He has nothing else to do all day but chat with neighbours, and yet he can't get home before curfew. We had peace when he was away."

"He'll soon get enough of the neighbours after a night or two. It's always like that after he's come home," Michael said. "You go on to bed, Mother. I'll wait up."

Reluctantly, at Michael's suggestion, the household retired and he waited alone. He gathered up his magazines and books, pulled the heavy curtains in case the light from the window could be seen by the Tans as they passed on the road below. Then he sat beneath the hanging lamp, leafing idly through the pages of a magazine.

Sally lay anxiously in bed, listening for the sound of Tom's footsteps. Deep in her heart, buried beneath the show of confidence she had displayed before her mother, was the fear of Tom's renewed activity in the Shinners. When he was with the Fallons and the Duffys he was bound to be implicated in it. She got out of bed and looked out into the quiet leafy June night. The whole world seemed a lonely empty place. The screech of a fern owl cut the veil of silence, like splinters of broken glass. Silence folded again over the echo. It was again split by the bark of a dog. It was a high, hysterical sort of bark, like that of a startled terrier, not the foolish hollow night-time sound of a dog barking at the moon. Perhaps, thought Sally, it was barking at Tom on his way home. It ceased, too, and silence reigned again. The rake of the corncrake's single note filled the vacuum. A great white moth flew in through the open window and became caught somewhere in the lace of the blind. It flapped and flopped, and made a noise that seemed louder than that of the screeching owl or the barking dog. Sally released it, and then, slipping her dressing gown over her nightdress, she tiptoed into the kitchen. Michael had discovered something interesting in his paper and sat reading beneath the lamp. Two or three small moths beat noisily against the globe of the lamp. Michael did not hear Sally coming behind him, and he raised his head with a start immediately he became aware of her presence.

"I wonder what's keeping him," she whispered. "Have you any idea?"

There were doubt and hesitancy in Michael's reply. "Don't worry about him, Sally."

It was then they heard steps in the yard. Sally sighed with relief. They were Tom's light and hurrying steps. When the footsteps reached the threshold of the back door, Sally nodded to Michael and then silently and more contentedly went down the passage to her bedroom. As she slipped into bed she heard her mother call from her bedroom.

"What happened, Tom? We've been worrying."

Sally knew her mother had not been sleeping but had been lying, like herself, straining her ears in the silence, to hear Tom's footsteps.

"We were playing cards," Tom called back. "I didn't realise it was curfew time till it was too late – 10.30 it was. I'm sorry."

"It's half one now."

"I beat the curfew, anyway, and if I had been caught at 10.30 it would have been just as bad as 1.30 – might as well be hanged for a sheep as a lamb."

"It would have been much better to come home early," his mother said firmly.

"We'll talk it over in the morning," Michael interrupted.

Sally heard her brothers talking together for a time in a quiet whisper, before they went along the corridor to their rooms.

14

Four More Days

Sally drank a cup of tea and left for Cloona. Her father was sitting in the shade of the rhododendrons, reading the paper Tom had bought. As she passed on her way down the drive, she reassured him she would not forget his tobacco, as Tom had done.

The town had a tropical air. The few people who were on the streets kept to the shady side, while the dogs prowled away on the sun-baked pavements and lay in the shady doorways. As Sally passed Matt Heaney's bicycle shop, she saw the empty place by the window where Matt often worked. The door was closed, and so she could not leave her bicycle. She thought that Matt must be upset, embarrassed or even ill, because of the fright he had had the previous night. She hoped it had nothing to do with the letters left in the saddlebag of her bicycle or the friendly little warnings he gave her about being seen talking to the officers.

She wheeled the bicycle along and left it outside Mr Pratt's office. Mr Pratt's attentions upon her had become even more pressing. More objectionable. She hoped Mrs Brigson would see her bicycle outside and come in and liberate her from the embarrassing position of listening to

Pratt's petty compliments. She usually bounced in whenever she saw Sally's bicycle outside. She ignored Sally and monopolised the conversation. Could she be jealous? Sally thought. Did she resent his increased attention to Sally since the ball in Clanratty? Sally could reassure her she need have no fear.

Sally sat at the typewriter, facing the window, clattering out the few letters while keeping an eye on the wire-mesh window for the great Leyland. She saw it draw up outside Matt's. As Sally watched through the window, she saw the gradual activity of troops stirring into action after the previous night. A military patrol was parading the streets. Sally was amused at the stupid and oft-repeated action of the British forces locking the stable when the horse was gone, sometimes as much as twenty-four hours after ambushes and incidents got underway, when those responsible were as many miles away as time and their knowledge of the countryside would allow. She spotted Dave and hoped he had a letter for her. He might leave it at Matt's. Finishing up her typing, she made an excuse to get to the post office before the mail left.

Indeed Matt had a letter, which he handed to her. She popped it into her pocket and hurried along. Turning the corner, she bumped into Tom with Kitty.

"How did you get here so soon? I didn't know you were coming into Cloona. Where did you get that bike?"

"I borrowed it from Frank Fallon. He arrived just as you left. I came in for confessions for tomorrow's holiday," Tom explained. "You're about an hour too soon."

"Well, I'm going home," she announced.

"It's a pity you can't concern yourself more with what people think!" he said. "Who are you after posting that letter to? Barclay?"

"There are other people in the world besides Barclay," Sally replied, glad to know that he had not detected her receiving the letter but had mentioned only the posting of one.

"I hope it doesn't get mixed up with your officer friend's dispatch or his letter to his wife, or whoever it was he posted to the same time as you did."

"Cloona post office is not as bad as that. In its own way it's just as efficient as Maynooth. Now I must get the tobacco you forgot this morning. Don't get caught in curfew tonight," she warned.

She jumped on her bicycle and pedalled down the centre of the street between the rows of patrolling tin-hatted soldiers. She didn't go back to Pratt's office but continued her journey home, calling at the small huckster's shop on the outskirts of the town for her father's tobacco. She cycled quickly past the Clanratty gates. The lorries were coming and going, disturbing the peace and quiet of the country road. When she got out of sight of them at the bend near the bridge, she stopped to read Peter's letter. She was impatient to know its contents. She propped her bicycle against the wall and glanced cautiously around, keeping a vigilant eye on the road. She feared that Tom would come sneaking around the bend, for she doubted the truth of his statement about going to Confession. She had a feeling he had followed her deliberately, dogging her and watching her every move. There was an ever-growing barrier of suspicion arising between them. She somehow linked up his absence last night with the Matt Heaney affair, and his attitude did not help to change her opinion.

The roads to right and left of her were empty. Along the riverbank below, a few cows lay chewing their cud in bovine contentment. Where a whitethorn hedge met the end of the bridge wall, a pair of fettered goats stood on hind legs to nibble its succulent tops, their faces on a level with her own, their square-pupiled eyes staring uncertainly at her. She read Peter's letter quickly, between furtive glances cast down the Cloona road. Then she thrust it back into her pocket. She leaned lazily over the bridge to relax and to slowly go over the words of the letters in her mind. It was almost a week since he wrote this letter. He said he was coming home on the twentieth. When would that be? What date was today? She could never remember dates when she was writing a letter; she just put the day down. Excitedly she began to count up. Tom came home on the fourteenth – that was the day before yesterday. Tomorrow would be Corpus Christi, the seventeenth. Then today was the sixteenth.

"Only four more days!" Only four more days until she saw him – perhaps! The stream beneath the bridge seemed to whisper the good news as it tinkled over its gravelly bed, and her words echoed through the rough stone arch. She skipped gaily across the road to lean her bare arms on the warm stone parapet on the other side, and to hold her face up to the setting sun. Beneath the bridge, trout darted swift as shadows, streaking across the pebbly, sandy bed. Down in the middle, corncrakes answered each other.

The shadow of the Crag was mirrored clear as a cameo in the smooth unruffled surface of the lake. The Sheep Slopes, with their forest of fern, grew luxuriant again in the make-believe of reflection. She moved along the bridge to where the water was trapped in static little pools between boulders and little sandbanks, like bits of broken mirror strewn across the riverbed. She leaned over the wall and caught her own reflection in one of the smooth little pools. Her face appeared radiantly happy against the bunch of golden ringlets falling over her shoulders and the cool freshness of her summer dress. Lines from Peter's letter drifted through her mind.

> Michael knows we are going together, and Michael wouldn't mind you marrying me. Nor does your father. I don't suppose your mother would, either, if it weren't for Tom. It's Tom's fanaticism that is the spanner in the works. It's Tom we have got to change and convert to kindness, tolerance and thought for other people's feelings. We must have it out with him. We can't go on meeting in this hole-in-the-corner fashion for a whole month. You talk to your mother about it, Sally.

It's easy for Peter, Sally thought, as her high spirits flagged a little. He can say things like that but he doesn't know Mother nor Tom as well as I do.

The thought of putting her love affair with Peter before her mother and Tom brought her back with a jerk from her flight of fancy into her dream world. To discuss it with her mother was to meet with open disapproval, which she had not yet come up against. And to discuss it with Tom – well, Tom just would not discuss it, so there was an end. She would wait and talk it over with Peter first. In his letter he had made a plan with her, suggesting alternatives in case the first should prove impossible. He would see her here at the Hazel Bridge on the first evening of his return. Or on the second evening he would meet her down by the lake's edge where the alder spinney ran along to the boathouse. It would be easier to meet him on the first evening, Sally thought hopefully. No one would then really know he was home, and there would be no vigilance on Tom's part. It was here she was going to see him. Here, with the western sun beaming gold across the pink-purple of the blossoming heath and the bracken beneath the Crag.

The shimmering summer mist was now rising from the warm earth in the lower meadows and the Crescent Acre. She put her hand into the pocket of her cotton dress to feel Peter's letter, to reassure herself of its reality. Then she touched the heart little square of her father's tobacco. It's time he had it, she thought. Tom had already disappointed him. She blamed herself for her unwarranted delay. She crossed the road to her bicycle. The two goats were still intent on their work of destroying the whitethorn hedge. They had climbed higher to feast on the fresh red shoots. She jumped on her bicycle and rode off, leaving a little white trail of dust where the tyres cut into the road.

15

The Question

Frank Fallon and Michael were playing draughts in the kitchen when Sally entered. Her father was engrossed in watching the game, scarcely missing the tobacco. Her mother was ironing white shirts belonging to Tom.

"Did you see Tom?" she asked, as she looked up from her smoothing.

"Yes," Sally replied. "He's gone to Confession."

"Why didn't you go?"

"It's only a fortnight since I was there," Sally said, feeling rather guilty.

"It's not a fortnight since Tom was there," her mother said reprovingly.

"It's different with Tom. He's going to be a priest and it's expected of him."

"It's expected of you, too, because you're his sister. Michael was there this morning."

"I didn't go because it was expected of me," Michael said, amused, raising his eyes from the draughts board. "That's not a motive to be recommended for going to Confession."

"Hope he doesn't stay away too long with my bike," Frank said, "maybe have my only means of transport taken by the Tans. I'd as soon do without my legs as without that old bike."

"What good would your old bike be to the Tans?" John Glynn asked.

"What good is many a thing they take?" Frank was philosophical.

They played game after game, John, Michael and Frank, while they waited for Tom's return. Sally took on the ironing of the shirts, while her mother made scrubs from the armful of heather she had brought from the bog.

"He's not leaving me much time to get home before curfew," Frank said eventually.

"You can stay all night," Sally said. "Same as Tom did in your house."

"Same as Tom did in our house?" Frank repeated, puzzled. "Tom has never stayed after curfew in our house. When is he supposed to have done?"

"When do you think? He only came home the day before yesterday."

"Listen!" said Michael. "There's Tom now. Better go out and take the bike from him."

Frank lost no time. He grabbed the bike as Tom dismounted outside the door and dashed off.

After the Rosary Sally waited a long time round the kitchen. Frank Fallon's surprise, which amounted to a denial of his card game with Tom, filled her with suspicion. Now she became more convinced Matt Heaney's midnight ride was connected with Tom's absence.

At last she and Tom were alone in the kitchen. "Are you going to Communion in the morning?" she asked.

"Why do you ask?"

"Because I want to ask you a question. Indeed, I want to ask you a lot of questions, and if you're going to Communion in the morning then you must answer them truthfully."

"I need not answer them at all if I don't want to," Tom retorted. "Going to Communion places no obligation on me to break the silence."

"I haven't forgotten your shady manoeuvres at Easter, and now you're acting very suspiciously. Are you in the Shinners – an active member, I mean?" she demanded, looking Tom straight in the face.

He looked at her without answering.

"Had you anything to do with that Matt Heaney affair? If you had, you'd better come out in the open and tell us all about it. You'd better give up Maynooth and stay at home, or go out and work honestly. Then you could let Michael go into the religious life and joined the Franciscans or whatever it is he wants to join. If you have all the courage you need to take orders from the Shinners, then bring your courage to help you out of the pretence of a vocation to the priesthood that you do not possess. Are you in the Shinners?"

"No!" Tom said flatly. "I'm not. I wouldn't be trusted in the IRA, not while my sister moves in Imperial circles and takes messages, even written ones, from an officer of His Majesty's army stationed at Clanratty Castle."

"Take messages? What are you insinuating? Just what are you hitting at?"

Tom, now that he had changed the situation and swung his opponent around on the defensive, pressed home his advantage. "I'm hitting at a serious charge of which you are suspected. You are known to be, and have been seen, giving or receiving messages to and from an officer from the castle."

Sally leaned against the table. She picked up some wooden draughtsmen and toyed with them, clicking them together in her hands. She never took her eyes off the almost cruel line of Tom's thin lips, now closed firmly after his accusation.

"Who told you that?"

"It doesn't matter who told me, it's true, isn't it?"

"Yes." Sally gathered her courage. She knew she was going to make a clean breast of it, for the truth was not as bad as the rumour. "I gave no message whatever, but I did receive letters from Peter Barclay." Suddenly she felt angry. "If you hadn't, by your bigoted intolerance, made Mother hostile to Peter, there would be no need to receive letters by those means."

"You are corresponding with Barclay, then?"

"Yes, I am. It's a crime, too, I suppose, so you'd better tell Mother, tell the Shinners, tell everyone and anyone you like. He's going away! He's going to Africa! So you won't have to worry about him much longer!"

"Well, that's the place for him. Out there with the blacks. I hope it's hot enough for him, nearly as hot as Belfast on 12 July. I hope he learns a few new war dances to show the Orangemen in Belfast!"

"Don't sneer at the blacks and their war dances."

"I'm not sneering at the blacks. I'm sneering at the British."

"You're losing your grip on Christianity, Tom. To say nothing of Catholicism. I wish Fr O'Rourke could hear you say that. You'd get a lecture, all right. But above all, I wouldn't like Michael to hear you – he'd be shocked."

"Are you shocked?" Tom sneered.

"No! But my skin is thicker than Michael's."

Tom's lips curled in contempt. "If all Irishmen were like Michael, the Irish would have been ground into oblivion centuries ago. His idea is peace at any price, even at the price of slavery. It's not my idea, though."

"If all Irishmen were like Michael – and indeed all men everywhere – the world would be a wonderful place to live in," Sally said.

"A wonderful place for the British, a regular Garden of Eden."

"With you the serpent."

"And you, Eve, the eternal mischief-maker."

"You or the Shinners aren't doing much to make it a Garden of Eden, it's more like hell let loose. Curfew and ambushes. Half the country on the run and the other half shivering in its skin from dawn to dusk and back again around the clock."

"Who's making it like hell? Nobody but the Black and Tans, and the British Army, and people like you and Barclay!"

Sally threw the draughts down on the table. She came closer to Tom and stared into his eyes. "Don't accuse Peter or me of anything dishonourable. If you do, I'll strike you across the face, even if it is looking across from a Roman collar. I'll take that smug smile off your face!" she hissed, her eyes blazing.

"Easy, Sally. Don't lose your temper. You may get an opportunity to flay all about you some other time. I admire your courage. You know, you have more than Michael and me put together. I think it's you who has Uncle Batt's fiery temper and not me, as they all seem to think. All I have of Uncle Batt is the red head and the love of Ireland. Thank God. Thank God for my love of Ireland, I mean, not for the red head."

"You and Uncle Batt!"

Sally turned to leave the kitchen lest she be further provoked. She was pleased she had refrained from telling him that Peter was coming home, and she was glad that there was no need to receive further letters for him through Lieutenant Sternitt. Tom's disclosure that she had been seen giving or receiving letters bothered her, for although Matt Heaney had warned her, she had taken no notice. It was a rather indirect sort of warning, which didn't actually mention the letters. But for Tom and others to know was a different thing altogether.

For now, she tossed her worries through the open window and thought of the three days – only three days – until Peter was home. If Tom and her mother made it impossible for her to see him, then she would enlist her father and Michael's support, and discuss the whole affair frankly. She knew, of course, that it was her mother and Tom who ruled the household. She alone opposed them. Both her father and Michael's peaceable natures were not much support in a crisis.

But she wouldn't think of that now. She would leave it until Peter was here. Then she would talk it over with him on the first evening they met, and together they would find a way to smooth the path for the coming months.

16

Summer 1921

The sweltering summer of 1921 left little leisure for the farmers. Many of the young men were on the run. To those who remained, and to the women, fell the task of carrying water from sorely depleted sources to the thirsty animals and withering crops. Cattle stood by the field gates, saliva dripping from their thirsty jaws, their tongues lolling out as they awaited the bucket of water that tired hands might bring. They lowed impatiently by the empty field troughs or stood in the shade of the trees, flicking ticks and flies from their tortured hides.

The pump in Glynns' yard had been dry for almost a month. The water for the household now came from a little spring well in the garden. It, too, gave grudgingly, little more than two or three buckets daily. Water for the animals had to be carted in barrels from the lake. Sally's arms constantly ached from filling and refilling and carrying. Sometimes Tom came to help, but more often he had not returned from early Mass, when Michael, Sally or Trooper, or all three of them, set off to fill the barrels before the heat of the day. It seemed an endless task that made them almost grateful for what they had previously considered a plague – the rising lake and the flooded meadows. Each autumn found them battling the same floods. The rain that had hitherto been a curse would now seem like a blessing. Morning after morning the same work went on. It was a ritual now. Michael and Sally fetching, Trooper tipping the water into the barrels and Chess flapping about in the water, his questing nose sniffing the algae on the stagnant surface.

The morning air was fragrant with the scent of white clover, sweet briar and woodbine. The line of the dried-up rivulets was marked by a purple line of loosestrife. The orchid-like blossom of the wild iris had been already replaced by angular seedpods peeping through the trembling plumes of meadow grass, all creeping down from the meadows away from the company of the silken-tasselled knapweed and sturdy-stemmed moon daisy. Sally watched them all bravely fight the drought by taking from the night dew their meagre ration of moisture.

The morning after Sally's quarrel with Tom, the sun had broken through the heat haze when they unharnessed Scarva and turned him loose. The morning's work had whetted the appetites of all – even the horse, who turned immediately to his grazing. Sally, Michael and Trooper went in for breakfast. Tom came in from Mass in time to join them. He sat silently and glumly at the table. Neither of them made any reference to the previous night. The conversation drifted around and occasionally over to Trooper.

"I never was as sick of good weather. But just wait till we start to mow the hay. It'll rain then 'till it doesn't know when to stop."

"That may be tomorrow," Michael announced. "I think we'd better start at the Long Meadow. The crop is poor, but it won't get any better now it's getting brittle."

"Good idea," Sally agreed. "I'm going to work at the office this afternoon and tomorrow afternoon, but the next day we can all get at it. Even Tom," she said, drawing him into the conversation.

"Miss Sally is determined to make Fr Tom work," Trooper said. "Wouldn't do him any harm, either."

Mrs Glynn immediately came to Tom's rescue. "Tom does work, you know, Trooper. His mind has to work even if his hands haven't."

"Well, can't he give his mind a holiday and work his hands for a change? That's what I do on a Sunday. I make me mind work more when me hands are at rest. It's not a bad idea to keep them both workin'."

"Is that what you do, Trooper? There is more wisdom in that old head of yours than in a dozen like Tom's," Sally said.

"There's not as much religion in it, Miss Sally. I hadn't much time for religion when I was soldierin'."

"That's the time you ought to be really religious, when there is danger of any sort threatening. Prayer can be a great weapon to a soldier," Michael added.

He did not add that this had been his experience, because of his mother's disapproval of his Easter week activity in 1916. Trooper knew this and did not pursue the subject.

"It's great weather for the lads on the run – that's the only thing we can be thankful for. I suppose we shouldn't grumble, even if we do have to carry a few barrels of water before breakfast every morning. We can come home and eat and sleep in peace."

"I'm glad someone in the house has a thought for them," Tom said, getting up from the table.

"We all have a thought and a prayer for them," Michael said.

"Not all."

Tom glanced back across his shoulder at Sally as he left the kitchen.

Sally could have flared up at him again. Her feelings of the previous night were not yet dormant, but she pushed back the smouldering resentment and ushered thoughts forward one day to Peter's return.

The dewy heat haze of the morning dissolved beneath the almost tropical midday sun. Insects and animals browsed and basked in the shade of leaf and blade. But there was no rest for Michael and Trooper as they made preparations for haymaking. They pulled the mowing machine from its hibernation into the shade of the hay shed. They trotted backwards and forwards with spanners and oil cans and long serrated blades. John sat on an upturned water butt and offered the sound advice born of years of ownership and experience of the mowing machine, regarding replacements and adjustments.

"There's no hurry. This weather could go on till August."

"There's always hurry at hay," Michael reminded him.

"It could go on until August or it mightn't last a week, and once the rain comes 'tis fare you well, Killaley, to the haymakin'," Trooper added.

Hearing them talking, Sally left her work in the kitchen and went out to the cool hay shed. It was a sign of advancing summer to see the old mowing machine pulled out. She liked to hear the buzz of the wheels and the call to the horses and the click when the blade was lifted. She liked to see the swathes going down, and in the silent intervals to listen to the little echo of the grasshoppers. She liked to smell the warm spicy scent of the hay and the honey from the nests of the wild bees. She sympathised with the timid little black bees retreating while the red bees defended their stores vigorously and viciously. Sally preferred to rob the red bees' nest because of the thrill of the chase, but to rob the little black bees seemed to be sacrilege indeed. Trooper promised to bring back honey from the meadows if he found a nest.

"It must be a red bees' nest," Sally warned.

Trooper's fight with the bees was a source of the greatest amusement to her. She often forgot all about the honey as she watched him swipe at the attackers with his cap and call them outrageous and fantastic names as they darted around his billowing white beard or followed him in the retreat he beat, as fast as his legs would carry him.

Mrs Glynn came through the back door.

"Sally, Tom wants you to go for the paper," she said.

"They wouldn't be in yet," John reminded her.

With the uncertainty of trains it was sometimes afternoon or evening when the papers finally arrived in Cloona. There were many occasions when they didn't come at all but were suppressed because they gave an account of some incident of which the powers at Dublin Castle did not approve.

Tom crossed the yard to join the little group in the hay shed. The sun caught his fiery red hair and the copper-gold binding of the missal in his hand. "Go for the paper, Sally. They're sure to be in by now."

"Aren't you going to Cloona yourself today?" she asked.

She wondered why he had changed his custom of darting for the papers immediately after breakfast.

"No, I have to go over to Fallons'. They have hay down. I promised I'd give them a hand."

"Can't you wait for the paper till I'm coming home this evening from the office? Seems stupid going off now in the sweltering heat for the same paper with the same old news. So many ambushes. So many barracks burnt. You can't be all that thirsty for news."

"I'm very thirsty for that sort of news!" Tom said.

"What sort of news?"

"So many ambushes. So many barracks burnt."

"Then you better go for the paper yourself. Besides, going twice daily into Cloona in weather like this is too much like hardship, and I have to work in the office too. You're on holiday. You have nothing else to do but cycle around and read newspapers."

Sally saw her mother coming to the door and she knew that further argument with Tom would be futile. Reluctantly she left the hay shed and went into the house. She put on her pale green cotton dress and tied up her ringlets with a narrow ribbon. She loitered, furious at Tom's unreasonable demands on her. She slipped her feet into white canvas sandals. They were old and worn, with their rough places smoothed over with pipeclay. Her mother gave her a list of small items she needed and, at Sally's request, the money to buy a new pair of sandals. The prospect of the new sandals took the drudgery out of the trip to Cloona. Sally set off merrily on her bicycle down the avenue. Chess bounded along behind her.

"Go back, Chess! Back!"

But he darted ahead and sped along, determined to accompany her. She got off her bicycle and threw stones into the hedge in the hope of escaping when he retrieved them, but he refused to be drawn into her game and stood up the road, barking foolishly. She gave up trying to send him back and he dropped in behind her, plodding along in the dust. Perhaps he would tire and return home. She did not want him to follow her to the town, for it might give him the habit of straying which, in turn, might lead to his getting lost or stolen. She quickened her pace in the hope of making him abandon his pursuit. But he doubled his efforts, bounding on the grassy road verge down the hill and around the turn, out of sight. When Sally rounded the bend she found Chess standing in the middle of the road, staring back towards her with a puzzled look on his face, which seemed to say, "Now look at the fix we're in." She pulled up alongside him and got off the bicycle as her front wheel almost touched the edge of the yawning chasm in the bridge across the dried-up river. Together Chess and she stared in bewilderment.

They looked down on the stony riverbed through which a trickle of water wandered in a tortuous course, seeking the line of least resistance. Sally knew blown-up bridges often meant ambushes. As there was no sign of a recent ambush, she decided she had better move on quickly, in case one was due. Hastily she sought some means by which she might cross. With the riverbed almost dry she could scramble down the fallen masonry at one corner and carry her bicycle across. Or she could go by the meadow side. Either way would mean carrying her bicycle. She could also scramble along the turreted ivy-covered parapet. In this case she would have to leave the bicycle and walk all the way to Cloona and back. She decided on the first course and was about to climb down over the tumbled stone and mortar when two men approached her simultaneously from opposite sides of the blown-up bridge.

One was tall and handsome, with blue eyes in a bronzed, unshaven face. His fine physique was not flattered by the saggy, dirty grey suit he wore, and the grey, shapeless cap with its peak askew. The other man was small and dark. His shifty ferrety eyes glinted from beneath a slouch hat. Sally thought she had seen the hat somewhere before. She caught a glimpse of a hole in its side. More like a cigarette burn than a bullet hole. Quickly she remembered it was Chris Heaney's hat. Greasy and dirty and domed, like a straw beehive. The curved brim was like one big eyebrow designed to arch over both eyes. The little man's head appeared to be pushed up into it rather than the hat put on his head. His receding chin, dark stubble of beard and prominent teeth gave him a vicious snarling appearance that warned Sally of the hostile nature of the two men whom she had thought, for an instant, to be chivalrous escorts coming to help her across the broken bridge.

17

Shorn

"Are you Miss Glynn – Miss Sally Glynn?" It was the tall man who addressed her in a manner demanding a hasty reply.

"Yes," Sally answered promptly, as eager as he was to have the mysterious interview over.

"Then follow me," he commanded. "I have something to say to you."

He turned to lead the way behind the broken parapet of the bridge towards the Crag.

"No," Sally said stubbornly. "I will not leave the road. What you have to say I can hear now."

"Follow me! Offer no resistance. It's better for you," he warned.

"Go on. Get off the road!" the ferret-faced man barked as he moved towards her, his hand out to give her a push. Sally turned and stared at him. She drew back a little. She thought of the frightened-eyed newt she had, as a child, seen in Tom's hand, and of Michael's words: "Don't be afraid, Sally. He's much more frightened than you are." Hesitantly she followed the tall man through the ragged opening in the low wall. Ferret Face took her bicycle from her and left it inside the whitethorn thicket where yesterday

Sally had watched the goats nibble. He followed along behind her and they walked in single file over the rough path and picked their way over the path at the base of the Crag. The long green strips of the hearts-tongue fern growing on the shady wall licked Sally's face like slimy serpents. Briar and bracken barred their way but it was trampled down by the leading captor to make the path of his prisoner less difficult.

It was only a short distance from the Crag to the Witches' Cauldron but to Sally it seemed an endless journey until they left the shady path to emerge on the hot side of the Crag into the broiling sun. As she climbed, she had tried to conjure up a defence, for she knew from Tom's warning of what she would be charged. Now she stood close to the sun-scorched wall of the Crag, the two men on either side of her like executioners. Behind them, the rocky Crag towered, its open stone alcoves like the doorways of tombs. Directly below, the breast-high bracken, like a miniature forest, wandered down the Sheep Slopes to where the willow and hawthorn mirrored on the surface of the lake.

"Miss Glynn," the tall man said, finally, "you have been found guilty of giving or receiving messages from members of the British Army of occupation."

"No!"

At this moment Chess bounded through the bracken. Sally had forgotten him. The small man jumped nervously. Chess stood out at the edge of the stony cauldron.

"That your dog?" the tall man asked quietly.

"Yes."

"Call him in close to you."

The small man drew a revolver and pointed it at the dog.

"Oh no!" Sally shouted, jumping at him. "You can't shoot Chess! You can't!"

The tall man spoke again, addressing the other. "Put away that gun. What the hell are you up to? One shot here would echo around half the country."

He turned again to Sally, who had called Chess towards her and was now holding his collar with one hand and gripping her bicycle pump with the other.

"Haven't you given or received messages from the army of occupation? Haven't you?"

"No!" Sally said emphatically. "I have neither given to nor received messages from the army of occupation. I have received messages from an officer of the army who is an Irishman. I have received letters from Peter Barclay."

There was a pause, as though the tall man was unprepared for her defence.

"These men are not Irishmen. They are renegade Irishmen. Do not confuse the two!" He changed the charge. "You are, or should be, aware that a boycott exists on all members of the army and police, and you have ignored it by speaking to them. You have even accepted a lift in a car with one of them, and have attended dances in Clanratty."

"Yes."

"Then we must punish you. We have been given orders to do so to teach you a lesson. To set an example to other girls who might be so foolish as to take similar liberties or so flagrantly break our laws. Do you know what that punishment is?" He paused dramatically. "Your hair must be shorn!"

Sally stood, dumbfounded, as the sentence was passed. The word *shorn* sounded almost barbarous. She glanced quickly to either side of her, seeking an escape. Her hand slipped from Chess's collar and went slowly, instinctively, as a measure of protection, to her thick, golden ringlets. As soon as she took her hand away, Ferret Face, with one swift, nervous movement, whipped a pair of scissors from his pocket. He roughly seized her hair and hacked off two golden ringlets.

Like a wildcat awakened by the sudden approach of an enemy, Sally jumped into action from the daze into which the sentence had spun her. She raised the bicycle pump, and wildly hit out at her surprised attacker, raining blow after blow upon his head and shoulders. She took no aim but wielded the pump randomly.

Both men appeared wholly unprepared for such fierce resistance. The small man, bent almost in two, raised the hand holding the scissors to ward off the blows. Sally grabbed the scissors and clutched them firmly in her free hand, while the other hand kept dealing the blows to his elbow, now raised like a schoolboy attempting to protect his smarting ears and skull. The tall man leaned back against the hot stone crag and laughed at the ludicrous position of the girl turning the tables on her opponent and beating him mercilessly with a bicycle pump, a man with a gun in his pocket.

The little man grabbed wildly at the flailing pump but missed each time. He snatched his hand away as the pump cracked across his knuckles. After many unsuccessful attempts, he caught the pump handle, and sharply pulled on it. It did not offer the resistance he anticipated. The handle shot out from the case of the pump which Sally held firmly in hand. As he was standing with his heels against a stone, the extended pump gave him no way to adjust his balance, and he fell over backwards, rolling over the edge into the bracken.

Sally turned to flee back along the path to the bridge, but the tall man blocked her path.

"You can't go that way!"

Like a hunted animal, Sally looked around for another means of escape. She wasn't going to cringe and ask for mercy from these men who listened to stories and gossip from people like Gerty Fallon, for it was Gerty whom Sally blamed for the fuss she made of Chris Heaney's stories.

"You're a very courageous girl, Miss Glynn, and because of your courage, and your brother's patriotism, I will take it upon myself to disobey my orders regarding your punishment."

Sally didn't think he ever really intended cutting her hair; she had seen the way he flinched and raised his hand to stop the capering little monkey who had already snipped off two ringlets, and who was now on his feet again and prancing around like an excited terrier.

"Orders is orders! Who'll accept responsibility for disobeying them?"

"I will," the tall man said.

But Ferret Face went on protesting in a low growling voice.

Ignoring him, the tall man said, "You may go home now, Miss Glynn, on certain conditions. You must stick to the rules of the boycott on the police and on the army of occupation."

"Does that include Peter Barclay?"

"No, he is not a member of the army of occupation, but your association with him must not lead you into any contact with the army. You cannot now go on to Cloona. You must return home by the lake. There is a boat there, down at the end of that lane."

"Don't let her go. She'll get us shot! She'll spy on us, the little bitch!" the small man said.

"Can you row a boat?"

"Yes, but I'm going home by the road. I want my bicycle." Now that she saw escape was open to her, she wanted to choose her own means.

"You can't go by the road. Your bicycle will be delivered to you by some means. It will be left somewhere for you. We will see you get it. You must do as I say. If you cannot promise to do what I've asked, then you will remain here for some time as our prisoner."

Sally saw that it was useless to argue further and nodded her head.

"There is no time to discuss plans with you," the man went on. "You must do as I say. You get in the boat and keep close to the shore, in the shelter of the trees. You may row to where the lake turns and the road above the fields is visible. But you may not go around that bend after twelve o'clock. You will hear the Angelus bell ring from Kilalisheen and from Cloona, and that will be the signal for you. One other thing," he said slowly, "you may not discuss this incident with anyone outside your own family before nightfall. There is no need for me to stress the importance of silence."

"You're preparing an ambush," Sally said. She pointed to Ferret Face. "He's more likely to give you away than I am. He's a fool! And he'll shoot one of you as quickly as he will a Black and Tan."

"He's unaccustomed to women."

As he spoke, Ferret Face, who had been crouching between two boulders and looking towards the blown-up bridge, turned quickly.

"They're here!"

He jumped over the boulders and quickly disappeared through the bracken and briars.

18

Ambush

Almost before the sound of Ferret Face's voice had faded, a sharp volley of shots rang out from the bridge. Then lorries coasted down the hill from Clanratty, their engines in tandem with the shots, preventing any warning of their approach.

The tall man pulled Sally into the hot stone alcove in the wall. He pushed her behind him and stood in front of her, his revolver in his hand. They stood for what seemed an eternity in the hollow of the sizzling rock. The merciless midday sun blazed down upon them as volley after volley of shots cracked and echoed close to their ears and whined across the lake. There was barely room for them both in the narrow stone shelter, and as Sally stood behind the man, his left shoulder pressed against her. She could see the wave in his dark hair beneath the greasy curly unkempt growth on his neck. Beads of sweat ran down into his dirty collar. She could see his long white fingers and ragged nails. The slim hand holding the revolver was not the hand of a manual worker. The man cautiously edged a little forward. She pushed forward after him and hitched herself up a bit by leaning on the rough stone edge.

Peeping through, she caught a glimpse of the bridge below and the strip of green behind the silver army of birch trees. Everywhere now seemed alive with men, lorries and tenders. Black- and khaki-clad figures darted furiously between or crouched beneath the vehicles. Puffs of blue smoke came from the revolver shots and blossomed like magic flowers at irregular intervals along the base of the hedge beside the road. Sally's captor pulled her roughly down and pushed her with his broad, strong back into the alcove.

"Keep down!" he commanded. "For God's sake, keep down! You've made enough trouble. I ought to have been at my post by the bridge, not here. They came too soon. They weren't due for nearly another hour." He growled the words to himself in a low voice.

The shots now appeared to be covering a wider area, and were coming closer, spreading all around. They were being encircled. Spasmodic firing came from confusing directions. The tall man listened intently in an effort to place it, before he moved into action. Sally suddenly felt faint. Her heart was pounding and she could hear its dull pump in her breast. A saline taste was on her lips and her cotton dress was sticking to her body. The scorching sun was burning into her bare head. Her hand was scratched and bleeding where the point of the scissors had caught her when she grabbed them. The blood was smearing the dirty grey suit of the man, as well as her own dress.

"Let me go!" she gasped. "Let me out before I faint. I can hide in the bracken where it's cooler."

"No. When the bracken moves, it will give us away."

As he spoke, Sally saw the bracken actually move close to them at the edge of the Cauldron, and the top fronds danced in the sun. The man gazed towards it unblinkingly. Sally's eyes, peering from behind his shoulder, followed his gaze.

"It's Chess," she whispered close to his ear.

"Damn that dog!"

Sally noticed that he did not change his vigilance or relax his hold on the drawn revolver covering the moving bracken. And then, only a few yards away, the green bamboo stems parted, and a paw-like hand holding a revolver came into view. The sagging jowls of "Loper", the lone Tan of Gerty and Frank's wedding night, emerged. His tasselled Glengarry was pulled well down on his forehead, but he was still easy to recognise.

"He's harmless. He's—" Sally whispered.

But before the sentence was complete the man had fired. The Black and Tan's face disappeared and the bracken waved and crackled noisily as his body rolled through it down the steep incline towards the lake. Sally covered her face with her hands. She felt limp and faint, and only the man's back wedging her against the rock kept her upright.

"They're closing in on us." He spoke hoarsely, turning and pulling her trembling hands from her face. He jerked her down from the hot hole in the rock. "Crouch behind that wall when you can reach it," he said, pointing out an escape route. "Get down to the lake and to the boat as quick as you can."

He pushed her forward to go, eager to be rid of her. Sally slipped along from boulder to boulder, pausing at intervals to plan her next move, until she reached the shelter of the broken wall. She crouched beneath the ragged protection it offered, sometimes lying flat on the grass when she thought it safer. She could hear the shots in an ever-widening circle and, from the bridge, the occasional sharp command of a voice. As the shots struck the top of the wall close to where she lay, they skimmed the lichen from it like a swarm of green butterflies. Sally gasped in terror.

She reached the end of the wall and paused for a long time, loath to leave the scant shelter it afforded. Then, with a swift, almost animal-like, movement she streaked across the open patch of grass and bracken. Once over, she quickly thrust her way through the hazel and briar thicket into Folly Lane. It was cool. The dark hawthorn overgrew the lane, allowing a welcome respite from the sun-baked wall but offering less security. With the bicycle pump she beat a path for herself through the tangled undergrowth and ran down to the lake. The noise of the gunfire was now more spasmodic. The intervals between volleys and single shots lengthened like a receding thunderstorm.

In the silence of one of these intervals, Sally heard the Angelus bell ring at Kilalisheen church. She blessed herself and said a brief prayer as she made her way to where the boat was moored. She had not forgotten about the warning and the mention of the Angelus bell. She clambered into the boat, which she recognised as being their own, and manoeuvred it away from the shore. The long mooring rope was tied up to the rough alders.

It hurt her already torn hands to loosen its knot. She punted with one oar through the shallow water, keeping close to the edge. She could not see into the shallow depths. The surface of the water was covered by the yellow-and-black-spotted willow leaves, blighted and fallen as the marshy swamp had become dry and baked by the summer's long drought. Once, the boat stuck on a sandy shallow and she had to get out and wade in the water to release it and push it off. Cautiously moving out a few feet further from the shore, she continued punting with one oar. Her progress was slow and laborious.

Suddenly a burst of gunfire from the Crag rang out, echoing again and again across the water. She lay low in the boat and let it drift. Then, in the silence that followed, she mustered her courage and, putting both oars in the wooden oar locks, she pulled upon them and moved still further out in the deeper water. She rowed now with more ease and safety, but the wooden oar pins creaked noisily. She searched in the bottom of the boat and found a tin of worms. She emptied the wriggling mass over the side and, after filling the tin with water, she drenched and silenced the creaking pins. Then she skimmed in rapid strokes around the bend in the lake.

The shooting had ceased now, and a blessed peace seemed to fall on the lake and the woods. No sound came from anywhere. In the quiet seclusion of the tall reeds Sally shipped the oars and let her tense body relax while she reflected on all that had happened. She thought of Chess. Where was he? Dare she call him now? She longed to do so but prudence forbade such a risk. Memories of poor Chess's trusting face took her mind back to the Black and Tan, now lying dead or wounded in the bracken at the bottom of the Crag. And with all that shooting, God knows how many others as well. Maybe they included the tall blue-eyed stranger who had fired point-blank into a man's face and yet had flinched when he saw a girl's hair cut off.

She leaned over the edge of the boat and watched the reflection of the tall reeds dance when she stirred them. When the ripples subsided, she saw her own reflection in the water. Over one ear, from where the two ringlets had been snipped, a bunch of hair stood out. Stubbly and unruly. She took the captured scissors from the pocket of her dress and tried to shape her ragged tresses. But she seemed to be making them even worse. She washed the caked mud from her injured hand and, gathering a palmful of water, wet her hair and patted it into subjection. She pushed the boat out slightly from the reeds so that the mirrored surface of the water would not be distorted by the bending and waving columns of green. The clearer her reflection became, the more dissatisfied she grew.

How was she going to face them at home? What could she tell them, especially her mother? She could not tell the truth, which would mean telling the whole story leading up to today – the dance in Clanratty and the mutilated blue dress. She would have to think up a likely tale. But there were also the added difficulties of her bicycle and the missing Chess. How she hoped Chess would go on home and not ramble about searching for her.

A wild duck rose with a beating of wings from the reeds. The sudden commotion frightened her and her heart raced madly as the duck beat the air, seeking a balanced wing in its heavy, ponderous flight. Sally watched it cross the lake and her eyes returned to from where it had appeared, searching for the little yellow fluffy balls of deserted ducklings. Then, to her great delight and relief, she spotted Chess. He was sniffing along the water's edge.

"Chess!" she called excitedly, standing up in the boat and forgetting all dangers.

The sound of her voice in the silence was startling, and she quickly crouched down again in the boat. Chess stood, one paw raised. Then, seeing and hearing Sally, he eagerly bounded forward, splashing belly high into the water. Sally turned the bow of the boat inland and pulled in to meet him. He scrambled awkwardly over the side, and onto the seat beside her, licking her hands and face. She put an arm around the wet, wriggling, excited dog, speaking softly to him in the mutual joy of their reunion.

"Down, Chess, down!"

He reluctantly obeyed her and lay quietly at her feet on the bottom of the boat. Sally pulled slowly and easily along the edge of the reeds. There was no sound save the lap of the waves as they rolled gently back from the bow of the boat, the drip from the fettered oars making roles of rings on the jelly-like surface of the water. She skilfully manoeuvred the boat into the boathouse. Stepping out, she tied up the boat and left the oars lying along the seats.

Whoever brought the oars here to accommodate the Shinners can take them back, she thought. It must be either Tom or Michael, but she couldn't be bothered now to think about them further. She was so tired, so hot and so worried.

It seemed like a week since she had stood on the shingly patch, helping Trooper and Michael fill the barrels. She trudged up the rutted path as though an invisible load lay across her shoulders. Her old sandals were torn and the spiky thistles hurt her feet. She thought of the new sandals. She hadn't got as far as getting them. She hadn't even the money now. It was in her purse in the saddlebag of the bicycle.

As she walked, she wrestled with half-made excuses about the bicycle. Suddenly she saw Chess quickening his stride on the path before her. He bounded forward. Looking beyond him, she saw Michael coming to meet them.

19

Raid

"What happened, Sally? Where have you been? How did you get here? Where's your bike? We were so worried about you, Sally." Michael rushed on, giving her no time to answer any of his questions.

"There was an ambush. I got caught in it."

"Yes, we knew there was something wrong. We heard the shots and thought Clanratty was being attacked." He looked at her bleeding hand and the smears on her dress. He did not notice her lopsided hair. "Were you hurt, Sally? There's blood on your hand."

"It's nothing. Only a briar scratch." She wiped away the little oozing smear along the red line the scissors had made.

"Where's your bike? And how did you get up the lake?"

"The bridge was blown up when I was coming back. I left the bike at Matt Heaney's – the chain was broken. I got a lift as far as the bridge. I can get my bike this evening."

"Who gave you the lift?"

"I don't know. He was a stranger in a pony and trap. He had to turn back when the bridge was blown up."

"Funny you didn't know him."

"Isn't it?" she said, marvelling at how easily lies came to her lips, and at how very accommodating they could be. "He was going to buy pigs or something from someone up at the mountain."

"Pigs in a pony trap!"

Sally felt she was going to yell at Michael if he kept on tormenting her with unnecessary questions when she had already gone through so much. She tried to turn his thoughts away from the imaginary man and his imaginary pony and trap.

"I got the boat – it was anchored at the end of Folly Lane."

"Whose boat?"

"Our boat. The Shinners must have had it, oars and all."

"Who gave them our oars?" Michael was obviously surprised.

Now Sally concluded that it must be Tom who had given them to the Shinners. "Maybe they just commandeered them themselves, last night sometime. Tom had the boat out last night, maybe he left the oars in it."

"You look frightened, or something, Sally."

Sally did not like the *or something*. She knew it was her hair so she kept the shaggy side of her head away from him.

"I'm not frightened. I'm just tired after rowing the boat in the heat, that's all."

They entered the cool, shady drive leading to the house. Her parents were standing in the garden looking expectantly and anxiously towards the gate. As soon as Michael and Sally emerged from the rhododendrons, her mother threw both hands up in a gesture of gratitude and her father waved his stick. Tom came through the door. He had just arrived back from Fallons' when Sally and Michael came into view.

When they were within hailing distance, Michael shouted, "She got caught in the ambush."

"Are you hurt, Sally?" her mother called.

"No. She's all right!" Michael answered. "She had to leave the bicycle and row back by the lake."

"Anyone killed, Sally?" her father asked.

"I don't know. I didn't wait to see."

"I should hope not." Her mother was clearly relieved to hear this.

Tom was standing in the doorway, eyeing her critically. He had no rapturous greeting to offer. "What happened to your hair, Sally?" he asked, almost before he had time to look her over.

She had smoothed the rough-cut strands into place with water but it was dry again now and more limp and unruly than before.

"I got burrs in it. I had to cut them out."

"There are no burrs in June. The burdock isn't in blossom yet."

"Yes," her mother said nervously, coming closer to her and touching the shorn locks. "What happened, Sally?"

Sally pushed her mother's hand away and covered the shorn hair with her own hand, as they gathered around her. "It got caught," she said.

"Caught?" her mother repeated. "In what?"

"They … they … had to cut it."

"Who had to cut it?" her mother asked. For now that Sally was safe, there was nothing to worry about except hair.

"The men." Sally remained vague.

"Ah Sally, they surely didn't have to cut your hair, no matter what it was caught in?"

"Caught the trees – her beautiful hair – like Absalom!" Tom mocked. "What did they cut it with – a sword?"

All of them seemed prepared to make a joke of it except her mother, who considered it almost a tragedy.

"What a fuss about a lock of hair," Sally's father said, as Trooper came from the back of the house to hear the news. "Far worse if it had been Trooper's beard. That wouldn't grow again as quickly as Sally's hair."

They all moved into the house. Sally slumped heavily into a chair by the table. She was unable to eat the dinner her mother had ready and to which all of the others sat down contentedly.

"I'll have a cup of tea, that's all." She washed her hands. Wiping her face with a towel, she took a hasty, anxious look at herself in a mirror by the window. Then, sitting at the table, she took the cup of tea her mother had made for her. She sipped it indifferently and nibbled at a slice of bread. All the time the questions kept coming at her.

Did she see any of the IRA? Yes. Did she know any of them? No.

Where was she when the firing was going on? Behind the Crag. How did she get down to the lake? Down Folly Lane. Why didn't she come back by the road? Because the shooting was going on and the man told her to go back by the lake. What man? The Shinners man. How did the boat become moored at the end of Folly Lane? They must have commandeered it. But they couldn't commandeer the oars – they were in the trap house. Maybe they were someone else's oars.

At this point Trooper went out into the trap house and came back with the news that the oars were gone out of the corner. Michael looked at Tom, and Tom suggested they leave Sally alone and go and mow the meadow. After all, they had spent the forenoon preparing the machine. To Sally's relief Tom left the kitchen, and Michael and Trooper followed him to the back door.

Suddenly Michael raised his hand. "Listen!" he said.

All lapsed into silence, a silence broken by only the sizzling of two freshly cut logs on the fire. But this was quickly drowned by an even louder hum. Tom and Trooper edged back into the kitchen.

"Lorries!" Michael announced. "Coming from Cloona."

"Couldn't be," his father said, "not with the bridge down."

"They've had time to put planks across it," Michael surmised.

"Not planks to take a lorry," his father said.

As they listened, the noise grew louder and two army cars came up the drive and stopped in front of the house. Tom, Trooper and Michael stood hovering around the back door. Sally and her father sat near the table. Her mother stood looking nervously at all of them. Raids, no matter how innocent their victims might be, often brought surprising and sad results. For her part, Sally thought she'd had enough of this sort of thing for one day.

The soldiers, red-faced with heat and frustration, came belligerently forward.

"'Ow many men in this 'ouse?" the spokesman demanded, as he eyed each of the four men in turn. "There was a blinkin' ambush down the road. You know that! Any of you fellers in it?" He didn't wait for a reply but started his own process of elimination.

"You wasn't," he said to John, eyeing his stick and the old rocking chair.

"And you wasn't, ole Santa," he said to Trooper.

"And you, magpie!" he said, addressing Tom and going over close to him. "These your own workin' clothes or just borrowed ones?" he asked, giving the clerical collar a tug.

"They are my own," Tom answered.

One of the soldiers came forward and, taking hold of Tom's hand, compared the student clothes with the student hands.

The man in charge again turned to Michael. "Where was you all mornin', 'ansome?" he sneered.

"I was here, preparing the mowing machine to cut the meadow."

"Sure you wasn't getting a saw ready to cut the planks in the bridge, or a charge of gelignite to blow it up with?"

"No. I was here in the yard – never left it."

"Any Shinners 'iding about this place? 'Ave a look," he instructed the Tans standing around.

They prowled through the rooms. As they shuffled out to search the yard and outhouses, Sally thought uneasily of the Black and Tan's tunic and cap behind the rafters. Her mind went to the bridge and the thought of the Black and Tan lying dead or wounded in the bracken at the foot of the Crag. She shuddered but no one noticed. The soldiers found nothing incriminating, however, and they got back into their cars and swooped off down the avenue. Where the opening in the trees permitted, the Glynns could see Black and Tans and soldiers gathered in little groups around the fields and on the road leading to the bridge. They had even reached the Long Meadow and the Crescent Acre, ploughing through them heedless of the damage they might do to the crops.

"I'm going to lie down. I've a headache," Sally said.

She went into her bedroom and closed the door. She went to the mirror on her dressing table and at last found the energy and opportunity to study, without interruption, the devastation to her hair and to experiment with methods of camouflaging it. She took the hand mirror from her dressing table. After scrutinising the shaggy ends from every angle, she combed out the remaining ringlets on the back of her head. Then she tried to fit the scraggy ends into the bow, always with the same result. The long, shining ringlets fell back into their corkscrew line, and the chipped-off loose ends stuck out awkwardly. In the end she twisted the bits into curl papers.

The room was still warm from the heat of the midday sun when she got up and undressed. She cleaned the bloodstains from her injured hand in the deep basin on the washstand. She dipped a towel into the ewer of cold water and laid it on her burning forehead. Then she lay back on the flowery chintz counterpane. Her burning forehead seemed cooler now and she felt better. The fear and tension were slowly losing their grip. The bees were buzzing noisily where wall roses overhung the bedroom window. This was the only sound creeping in from the lazy, hazy heat. Her thoughts were shuttling backwards and forwards between the morning's confusion and Peter's return tomorrow evening. Their meeting place, the Hazel Bridge, would never again hold for her the many pleasant memories of meeting Peter there. Always above them and mixed with them would come the ghost of "Loper" the Black and Tan and that awful ferret-faced little thug. The tall blue-eyed man she somehow could forgive. There was something finer in him than revenge and retaliation and petty reprisals for petty offences. Indeed there was something about the tall man that she had pictured in Patrick Pearse. Something of the spirit that had captured Michael's admiration. Something perhaps of Michael himself. She hoped nothing had happened to the man in the melee because of her, and that he had escaped. She thought of Ferret Face. She hated him. She was sure it was Chris Heaney's hat he had on. There wasn't much danger of Chris getting into the fighting, though, unless, like herself, he got caught in it by accident. Chris carried on his fight for freedom by spying around the town or from a safe seat in the old Ford. It could be, she thought with almost malicious glee, that Chris had been about the bridge somewhere to point her out to the two strangers. After all, how could they have known her? If he was there, she hoped he got shaken up in the fighting. Perhaps a stray bullet found him.

Sweeping the sickening memory of it away, she began to work out her plans for the evening when she would face the family again. What about her bicycle? She would have to borrow one from Matt until she got her own back. She would tell the family that Matt was fixing hers as she had already told Michael. There was always the possibility, of course, that Tom might go snooping around Matt's, asking for it. She was due to go to the office that afternoon, but with the bridge up and the ambush, Mr Pratt wouldn't expect her. She decided she would go in the morning and fix up with Matt about the bicycle. She would ask him not to tell Tom anything about it. She would have to put Matt wise somehow without actually telling him the truth. And, of course, she would have to buy the sandals and pay for them somehow because the money her mother had given her was in the purse in the saddlebag on the bicycle.

When Peter came she would have to meet him in Cloona. It could not be at the bridge, because for the next few days people would be dodging about having a look at it. All Cloona would want to be out to see where the ambush had been, even though they had seen it all before and there was nothing new about this one. But until something else happened, the Hazel Bridge would be the news. What would Peter think of her hair? He would laugh, perhaps, when she told him. Of course she would tell him the whole story. She kept few secrets from him.

Except the one about the blue dress belonging to Lady Isobel that she had purloined from her mother's trunk.

20

Captured

The long June twilight lingered through the leafy shadows and night came slowly into the Glynn kitchen. Indeed, but for the green curtain of the trees surrounding it, the house could have gone to bed without lamp or candlelight. Mrs Glynn liked the lamplight to end what she called the "too-long day". It marked a visible link between day and night, bringing the cosiness of winter to the summer-weary workers. Suppertime now seemed the only time when appetites rose above the constant thirst for long cool drinks. Those who had found food in the daytime almost nauseating, now, in the cool of the evening, became gourmets, indulging freely in the farmhouse fare Mrs Glynn provided. Crisp green salads, fresh soda and wheaten bread, scones with honey or homemade jam, rhubarb and gooseberry tarts. Sometimes a few fried trout or an eel bouncing on the pan were offered.

Mrs Glynn fixed her husband's chair in its customary place at the top of the table. The others were just settling down to enjoy the supper, which the day's hasty and irregular meals had prepared them for, when the front door opened and the tramp of feet filled the tiled porch and corridor. No one spoke as the dark wave rolled in like a noisy menacing tide of stampeding animals. As the soldiers marched over the kitchen floor, Sally stood with the big brown teapot in her hand, gripping its glossy hot handle. The handle was burning her hand and she put the teapot back again on the hearth. She stood slightly behind her father's chair. Trooper sat in his chair near the back door. Tom sat opposite his father at the other end of the table. Michael was standing across the kitchen, his hands gripping the chair he was carrying. His mother stood, holding the milk jug she was about to place on the table. All were immobilised like marionettes on a broken string. Chess ran forward in his foolish, friendly way to welcome the invaders. One of them pointed a gun at him.

Mrs Glynn spoke quickly but coolly: "He's all right. He's quiet. Down, Chess."

Sally thought, it's the second time today that Chess has had a gun pointed at his head. Or is it today? she wondered. She was confused, considering the elapsed hours and the events with which they had been packed.

"There's that dog! I saw 'im there, too, gallopin' around the fields as if 'e was lookin' for som'at or somebody."

The commander of the party ignored the acute observation of his lackey and started his own line of enquiry. It was pretty much the same as it had been with the others who had raided the house that afternoon.

"'Ow many men in this 'ouse?"

"Same number as you see," Mrs Glynn replied.

He eyed them shiftily, his eyes flitting around them before finally settling on Michael.

"Where was you all day?" he demanded.

"I was in the yard in the morning preparing the mowing machine, and in the afternoon I was cutting weeds with that at the back of the house, so as to get the oil worked into the machine, and to get the horse accustomed to it."

"'Oo was with you in the yard?"

"All you see here." Michael waved his hand as he identified and introduced each member. "My father, my brother, Tom, our help, Trooper. My mother and my sister, who came out for a while," he said.

"Hm! Quite a jolly family party," the Tan said sarcastically, his eyes fixed on Tom. "What are you supposed to be?"

"I'm a student – a clerical student."

Ignoring Tom's reply, the Tan turned to John and ordered him to stand up. As John struggled to his feet, the Tan seized the lapel of his collar and pulled him roughly from his chair. Without his stick, John wobbled and would have fallen but for Sally's supporting hand.

"Can't you walk?" the Tan asked. "Sure you're not acting?"

"Wish to God I could walk," John growled. His family sensed the hidden threat in his wish.

"You," – he turned his attention to Trooper – "is this thing real?" He tugged at Trooper's white beard.

Trooper jumped to his feet. "If you raise a hand to me again, you spawn of English jails, I'll show you what a soldier is! I've soldiered in more wars than you could count. I was mounted on me charger when you ... when you—"

"Shh, Trooper! Shh!" chorused each member of the family.

Trooper's explosive temper would not have been of any use against these armed marauders.

The leader again turned his attention to Michael. "You knew – or maybe you didn't, like the rest," he sneered, "that there was an ambush down the road today? I must arrest you as a member of the ambushin' party. You was there, wasn't you?"

"No!" Michael said firmly.

"A bicycle from this 'ere 'ouse was found beside the bridge, an old Rudge-Whitworth bike with new links in its old chain. There was such a bicycle 'ere before. Where is it now? Don't suppose you know anything about it!"

"Yes, it's my sister's bicycle. She left it—"

Sally moved quickly to Michael's side. "I left it at the bridge. I swear it was me!" she cried, panic-stricken.

"No use taking the blame, noble little sister," the Tan said, and turning to Michael he continued his interrogation. Michael became confused regarding the bicycle. He remembered Sally saying she had left it at Matt's because the chain was broken. He wondered if Tom could have collected it and have been in the ambush, instead of helping Frank Fallon with the hay as he had said. Michael didn't know what to think. Was Sally trying to save him or cover up for Tom? Torn with doubt, he remained silent to further questioning.

Michael's silence provoked the Black and Tans and they gathered closer and more menacingly around him. One of them struck him a blow with his open hand across the face.

Sally jumped in between them. "Ah, no! You can't do that!" she cried.

But the protests of both Sally and her mother were met with sneers and pointed revolvers. The Glynns could only stand helplessly by while, at the point of a gun, Michael was pushed through the door to the waiting lorry.

Michael turned in the shadowed hall and called, "Don't worry, Mother. Don't worry, Sally."

The Tans echoed his words in mocking parody. Trooper followed them out, shouting and cursing at them and the British Empire. As the lorry was slowly moving away with Michael, under heavy escort, two of the Tans grabbed the noisy and protesting Trooper.

"Come on, you too, you garrulous old Santa," one of them shouted. "We'll give you a faster ride then your reindeers." They threw him, still shouting, into the lorry with Michael.

Sally stood with her mother, father and Tom, watching helplessly as the lorry moved down the avenue to be swallowed up in the dense foliage of the rhododendrons. They saw it swing out onto the road. They followed the glow of its headlamps until they dipped into the hollow by the bridge. They heard it slow, almost to a standstill, as it crossed the temporary planking structure. Then, as the noise faded into silence and the light into darkness, they turned into the house, carrying with them the burden of their grief and suspense.

Sally sat on the chair Michael had been holding and laid her head on her arms across the table. Her forehead ached. It felt as though a hot vice was squeezing it. Her eyes burned but no tears came to take the dry smarting from them. Her mouth was hot and dry. Her heart was frozen with terror – terror for Michael. Where was the journey he had now started going to end? Tonight in Cloona jail. From there, Mountjoy, Ballykinlar, Spike Island – or maybe the firing squad? She thought with pride of the way he had accepted the insults. He was like Christ with the Jews, she thought. If it had been Tom he would have lost his temper. He would have kicked, scratched, and bitten them in an effort to escape. Maybe he would have been shot there and then. Even this might have been more bearable than to watch Michael's accepting martyrdom. Why did he not deny these accusations more vehemently? Or was he sheltering Tom? Was Tom in it? She wished now she had told the truth about the bicycle and her haircut.

Out of the welter of confusion, she thought of the person most likely to have identified the bicycle. It must have been the orderly who had lifted it into the back of Lieutenant Sternitt's car the day the chain broke. She saw a glimmer of hope. Perhaps Lieutenant Sternitt could help them to proclaim Michael's innocence. She raised her head from the table and looked at her mother who was crying silently with her back to the lamplight, her face in the shadow. Her father put a hand out to her mother and whispered with a broken unfamiliar voice, "Don't fret, Nell. They won't keep him."

Tom sat near the smouldering fire, nervously fingering his closed missal.

Sally looked at him. "Were you in on this thing today? Tell the truth. Has Michael gone to jail to save you?"

"No. Michael has gone to jail because you left your old bike at the bridge when the IRA took you around the Crag to cut your hair. That's why he's gone to jail! That's where Peter Barclay has landed all of us."

"How do you know they were going to cut my hair? You knew they were going to cut my hair and you wouldn't even warn me? You sent me for the paper."

"Warn you! How many times did I warn you? Even Matt Heaney warned you – and you know what happened to him. They had orders to cut your hair." Tom's attitude was cool and matter-of-fact.

"Orders from whom? From you, maybe." Rising to her feet, she went quickly towards him, as though she might strike him.

"Easy, Sally." John made an effort to calm Sally's rising temper.

"It's Peter Barclay who's at the root of it all," Tom said, turning to his mother. "I always knew something unwholesome would come of his friendship with Sally, but none of ye would listen to me."

"You're talking nonsense, Tom," his father said. He seldom went against Tom, or, indeed took any side in family feuds. "I can't see how he comes into it at all, and there's no use conjuring up a scapegoat out of someone a thousand miles away."

"It's a pity he's so far away. Maybe he could do something. Maybe he could get Michael out if he was here. He could use his influence," Sally's mother cried, desperate for a solution.

"Do something? Use influence? You don't think he would have any influence! Even if he had, we're not going begging favours of the Black and Tans," Tom sneered.

"Not when it's not your skin that's in danger. I would beg favours of the devil himself if I could get Michael out of jail," Sally said.

"You would! But Michael wouldn't. He has more spirit, thank God."

"Please! Please, children," their mother cried, raising her apron to her face. "Don't quarrel. There's too much quarrelling all around us without bringing it into the house. We can hope and pray for his release."

Sally was now praying for Peter's return. Maybe, as her mother said, and despite Tom's sneers, he could do something. Even Lieutenant Sternitt might find a way to help. After all, she thought, he's Peter's cousin and an Irishman too, and can't be wholly deaf and blind to the injustices that are being inflicted now, especially on Michael. And certainly she could convince him of Michael's innocence regarding the ambush. She gathered some comfort from this, and tried to console her mother and father.

"He'll be out tomorrow night, maybe even tomorrow evening," she assured them.

But neither of them answered her hopeful prediction. She reflected on the outrageous situation in which Michael and she were in. The silence that had descended on the kitchen was broken by the sounds of footsteps coming up the drive – slow, plodding footsteps. Tom moved towards the door and Sally followed.

"There's someone coming," she said in a whisper. "Maybe he's back! It's Michael, I bet it is!"

Her mother came and put a trembling hand on Tom's shoulder as he drew near the door. "No, no!" she cried, tension still in her voice. "Don't open the door yet. You never know."

Nervously they stood waiting, expecting a knock. They were startled when the door opened as though a battering ram had struck it.

"Trooper!" they all exclaimed together and then looked past him through the open door.

It was his mother who asked, "Where is Michael?"

"I escaped! I escaped!" His face was scratched and bleeding and his shirt was torn. "I jumped out of the lorry when it slowed down for the broken bridge. They threw me out! They said I was too noisy." He was excited and feeling very heroic. He contradicted his statements in every second sentence. "Threw me into the briars and bushes, they did!"

"You don't call that escaping," Tom said.

"Oh, the damn blackguards!"

"What about Michael?" Sally screeched at him. "Where is he? Tell us about him!"

"Dammit, there's nothing to tell about him, 'cept he's gone on in the lorry – and you know that. Look at the state of me, knee-deep in me own blood!"

"Oh, shut up, Trooper," Tom said. "There's nothing on you, only a few scratches. I saw you worse after cutting a hedge."

"Come on, Trooper, and wash yourself," Mrs Glynn said, picking up an enamel bowl and taking the kettle from the fire. She carried them out to the back scullery. Trooper followed, growling into his beard at the Black and Tans and those who did not appreciate his heroic exploits.

The uneaten supper was cleared away. No one, except Trooper, appeared to have any interest in it. They knelt and said the Rosary, each member of the family remaining on their knees a long time after its completion, saying their own private prayers before going to bed. Tom took out his breviary and his little leaflet prayers and continued reading far into the night while the other heads in the house tossed uneasily on their pillows, each thinking feverishly of Michael and his lost freedom. The lost freedom of many, in the cause of this greater freedom of which they talked – now it seemed as far away as in 1916, when Michael fought his first losing battle.

21

Politicised

Sally stood before the mirror in her bedroom, trying to conceal the ends of her shorn locks. She combed and twisted them into strands she took from the remaining ringlets and, crowning them with her straw hat, she set off to the railway station to meet Peter and visit Michael. She now considered that Michael's arrest had cancelled out any promise she had made yesterday to ignore and refrain from talking to members of the British Army of occupation. She no longer feared Tom's or her mother's disapproval of her friendship with Peter. They had bigger problems on their minds.

She had no bicycle now. She would have to walk all the way to Cloona, unless she managed to get a lift in the Barclays' trap. She trudged along in the dust as far as the bridge. It had all been changed now. It was not the bridge she had known all her life. She leaned on the parapet that had been the scene of the previous day's ambush, the scene where she herself had been the first victim and where the incriminating bicycle had been left. She watched for the trap coming down the side road from Storm Hill on its way to the station to meet Peter. If Mrs Barclay wasn't in the trap when it came along, she was going to get into it with Corney Thornton and boldly go to meet Peter in broad daylight at Cloona railway station. Peter no doubt would be amazed at the change in her attitude and conclude she had put the matter to her parents as he had suggested in his letter. But she would not keep him long in doubt. Peter must find a way to get Michael out.

She leaned over the bridge. The surroundings had changed much in the past twenty-four hours and were scarcely recognisable. The long, lush grass by the riverbank was flattened to the ground. Great boulders and planks from the bridge were damming the small stream, diverting it and forcing it up on the gravelly sandy beach from which it had withdrawn in the drought. The whitethorn hedge where the goats had nibbled was splintered. Its crudely amputated limbs lay on the ground, their leaves already wilting and their crop of little green haws drooping on thread-like stems. Sally took in the scene, tracing in her journeys around the Crag, her trip up the lake and the whole chapter of events up to now. Just then she listened as the clip-clop of horses' hooves on the dusty road became clear above the sound of the rubber-shod wheels of Barclays' trap.

She covered her face with her hands and said a prayer to herself: "God keep Mrs Barclay at home today."

She crept out to the end of the bridge and climbed onto the rickety parapet. She caught sight of the trap through the gap in the hedge, and as though her hasty prayer had been heard and answered, she saw, to her relief, a solitary head. No trailing plumes or rose-coloured veiling. She could see only Corney's dirty old panama hat. She skipped across to the little triangle of grass where the Storm Hill Road emerged onto the Cloona road and waved her hand to Corney.

"Hello, Corney! Would you give me a lift to the town?"

"Whoa!" he called, pulling on the reins. "Surely, Miss Glynn, surely. You're going in to see Michael, I suppose?" He could scarcely wait to hear the news first-hand from Sally.

"Did you hear about him? Wasn't it awful, Corney?"

"Indeed, it was a fret altogether, and him not having a thing to do with the ambush. Oh, 'tis terrible times, terrible times altogether, Miss Glynn! But maybe they won't keep him long. If they don't take him away from Cloona jail, it'd be all right. I'm sure we can all drop in now and again, to have a yarn with him."

"The danger is that there's not much room for prisoners in Cloona, and they don't keep them long. What little accommodation they have seems to be reserved for emergency cases, and I'm afraid of him getting shifted off. I suppose you heard Chris Heaney was arrested too?"

"Indeed, aye. They'll have to get a new porter in the bank and a new groom for your boss, Mr Pratt. A man of many parts was Chris."

"Very many parts."

"Wait till I have a good look at the bridge. You take these?" Corney said, tossing her the reins and clambering down. He stomped over to survey the broken bridge, and the crude but solid-looking temporary gangway thrown across it. "I suppose you were afraid to chance the bike across."

"I'm … I'm … I was!" Sally hesitated, glad of the excuse for her asking for the lift.

"You needn't be a bit afraid. That could hold up a train. You know, the English army is powerful at puttin' up bridges."

"And the Irish army is powerful at knocking them down," Sally added.

Corney returned to the trap and took over the reins. "Takin' it all round, it's a bad job, Miss Glynn, a danged bad job! Who's going to pay for puttin' the bridge up again, and who's goin' to compensate the wives and children of the poor fellows that's killed?"

"If they stayed at home in England they wouldn't get killed," Sally said. Her political outlook had taken on a sudden but clearly defined shape overnight. Since Michael's arrest, she had become decidedly anti-British.

"I didn't think you would condemn them, Miss Glynn – you that's always been so great with them. Sure, apart from the aristocracy, you're the only girl around the country that would let a British officer put his arm around her."

"I never let a British officer put his arm around me!"

"And what's Captain Barclay?" Corney asked slyly, eyeing her from under the brim of the old panama.

"You're an awful old tease, Corney."

"Maybe you'll be the next lady of Storm Hill. And there's no one I'd like to see in it better than yourself. And there's not a nicer fellow you'll find anywhere the length and breadth of Ireland than Captain Peter."

"But it's Geoffrey's widow who'll be the lady of Storm Hill."

"I don't think Mrs Geoffrey has any interest in it at all."

"I don't think Captain Peter has, either."

"Indeed he has! He comes home to see it very often ... unless it's yourself he comes to see," he added with a smile.

Sally didn't say anything about Peter's impending departure to Africa, nor did Corney. It was possible, of course, that Peter had not told his mother about it at all.

They trotted along past the Clanratty gates. Corney told more stories of the lovely Lady Isobel and the heartbroken earl. He told of how lucky her father was in his choice of a wife. "Your mother was a lovely girl when she came to Clanratty," he said.

As they entered the town, Corney asked, "Where will I let you off, Miss Glynn?"

They were near Daltons'.

"I'm coming to the station with you," Sally said.

"I had an idea that was in your mind."

They clip-clopped along the sun-baked streets to the station. They had not long to wait before the train came in. Sally rushed along the platform to meet Peter while Corney held the horse on the gravel square outside the high station walls. There was surprise and pleasure in the broad grin on Peter's handsome face as he caught sight of Sally zigzagging through the crowd towards him.

"This is a pleasure, Sally! So you have triumphed, I hope!" he said.

"Oh, Peter! No, it's Michael. He was arrested last night. He's here, in jail, in Cloona."

Peter's smile quickly disappeared. He stood looking with a fixed stare at Sally, seeing the depth of her distress as the disembarking passengers eddied and whirled around them. She went on talking, not giving him time to say anything.

"There was an ambush at the bridge yesterday. They suspected Michael – they came last night." She was breathless.

Peter took Sally's arm and began to escort her out of the station. "Don't worry, Sally, we'll find some way out for him."

Sally was aware of many eyes upon her, but she did not care now.

"Who's meeting me, I wonder?"

"Corney. I came with him in the trap from the bridge."

"You don't mean to say you haven't your bike?" To him, Sally's bike was an indispensable part of herself.

"No," she replied.

She couldn't start now to tell him the long story of the bicycle, because soldiers and police were posted all around the entrance to the station. She couldn't talk freely for fear of being overheard. Nor did she want to be holding Peter back now that he knew the worst. She reminded him that they would have to find a new place to meet and told him that there had been no change of heart on the part of her mother or Tom. They would still have to meet in secret. And so they arranged to meet in the boathouse in the evening. This suited Sally, for after they had carried the water up, and Trooper and perhaps Tom had gone to fill the drinking troughs, she could remain by the lake and later go to the boathouse.

In the meantime she would visit Michael. Peter said he would think about what steps, if any, could be taken to release Michael or at least not move him from Cloona prison. Peter knew that Michael would have no wish to be a privileged prisoner in Cloona, or anywhere else for that matter.

22

Prisoner

Sally's anxiety over Michael somewhat lessened after talking it over with Peter. She made her way along the streets to Daltons' to meet Tom. She wanted to hear from him if it was possible for her to visit Michael, or if there was any danger of his transfer from Cloona barracks. She found Tom and Jack stamping about uneasily. Sally entered the shop, and through the open door into the kitchen, she could see Ella Rogan crying into a dirty white apron. For one awful moment she thought Ella's tears had something to do with Michael. Ella raised her head as Sally entered. She had a look of pure misery. "Ella, what are you crying for? Is it Chris?"

"It's Chris. I never knew he was going out ambushin'," Ella sobbed. "He promised he'd marry me, so he did, the dirty scut!"

Sally couldn't quite understand Ella's attitude toward her imprisoned lover.

Mrs Dalton quickly explained: "She's going to have a baby," she whispered. "Disgraceful to think of this happening in my employment! In all my years in Cloona I have never had this sort of thing to cope with. What will people think? What will Fr O'Rourke think?"

Sally felt embarrassed. However, she soon forgot her embarrassment in her sympathy for Ella. Mrs Dalton continued to chastise Ella for the disgrace she had brought on the house of Dalton and the task that lay before all of them: finding a means to have Chris and herself married immediately, in jail or elsewhere, in order to mitigate the disgrace of having a child born out of wedlock. Ella continued to sniff into her apron and, when Mrs Dalton stopped talking, she raised her eyes from the dirty apron and began further loud lamentations and accusations.

"To think of me going out with him for six months and he never telling me he was in the Shinners. To think of all the cigarettes I gave him."

Mrs Dalton raised her head again, like a setter on the scent of game. "Cigarettes! You gave Chris Heaney cigarettes? Where did you get them?" Then she answered her own question. "You sneaked into my shop and took them, didn't you?" Now that she had found Ella guilty of one sin, she saw no reason why she should not be guilty of every sin.

"No, ma'am, I done nothin' of the sort. I paid for them."

At this Mrs Dalton added the sin of lying. She relentlessly pursued the source of Chris Heaney's cigarette supply, her concern for the reputation of her house or the illegitimacy of Ella's child forgotten.

Sally thought Mrs Dalton was harsh with Ella. She herself did not believe that Ella had stolen cigarettes. Ella wasn't clever enough. If there was any stealing done, Ella would be the one to be stolen from. But for the worry of Michael and the tragedy all around her, Sally would have laughed at it all. She went into the dining room to Tom and Jack. They had both been to the barracks but had been refused admission. This news disheartened Sally. It did not deter her, however. She left them and made her way to the barracks. Two sentries paced up and down behind the high barbed-wire-laced gates. After a lot of explaining by Sally, they called a third man who stood as still as a waxwork figure beside the inner gate, across the wide gravel square. He stirred into action and moved forward to question her. At last she was admitted.

"Come this way," he said, turning sharply and leading the way.

She trotted after the silent figure, across the square into a bare, cheerless room. Its only virtue was the cool shade it offered after the heat of the sun-scorched barracks square. Into this room Michael was brought to see her.

He appeared cheerful and unperturbed. What little anxiety he showed was for his family at home, left to cope with uncut meadows while the summer climbed to its peak of intense heat. He was of the opinion that he would not remain long in Cloona. Out of the five who had been arrested after the ambush, three had been taken to Sligo that morning, Chris Heaney being one of them. There now only remained himself and another, a stranger to him. He spoke freely with Sally within earshot of the sentry. Their conversation was noncommittal. There was no bitterness in Michael, no blame on anyone for the predicament in which he found himself. He was anxious about Trooper, and wondered how he had got on. He told Sally of the way the Black and Tans threw Trooper out of the lorry because he kept haranguing them. Michael laughed when he knew Trooper was safe and none the worse for his experience.

"Wish they'd thrown me out too. Don't tell him I told you he was thrown out. Let him have his little boast."

The news of the other prisoners was not comforting nor reassuring to Sally. She turned it over in her mind, balancing the possibilities for better or worse. Perhaps they intended keeping them as hostages, taking them around in the lorries as a protection for themselves.

If only I could find some way of getting him outside these grim awful walls, she thought as she returned wearily across the barracks square.

She pinned her hopes on Peter, feeling that there was bound to be something he could do to keep Michael here in Cloona. Then they could visit him, talk to him, and bring him things to make his captivity less burdensome, less isolated and less lonely. She asked the soldier who escorted her back across the square if it might be possible to see her brother again tomorrow. His reply left her even more depressed.

"Could be moved from 'ere any time. Might not be 'ere tomorrow."

With the soldier's words ringing in her ears, she could only hope that she might soon see Michael in happier surroundings. As she walked through the big iron gates into the freedom of the street she considered the doubtful freedom that the laws of the time permitted. When she arrived back at Daltons', Tom was sitting with Jack and Kitty on a seat outside the shop, awaiting her return. Her visit to Michael gave them hope. She suggested Tom go home immediately to bring the good tidings to her parents, but not to tell them that he had been refused. Kitty offered to drive him home in the car.

Sally decided she would go to Mr Pratt's office and tell him she would not return until Michael was released. He offered his sympathy in an embarrassed manner, but she doubted his sincerity.

Pratt took her hand. "I cannot do without you, Sally."

He had never called her Sally before. He did not release her hand but kept drawing her towards him. He was about to put his arm around her. As she recoiled from him, Mrs Brigson bounced in, foiling his attempted embrace.

"Good evening, Miss Glynn. What's this I hear about your brother being arrested?"

Sally did not reply.

"I'm afraid Miss Glynn will be leaving us until her brother is released. I hope it will not be too long. In the meantime, where can I find a typist?"

"Don't worry, I can do a bit of typing. Enough to take on Miss Glynn's work," Mrs Brigson offered.

As she closed the typewriter and left the office, Sally could see the triumphant grin on Mrs Brigson's face and the uncertain stare on Mr Pratt's. She didn't know which amused her more.

Sally went down to Matt Heaney's to borrow a bicycle. There was no need now to enter a conspiracy with him about her own. All she wanted was to hire one to take about until her own was returned. She told Matt she was sorry about Chris. Sympathy seemed wasted upon him. Her sympathy about Chris was as insincere as Mr Pratt's had been about Michael.

"'Twill do him good," Matt said. "And 'twill do Mrs Brigson good too! She'll have to find another spy. That's what she made of Christy – a spy! That's what landed him in Sligo jail, not patriotism."

"Shh!" Sally warned. "It's dangerous to say anything."

"Not when Christy isn't around!"

Matt appeared to be delighted with the freedom Chris's absence afforded him. He pulled out an old bicycle for Sally from a stack of machines with crooked handles and buckled wheels. He pumped up the tyres and was giving her the pump to carry in her hand, as there were no clips to hold it on the bicycle, but Sally assured him she did not want the pump. She remembered the pump was the only part of her bicycle she had salvaged at the ambush.

She wasn't quite sure if it still worked, since she had used it to bludgeon her assailant at the Crag.

As she left the town, the evening grew dark and threatening. Grey clouds dropped lower in the darker grey sky. They had gathered intensity from the sullen background above the horizon. They moved like sinister battleships manoeuvring slowly into position before the flash and draw of the storm. In the fields, men, women and children worked feverishly at the brittle, over-dry hay. If the weather broke, as now appeared likely, after the long drought, it might be the end of the summer and of the haymaking. Past experience of fierce, brief summers had taught them to take no chances and to make the most of dry spells. And so they sweated even as they prayed for the rain that enforced their labours, and hurried through the meadows. Their bare feet were protected from the stubble by old sandals as they gathered the flat swathes of hay directly into cocks. Its rapid ripening and drying eliminated the need for stacking.

23

Decision

Their parents waited anxiously for Sally and Tom's return with news of Michael. They feared it could not be good news, because of Tom's delay in returning. They didn't know whether to feel relieved or fearful when Sally eventually arrived.

Sally had taken care to shake off all fears and anxiety when she entered the avenue to the house. She now told a heartening story to her parents. She told them how Chris Heaney, with two other prisoners, had been removed to Sligo. She said the lad who was left with Michael was rather a nice sort of fellow. They were having quite a good time, she reassured them, and would likely be out in a day or two. She told them that they could get in to see Michael any time. She had had no difficulty at all and that when she left, Tom was going in to see him. She didn't disclose the brutal truth that Tom had been refused permission that morning. She suggested her mother go tomorrow if Michael wasn't released by then.

Her news brought hope and peace of mind to her distressed parents. To them the sultry evening seemed less depressing because of Sally's lively company. Tea was the most cheerful meal since Michael's departure.

Trooper came through the back door, brushing the flying ants from his beard and clothing. "Pismires! Sure sign of rain."

He asked anxiously about Michael, and Sally went over it all again, trying desperately to keep to the same story she had already told her parents. She hurried through it, all the time hoping that it wouldn't rain until after Trooper and she had filled the barrels. Then she could meet Peter by the lake.

"There won't be any cadgin' of water this evenin', Miss Sally," Trooper said, unconsciously driving the thin end of the wedge into her plans. "There'll be more than enough water before nightfall," he said confidently.

"The storm may drift off in some other direction," John said. "It's heavier back of the mountain. I've known a good many summer storm to go around Glenbrae, rather than cross it."

"Aye," Trooper agreed, "especially when ye badly wanted it here."

"We can't depend on the chance of a thunderstorm to fill the troughs. We have to fill them ourselves, Trooper."

"Right enough. Michael wouldn't think much of us if we left the cattle lowin' their heads off just because he wasn't here. We'll fill the troughs, and if the rain comes during the night, all the better."

Sally rushed through the evening's chores, spurred on by the prospect of meeting Peter. The rain still kept off, and the darkening sky had almost ushered out the long June day. It was getting near curfew time when Sally told Trooper to harness Raverty.

"Hurry!" she urged him, for she wanted to get Trooper away to the lake before the rain started.

"I wish you wouldn't be so obstinate, Sally. Can't you see it's going to rain? There is no use Trooper and yourself killing yourselves drawing water this evening. Remember, there's only the two of you. Tom would have come home to do it, only he can see it's going to rain."

It was so like her mother's confidence in Tom to make excuses for him.

"He doesn't know everything. He can't even read the signs, like Trooper does, about chirping crickets and flying pismires!" Sally said impatiently.

The thirsty lowing of the young cattle in the home field at the back of the house broke the quiet of the sultry evening.

"Listen!" Sally said. "They'll break out and we'll have to go rounding them up all over the place. It's easier to fill the troughs."

She had proved her point, and with that, Trooper set off for the lake. The flying ants swarmed on their heads and necks. Trooper swiped them off with his cap, cursing furiously and beating the air. Raverty's bit and bridle rattled continuously as the old horse shook the bothersome insects off his head and ears. Swallows and swifts darted low across the dry rattle grass and ragwort down by the lake and gorged on the swarming insects. When the barrels were filled, Sally sent Trooper home.

She went along the lake's edge to the boathouse, making a pretence of going to tie up the boat securely in case the threatening rain should be heavy enough to raise the level of the lake and cause the boat to drift off. She walked along by the water's edge, looking back occasionally to follow Trooper as he plodded his way after the cart, up the track through the Long Meadow. She was sorry to insist on the task of filling the barrels, but she had no other excuse to come down here, apart from that of pulling the boat up. Her mother might easily have sent Trooper to do it and so cheat her of the opportunity to meet Peter. When Trooper had gone through the First Gap, Sally quickened her pace. Her feet hurriedly crunched on the china shells of the freshwater mussels. Where the stubby alder bushes became high enough to conceal her from Trooper, should he look back, she broke into a trot. She covered the ground in long strides like a hunted fawn, bounding over the lichen-covered rocks, leaving the tangled briars, clambering over and under the twisted alder branches that lay like barriers before her. When she reached the boathouse, she was breathless.

She entered the cool green cave. It was almost dark within. The light from the leafy roof threw strange ethereal glimmers. From behind the trailing curtain of ivy that draped the walls, Peter emerged, moving forward to meet her. Peter, with his comforting smile and his hands outstretched. How she had dreamt of this moment. She rushed into his embrace. All the misery and trouble and unhappiness melted for a brief while in this magic cave. All the little things didn't count: the drought, the empty cattle troughs, the stinging ants, the impending storm, and the thunder rolling along the horizon. Even the big things she could forget too: the ambush, yesterday's ordeal, and Tom's constant contrariness. Even her shorn locks, which Peter now stroked tenderly. But Michael, she could not put Michael out of her thoughts.

Raising her head on Peter's shoulder but remaining in his embrace, she asked, "Can't you do anything, Peter? Anything at all? We can't let him go! We can't let them take him from Cloona!"

"Don't worry, Sally, there's something we can do."

"Something Dave can do?"

"I'm afraid there is not much he can do, Sally. He has his career to think about. But he can give me his car, that's all. I want the old Leyland for a few hours tonight, and I'll have Michael out, all right. But, Sally – and it's a big but – you know what it will mean?"

"No, I don't. What will it mean? All I know is that nothing matters if Michael is out and safe."

"Being out won't mean he's safe," Peter pointed out, his smile now gone. He had Sally at arm's length, looking straight at her. "It means that he'll be on the run, and so will I."

It was as if she had been given a choice of two unspeakable alternatives.

"You mean to help him to escape? How?" she whispered, as though ears were listening in the green shadows all around them.

"It's easy. I can call at Cloona barracks and ask for prisoners to take a fallen tree off the road. Sternitt did it one night. They sent out two men, and it would have been as easy as falling off a log to let them escape, or to go with them on the run."

"You and Michael on the run." Sally frowned as though it were something fantastic, something utterly impossible.

"You must remember that Michael and I went through it together before, Sally."

All too well Sally remembered those awful days of 1916, when her mother wept and walked about all night as if in a dream, and her father got up during the night and made tea to while away the long, sleepless hours. All too well she remembered Michael's homecoming – a maelstrom of gladness, disillusionment and disappointment. She remembered herself and Tom listening to the chastising and the congratulations and the conflicting accounts that lashed her about in a sea of confusion and childish ignorance. It was then that she had given up struggling with the tide and had drifted happily with whatever came her way. But Tom had struggled on, always. He was still struggling.

"But you were both students then. Your future was uncertain. Now it's different. You're a doctor and you're going to Africa in the service of the British Army." She spoke this as though it was a new thought that had come to her. There was no more escape for Peter from his appointment in Africa than there was for Michael from Cloona jail.

Peter smiled. "Well, perhaps an Irish hillside is a safer place for me than an African jungle. Certainly I know it better, anyway, and the type of animal I'd be likely to meet. I would prefer it, even with the Black and Tans."

Sally shuddered.

"Please, Peter, please—"

"Have no fear. I'll come back to you, Sally, when it's over. Maybe then Tom wouldn't think so hard of me."

"It's a big price to pay for Tom's favour."

"It's not too big for your love – and for Michael's freedom."

Peter drew her close to him. He went over the details of his plans, talking slowly and softly, to allow her to follow each move he intended to make. It seemed easy, almost foolishly so, but Sally thought that things didn't always work out as planned. There was often a hitch that put things wrong, like the night the door was locked when she came from the ball at Clanratty. Suppose Peter and Michael were shot and wounded in the attempt? And what would happen when it became known that the escape had taken place and that Peter had effected it? Would he not be subject to extreme punishment for the traitorous behaviour of using the uniform of the army to which he belonged? And Michael, too – was he not safer in jail than on the run?

On the run seemed such an indefinite period. There was no given time – only day-to-day, waiting and the awful uncertainty, the same as in 1916. But then the period was short; now would be like a prolonged repetition of that time. There would be the same praying for news, and the same trembling at every strange step that sounded on the drive, or every knock that came to the door. Her mother's hair would grow greyer and the lines would be etched deeper on her face. She would have that distant, searching look in her eyes, like Mrs Duffy and Mrs Dalton and all the other mothers whose sons were on the run.

Peter's proposals were clear-cut. But was he being rash, with that Barclay irresponsibility that neighbours condemned him for, that love of adventure?

Sally's thoughts raced wildly. She didn't know what to do. Ought she to say, "No, Peter, you can't do that. You must put the whole idea out of your head."

But above this fleeting thought she saw Michael again, on his way to some distant prison or facing a firing squad. She saw him as the innocent victim of some reprisal for her indiscretion. For, as Tom had said, it was really Peter and she who had unwittingly landed him in Cloona jail. Now it was surely their duty to get him out. Freedom, even the doubtful freedom to which he might escape, was better than jail. Her mind was made up.

"Where will you go when you get out?"

"There are plenty of places in the mountains where the lorries can't follow. Even the bridge can't take big lorries. You would be taking a chance going over them."

"Then maybe it's taking a chance going over it with the Leyland."

"Not a bit of it!" Peter assured her. "I was just down now having a look at it."

With each statement, Peter gave Sally more confidence in his proposals. She resigned herself to them, but fear still clutched her heart.

"There will have to be two of us. Tom will have to come," Peter said.

"Tom!" Sally exclaimed.

"Yes. Officers don't travel alone, and it's most unlikely that a single soldier would drive up to the barracks gates and ask for a couple of prisoners to clear the road, no matter how well armed he might be. And apart from all that, I want someone in the old car to keep the engine running. It's a brute to start once it stops." Peter paused, as though thinking of the whims of the old Leyland. "I hear there's only one other prisoner there with Michael. You never know what sort of stuff he might be made of. Tom will have to come. He must come. We'll see if he's as brave as he sounds. He won't have to go on the run. We can drop him off at his own avenue as we pass. I'll get a soldier's cap from somewhere for him. He won't be getting out of the car, so it won't matter what the rest of him looks like."

"Tom, in a British soldier's cap!"

The idea brought a fleeting smile to Sally's troubled face. But it quickly vanished. With his freckled nose and girlish lips, she didn't think Tom could deceive even the most stupid sentry under the high, swinging, electric light over the barracks gates. And now a new fear was added to her old ones. If Tom should be arrested, what of her mother? Tom was everything to her, much more, Sally reckoned, than Michael or she. So for her mother's sake, and not by any means for his own, they couldn't expose Tom to any greater danger than the risk of being expelled from Maynooth. But she would have to tell Tom and let him make his own decision. Something cold and chill seemed to strike Sally in the midst of the suffocating heat. It was like a wet, deathlike hand reaching up from the dark water to touch her heart. Peter could not understand. He did not know how much Tom meant in the Glynn household.

"He'll come all right, don't you think? Do him good to let off steam." Peter laughed lightly. "I'll pick him up at the bridge at eleven o'clock tonight."

"Yes, he'll come. I'll fix it all up."

They stayed for a while in the dark boathouse, clinging to the last few minutes they might have in each other's arms for a long time. Their eagerly awaited month's holiday would have a brief and abrupt ending. Instead of the tropical seas and the African jungle, there would now separate them only the hills and glens of Ireland. Sally's dreams of intimacy and pleasure with Peter would have to wait.

As they parted, Peter whispered, "We'll get messages to you somehow, Sally. Don't worry too much about us. We know our ground and every trick of ours is worth ten of theirs."

Sally ran back along the path, not looking back, not daring to catch a glimpse of Peter's face, lest she read something disquieting in his look or in his smile. She heard him push the boat out through the willow branches, and then the echo of the creaking oars across the calm lake. She stood breathless at the Long Meadow gate. She caught a glimpse of the boat as it passed through an opening in the willows and then she waved wildly to Peter. It was not a wave of farewell but one of encouragement to this man who she believed would risk everything for her. She shuddered at the possibilities. Surely now her family would give their blessing to their love. She so longed to be with him. She ached. Then, turning, she continued her swift flight, each step keeping pace with their quickly ripening plans. Rapidly she made her decision.

24

Escape

When Sally entered the kitchen, her mother was lighting the lamp. Tom had returned home when he was refused permission to enter the jail. He sat with his breviary closed upon his finger, awaiting the light so as to continue his reading. Chess sprawled, panting, in front of the sparse turf embers. Trooper sat in his corner, eating his supper before setting off home. Her father sat leaning forwards upon his stick, holding his empty pipe between his teeth. A silent, thundery atmosphere pervaded the kitchen, making deeper the dark shadows of gloom and depression already there.

"You were a long time pulling the boat up, Sally."

Sally avoided replying to her mother's comment. Instead she asked, "Did you fill the troughs yourself, Trooper?"

"Tom helped him. He was here when Trooper brought the barrels up," her mother said.

"There's talk of them moving Michael tomorrow," her father said, as though his mind had no room for any other thought. "God grant they won't. God grant they leave him in Cloona," he went on, making prayers of his wishes.

"I'm going to ask them," Sally said.

"Ask who?" Tom snapped, quickly looking up from his breviary.

"Who do you think, the saints? Saint Sternitt and whatever you call the man in charge of the Black and Tans."

"You'll do nothing of the sort!" Tom snapped the book closed and slapped it on the table.

"We want no favours from them. I've told you that before!"

"Keep quiet, Tom, and let Sally try if it's any use," his mother put in, contrary to her customary alliance with Tom.

Trooper got up and put his cap on to go home. Sally threw a waterproof coat across her shoulders in anticipation of the rain. The coat was a creased, shapeless affair. During the summer it had been thrown around from one peg to another, getting more abused than used. Now she wore it like a cape. Slipping along the corridor to Tom's room, she grabbed an old pair of dark trousers from behind the door. She rolled them into a bundle under her arm, concealed by the cape.

"I'll walk a little way across the field with Trooper," she said. "It's cooler outside, and I can breathe there, at least. I might go as far as Duffys'. Mrs Duffy will be waiting to hear all about Michael."

"Don't stay out after curfew," her mother warned.

"The big lorries can't get over the bridge now," Sally said. "And the Tans won't venture out at night in the small ones."

"They ventured out last night! Don't stay too long in Duffys'. If the rain comes it will be very heavy."

"If it comes on heavy, I might stay until it's over. Don't worry, Mother, they won't put us all in jail."

She sauntered out with Trooper and down to the grassy path, where he left her to cross the fields to his own cottage. After saying good night, Sally slipped back silently into the haggard and through the stable door. She climbed the slippery stick manger, crooking her toes in the old white sandals around the top bar. With one hand she grasped the cobwebby cross-beam above. Her other hand reached to the hole in the wall and pulled out the Tan's tunic. Two swallows shot like twin darts from their nest in the rafters and swooped through the doorway like hawking bats. She jumped down and picked up the trousers she had left at the bottom of the manger.

She crept out along the avenue and into the dark summer house among the rhododendrons.

In the summer house she took off the green frock, and tossed it behind the rustic seat. She thrust her legs into the rough black serge trousers and stuffed her short white petticoat into the waistband. She buttoned the trousers around her waist. They were tight, and she felt awkward and restricted as the rough serge chaffed her legs. She shook out the dusty, creased tunic and pushed her arms into the sleeves that were too long for her. She recalled their brevity on the flailing arms of its one-time owner. The tunic gave her a sick, nauseating feeling. Her thin undergarments stuck to her back with perspiration. This sick feeling quickly passed as she gathered her thoughts from the past and sent them spinning ahead. She rolled up her hair but the obstinate ringlets kept escaping from the cap. She picked up the green dress from behind the seat and, taking the scissors she had snatched from the man at the ambush, snipped the remaining ringlets from her head. These she bundled, with the scissors, back into the pocket of the dress. The cap fitted now and this seemed to give her more ease. She felt more in uniform and less in fancy dress. She felt sure of having made a good job of it so far and she was confident of making a good job of the task she was setting out to do. She tiptoed silently from the summer house onto the avenue. Each step she took seemed to better settle the heavy clothes on her. But the heat became unbearable. The heavy fabric on her arms and legs felt stifling after the freedom of her summer dress, and the high throat-fastening of the heavy tunic was constricting.

She toiled along as far as the bridge. There she waited in the shadows for the purr of the Leyland's engine. The rolling thunder gave her a few false alarms. Intermittent lightning flashed across the sky. Then, gradually, she saw the lights tip the hill and come slowly down towards the bridge. Fear at disappointing Peter ebbed and flowed within her. Would he have enough confidence in her? Or would his lack of it spoil his plans? Or would he have more confidence in her, whom he loved, than in Tom, who was always hostile to him and unlikely to want to cooperate with him? And was her appearance convincing enough? Would the tunic and forage cap make her more like a Black and Tan? Peter's officer's cap and military coat would make Tom look like a soldier. As the car approached, her courage flagged. Suppose it wasn't Peter at all but soldiers or Black and Tans? This last thought vanished quickly, for she recognised the old Leyland. She crept closer to the hedge, where she would have a clear view of the driver as he turned at the crossroads.

There was no mistaking him. It was Peter all right, and he was alone in the car. He stopped and sat over the wheel. Now she could make out the peak of his cap and his profile as he looked uneasily up the road. She moved out of the shadows towards him. She stood looking straight into his face, on which there was a blank look. It was evident he did not recognise her. This gave her courage, as she looked through the open car door. The blank look gave way to a puzzled stare.

"Peter! You don't know me! You told me officers didn't travel alone. I'm coming with you. I'm much better than Tom."

"Sally!" Peter gasped, drawling out her name. "I ... I ... didn't know you!"

"I know you didn't. I'm coming, not Tom."

"You can't do this, Sally. I won't let you take chances."

"But you said it was easy, and that there were no chances. You can drop me off at the gate, like you intended doing with Tom."

Peter was still bewildered. "The uniform, where did you get it?"

"It's the one they took off the Tan at Gerty's wedding. I told you about it at the boathouse. Don't you remember?" She rushed on. "But I didn't tell you I had it hidden."

Sally had a lot of arguing and persuading to do before she finally convinced Peter of her suitability as a partner in the mission. Eventually Peter gave in and she climbed into the car.

"What am I supposed to do? I know as much as Tom does about driving a car, and I'm prepared to take orders from you. Tom never would."

Peter showed her the way to keep enough petrol supplied to the wheezy, obstinate engine, and how to keep it turning over. They drove past Clanratty under the cover of the leaden sky that was grudgingly holding the rain from the thirsty, parched earth. The growling thunder seemed to have sprung from its distant lair, and the lightning's vivid claws tore the clouds apart. As they drew nearer the barracks gate, thunder cracked like rifle shots across their heads and the first drops of rain ping-ponged on the bonnet and roof of the car. Faster and faster the drops came, quickening their tempo to the thunder's roar and zigzag lightning flashes. Now light, sound and water rushed in one wild tumult from the opening of the heavens.

"All our prayers for rain are answered. Not frightened, Sally, I hope?" Peter said, concerned, turning to where she sat silently beside him.

"Not of the storm. I wish it was over though," she whispered.

"Wish what was over?"

"The whole thing!"

There was a trace of tension in her voice now as they were nearing the gates. They stopped talking, for it was no use. Either it came off or it didn't.

Down the wide empty street before them, the rain bubbled on the cooling pavements. Water spluttered through broken gutters and jostled in eddying whirls through gateways, tossing matchboxes and cigarette butts and little bits of street refuse like small crafts on a tidal wave. Peter turned the car at the barracks gate, ready for a quick getaway. Sally kept the engine running, while Peter jumped out and ran towards the gate.

"Halt!" the wet sentry bawled.

"It's all right. It's Captain Barclay. Any bloody Shinners here? Tree down on the road near Clanratty!"

"Only two, sir."

"Two will do, if they're strong enough," Peter said, walking through the gate the sentry was opening for him. "Bad night."

"Filthy, sir. Maybe the lightning struck the tree, sir."

"And maybe it didn't. I'll get the men. It's not a night to stand around speculating on what knocked the tree down."

He waited for no further action from the wooden-looking sentries but dashed across the square and entered through a doorway. A shaft of light was streaming onto the wet gravel. Two young officers, their heads together over a map, looked up as he entered. Peter had been introduced to one of them by Dave at Clanratty, a few hours previously. Both greeted him in a friendly manner.

"I want a few prisoners to clear a tree off the road. There is one down near Clanratty. I have Captain Sternitt's car."

"There's only two in the place," one of the officers said.

"Send them out and be damned to them!"

"Anyone with you?" the officer asked.

"Only an auxiliary I picked up at the police barracks – young, but can handle a gun. Sternitt is down there arranging for an armoured car to come with us. Hurry! Better fetch them before the road gets flooded."

One of the young officers went away and came back with Michael and his fellow prisoner – a weedy looking specimen.

"Come on. Step on it!" Peter urged as he pulled out his revolver.

He and Michael stared at each other with mutual blank understanding. He followed the two men across the square, the small man trotting at Michael's side and keeping close to him. One of the officers, revolver drawn, walked with Peter.

"Any tools to clear the road with? You need to fill up the car with saws and hatchets. You need them all in this damn country."

Peter merely grunted. The rain pelted off the bare heads of Michael and his fellow prisoner, plastering their hair over their forehead and ears, as they were bundled into the back of the car at the point of Peter's gun. The young officer then bolted back across the square to the shelter of the lighted doorway. The sentry closed the big gates and the Leyland drove away down the main street, passing the rainswept, indifferent military patrol, which cast no suspicious glances at the familiar army car.

Sally's mouth was dry, her heart pounding, and her body seemed to have grown limp. They all sat silently, afraid to speak in the uncertain and dark interior of the car. The presence of the unknown prisoner made them cautious.

After a while, Peter said, without turning his head, "Hello, Michael! So we're together again."

"What is this?" Michael asked suspiciously.

"Escape! Would you even say thanks?"

"I ... I ... don't understand." Michael's eyes fixed on the little Black and Tan at Peter's side. "Where are we going?"

"That's what I'd like to know!" Peter said. "The mountain first, I suppose. After that the choice is yours. Has your friend here anyone he could introduce us to?"

The man remained silent.

"You'd better convince him we're on the run! We've learned a lot since we were together before, Michael. Times have changed and we're not the students of Easter week. We haven't Patrick Pearse around, or other leaders, so we'll have to find one or lead ourselves."

Peter spoke conversationally, but Michael and his comrade were still cautious as their eyes drifted in the darkness from the back of Peter Barclay's head to the narrow shoulders of the black tunic.

They shook off the last lights from the town. On the outskirts they met a military car from Clanratty. With grave misgivings, Peter thought of the likelihood of it going to Cloona barracks. Indeed it could have no other destination and would immediately explode the story of the fallen tree. Suspicion and action would swiftly ensue. He put his foot down and the car sped on noisily.

Sally took the Glengarry off and turned to look at Michael.

"You didn't know me, Michael. Don't I look well in uniform?"

"Sally!" Michael exclaimed.

"You better be getting out of that rig, Sally," Peter advised. "Leave it in the car, and we'll dispose of it with my uniform when we abandon the car and take well and truly to the hills. Know where any of the lads are, Michael?"

"No, but Johnny here does."

"That's good enough ... if they're prepared to accept me, one of the enemy, in their ranks," Peter said.

He slowed down the car to take the rickety makeshift bridge and navigated cautiously over the rough planks. The lightning lit up the dark woods and the wet, dripping bracken slopes at the Crag. It played with fury on the leafy background, and the cracking echo of the thunder across the lake made yesterday's ambush appear a mere frolic for show. The cloudburst had turned the little trickle of the river to a frothy cascade, plunging hurriedly over the fallen timber and stones of the bridge, which now dammed the water on its rush to the lake. Sally turned to catch a glimpse of the face of Michael's comrade. She was anxious to establish some sort of picture of him before she left them. But her gaze was fixed elsewhere. Through the rain and mud-spattered back window of the car she saw lightning sweep the sky and vanish, leaving behind it only the glow of the lights of Cloona. A narrow beam, which seemed to grow brighter and fill the sky, emerged from the darkness they had left and, travelling quickly, it pursued them. Instinctively Sally knew that the beam was the headlamps of a car.

"There's a car coming!" she told them.

"Just watch it," Peter said quietly.

Michael and Johnny turned to look back.

"It's coming on! It's following us!" Michael cried.

"Must speed up our plans," Peter said, without showing any sign of alarm. "Get off those duds quickly, Sally," he instructed. "I'll slow down at your gate and you must jump for it. Take the trousers with you. You wouldn't do to have Tom's trousers found with the tunic. And whatever you do, don't let them catch you dashing for the house."

"I'll manage."

Sally wriggled out of the tunic. She threw it, with the forage cap, to the two in the back. The newfound freedom she acquired with the discarding of the tunic permitted her to turn around fully to properly see the features of the man in the back. Even in the dim light, she recognised him immediately. It was Ferret Face, who she had flogged with the bicycle pump! But now the car was passing the gate to the drive. Peter slowed down, but he dared not risk stopping completely because of the pursuing lights.

"Good luck, Sally," he said. "Mind yourself, and be careful."

"Tell Mother I'll be all right," Michael said as Sally dived from the moving car into the dripping shrubbery near the entrance gate.

25

Bucket

She picked herself up and hurried into the darkness of the trees. The lights were rapidly approaching and she didn't know whether she ought to shelter in the trees or make straight for the house. Perhaps, however, they would follow on after the Leyland, and not come up the avenue. As she looked, the lights puzzled her by their irregular spacing. She didn't wait but hurried into the summer house, where she peeled off the dark trousers and threw them into the rhododendrons.

The lights were now almost at the end of the drive. She saw one light, then another, piercing the darkness. For the first time she realised that they were motorbikes. Panic almost overcame her. At their present speed they would almost certainly catch up with the lumbering old car, fire on it, perhaps, and wound or kill Peter and Michael. The bikes slowed down and turned cautiously up the drive. Behind them a car followed, and it, too, drew up at the entrance to the drive. Soldiers got out and moved in a solid group, making no attempt to fan out to comb the grounds in their search. Sally knew she could not now reach the house. She groped for the green dress she had discarded, but it was sodden and she had no time to put it on. She wore only a short white petticoat that stopped several inches above her knee. The soldiers moved towards her. They must see her. What excuse could she have for being out at this time of night, half-dressed, long after curfew?

Crouching low, she crept out of the summer house and skirted along the hedge towards the well. The rain was pelting down on her bare shoulders and her ragged hair dripped miserably about her face. She fumbled about the low stone wall around the well, searching for a vessel of some sort to offer the pretence of filling it. There was nothing. She groped in the flattened grass at the back of the well, where old cans for cleaning up the dead leaves were often left. She found an old bucket. The handle had come loose from one side and it had no bottom. Hastily she scrambled down the wet slippery steps to the well. The soldiers approached. Sally knew they saw her. She was not afraid. She only wanted to put them off chasing the escape lorry. They flashed a light upon her.

"Hey, you!" one of them shouted. "What are you doing out this time of night? Don't you know there's a curfew?"

"I came out for a bucket of water to make tea for my mother. She has a headache."

Sally leaned the bucket on the grass. In the gleam of the flash lamp trained upon her, she could see the wet grass shining through the bottomless bucket.

"Why couldn't you have fetched the water before curfew?" another voice demanded.

"There wasn't any water in the well. I had to wait for the rain to fill it."

"Couldn't you catch it in a bucket, and save carrying it," another asked, but he didn't wait for an answer. "Seen a car pass this way just now?" he asked.

Sally did not answer.

"Aw, don't waste time asking these Irish wenches anything! Couldn't tell the truth if they was paid for it. They never see nothing."

One of the soldiers came closer to the wall. Sally grabbed the bucket. It swung askew on its one handle. She plunged it into the shadows of the well and let it sink into the darkness of the muddy surface water that was running down the steps into the spring.

"My bucket!" she wailed. "It's gone! I must go home for another."

"We are coming with you, Missy."

The soldiers followed her along the path and through the back door into the kitchen. Sally did not know whether her own family or the soldiers caused her the most embarrassment. Her mother, her father and Tom stared at her as though she was some strange creature who had descended with the storm. Speechless, they asked for no explanation. They knew there must be more than she cared to explain about her bedraggled appearance.

"I lost the bucket! It fell into the well."

They stared at her as though she had lost her senses.

"This the mother that's supposed to be sick? Couldn't you have fetched the water?" said one of the soldiers to Tom.

Before Tom could answer, they heard a car draw up, followed by another and yet another, until the house and garden were like an army camp. But it wasn't until the questioning began that John and Mrs Glynn and Tom learned that Michael had escaped from Cloona jail. They did not connect Sally's appearance with the escape. Rather they wondered if she had been a victim of a reprisal by the Tans. Even Tom's heart began to thaw into sympathy when he saw his sister.

Far into the night the road buzzed with activity in the effort to overtake the fugitives. There seemed no peace for the Glynns and no object in going to bed. The kitchen door was constantly banged open with rifle butts, and the room filled with uniformed men coming in and going out. Their repeated questions became monotonous, but through it all Sally sat as rigid as a Sphynx, awaiting the moment to tell her family all that she knew about the escape. It was almost dawn before she was given this opportunity, after the last belligerent and bleary-eyed Black and Tan had trudged out of the house. Hollow-cheeked and wide-eyed, Tom and his mother and father listened to Sally's whispered story, which she unfolded to hushed exclamations of praise and blame.

"Why couldn't you have told me?" Tom spoke as though she had deliberately cheated him of an honour.

"There wasn't time. Besides, Peter and you wouldn't have made a good team. I wore your trousers, though."

"I'm worried about Michael and Peter. Suppose they get caught." Mrs Glynn was anxious.

"Not a bit of it. Remember, there's the other fellow with them, and he knows where to hide," Sally said.

Tom was not so sure of "the other fellow" as Sally called him. "He may have no connections at all with the IRA," he said.

"He is a member of the Shinners."

"How do you know?"

Sally dared not say how she knew. Finally she blurted out, "Michael told me."

"But," Tom persisted, "Michael's only been in jail twenty-four hours. He couldn't know everything about his fellow prisoner in that length of time."

"Ah, stop harping on one string, Tom! Cloona jail is not Maynooth, and one doesn't have to be introduced by cardinals and bishops to establish an identity. Anyway, if Michael and Peter aren't satisfied with him, they can throw him in a bog or somewhere. He's only a little runt of a thing."

"And now I think we'd better go to bed for what's left of the night. What with the Tans and the thunder, this night is nothing short of bedlam." John pulled himself up with difficulty from his chair.

"It's as well to get all the noise over at once," Sally said.

"I hope it is over," Tom returned.

"I wonder what Mrs Barclay will think about it. I hope no harm comes to Peter for helping Michael. I hope Mrs Barclay doesn't blame Michael for everything, same as she did in Easter week," Mrs Glynn said.

"Doesn't matter what she thinks. It won't break any friendships, anyway," Tom said.

"It does matter, very much," his father told him. "He's her son, same as you and Michael are ours. And she has had hardship enough in her time, God knows."

"She'll likely set her heart against him for a while," Sally said. "Then, when she thinks there is a danger of him getting shot, she'll be ready to forgive him everything and welcome him home."

"Sure I remember your mother fattening the chickens for Michael's return in 1916," her father said. "Every handful of corn she threw to them she would say, 'I'll give him a bit of my mind when he comes home.' That's always the way with mothers. But, then, Mrs Barclay is accustomed to her son fighting."

"Yeah, fighting for the Empire – that would be all right with Mrs Barclay," Tom said, "but nothing so low as to be on the run in Ireland."

"He's very brave, and God save them both to come back to us," Mrs Glynn said.

She bent down to coax the dying embers into life, surrounding them with small pieces of turf and then putting the kettle over them. As the red flames licked around the kettle Sally sat waiting for the warm water to wash her hands and feet, and perhaps make tea. In a few minutes, as she listened to the kettle singing, peace and composure seemed to come upon her for the first time since the ambush and the arrest. Her tension dissipated, for hope came with the new situation.

Peter and Michael were together in the hills. She would get their messages in strange and mysterious ways, and meet them at all times and in unlikely places, perhaps. And all of them – her mother, her father, Tom and she – had found a new unity in Michael and Peter's sacrifice, a unity that Peter shared already, for he was now one of them.

Later, she went to her bedroom. There, discarding the bedraggled clothes, she put on a fresh, clean nightdress and tumbled, exhausted, into bed. She could hear the drip of water from the eaves. Through the window, she watched the light, scudding clouds come up in the wake of the storm. The air was fresh and clean now that the thunder had purged the sultry, clogging heat.

26

Truce

In the weeks following Michael's escape, the family adjusted to his absence. They worked with him constantly in mind. Tom accepted leadership, and Sally followed just as she had done with Michael. A new loyalty and better feeling arose between herself and Tom, born of their loyalty to Michael. And, if Michael's enforced fight for freedom was a losing one, it had at least won something very dear to his heart – an end to the cleavage between Tom and Sally, and Tom's acceptance, although grudging, of Peter Barclay as a friend and ally.

On this sunny day, Sally sat among the brown velvet buttons of the knapweed on the upland hill. She was gazing down on the Crescent Acre and looking forward to its reaping and harvesting. Beyond the field was the blue of the lake and the golden heat haze that lay over the hills. Somewhere, there in the purple folds of the hills, Peter and Michael stood together, as they had done in Dublin in 1916. "God saved them then. God save them now," she prayed.

The stream that had filled to overflowing with the torrential rain of the thunderstorm soon dried up again in the renewed and intensified heat of

July. Added to their persistent thirst, the animals now had the torture of the stinging horseflies. When driven almost mad by the pestering insects, they stampeded through gates and boundary fences and created new problems that required never-ending vigilance on the part of their harassed owners. Sally thought now of her father watching helplessly as she, Tom and Trooper wrestled with the burdensome tasks, and the mounting accumulation of work that Michael's absence and the tropical summer had thrust upon them. She knew he worried because he was of little use other than to help her mother around the yard and the kitchen. He would pick fruit for jam or might limp around with poultry and pig food. He was unable to give any assistance in the hayfield, where help was most needed. However, he couldn't remember ever having so much hay saved by early July. Tom and Sally's hands were blistered by the rough, hot handles of hay rakes and pitchforks. Sally's body was like the boys', as lean as the willow saplings from which her father had taken her name. Her face was as brown as a ripe berry beneath her cropped locks of sun-bleached hair.

Now, as she looked wistfully towards the hills, she saw the fields of neat haystacks, the blue-green of the sprayed potato leaves and the green of the flowering corn in the Crescent Acre. Mixed with the smell of the meadowsweet and wild blue scabious was the acid tang of the green haws, where the sun beat on them on the hedges at her back. Down by the lake's edge, the reeds provided their velvet cushions for the lazy dragonflies. In the rushes the copper brands of the flower were filling with seed. On the slopes of the hills down towards the bog, the heather glowed deep wine red. Everywhere there were signs of the advancing year.

But no real news came from Michael or Peter. They had to be content with the whispered snatches that they were all right, and the doubtful comfort of the hackneyed phrase "no news is good news". This was repeated with infuriating monotony. Sally was sick to death of it all. She wanted an end to this infernal situation. She was sick of wars and shooting. She could scarcely remember when war wasn't the principal topic of conversation. When two or three people came into the house to sit at the fire and chat, they talked of nothing else. And now, she was in the middle of it, with the two she loved best in the world hiding like wild things in the hills. She raised herself slowly from the rough, peeling bark of the cherry-tree trunk where she was sitting. Idly she pulled a bit of loose bark away, disturbing a colony of grey woodlice. She swept them away with an impatient gesture of disgust, displeased at the promptness of their discovery of the fallen tree – her tree.

Tom had gone to Cloona for the paper. She wished he was back; he had been a long time gone. Not that she was in any hurry to read the news. She could guess that another barracks had been burnt to the ground somewhere; another ambush carried out, to be followed by the customary reprisals. She had learned to dread the look of the paper for fear of what she might read in it now that Michael and Peter had gone. And she was afraid for Tom when he was too long away. Even as it was, she could scarcely understand the miracle of his escape, while Michael, who was so quiet, tolerant and peaceful, had been punished. She had not liked the way the officer in charge of the Tans had eyed Tom the last time they had called at the house. He seemed full of suspicion, she thought, and she had the terrible idea that he was contemplating Tom's arrest. She dared not think about it.

She had begun to doubt the wisdom of helping to effect Michael's escape. Perhaps Peter would have stayed at home and never gone to Africa at all. She would have him, regardless of what the Shinners said or did. How she longed for him now. She drifted to the sweet memory of his embrace and to her passion for him. Impatiently she shook off her regrets. They were bad company and piled up clouds of depression around her. What was done could not be undone. She trudged a little wearily through the dry, cracking meadow grass, which lay flat around the fallen tree, and out through the hoof-pounded gap on the dusty road. She reached the drive and walked along the path to the front door. There she stood looking at the flower beds in the scorched lawn.

The stumps of the herbaceous plants, which had been trampled on the night of Michael's escape, now poked up like a miniature windswept forest, their broken, hollow centres a haven for earwigs. The asters, which Michael had planted, had made poor progress; even the deluge that had accompanied the storm had done little more than revive them from the shock of transplanting. They had been attacked by slugs and now looked wilted and parched. Sally decided to find water for them somewhere. She would not let them die. She went around to the back of the house to where the tub was half-filled with water that had been used in the house during the day. As she went through the gate, she saw Tom coming up the drive.

He was walking briskly and broke into a trot when he saw her. Oh, how she hated his excursions to Cloona. How she feared the news his return might bring from Daltons' or other more mysterious sources of information. Now she saw him wave his hand in a gesture that seemed to say, "Wait, I have something to tell you."

She stood waiting, holding the cans of water. Their weight seemed to steady and balance her.

"There's a truce, Sally!" Tom said as he came across the grass towards her.

"A what?" She was puzzled by Tom's strange expression, registering neither sorrow nor joy.

"A truce! It's over! The fighting, the ambushing, the raids. They'll be home now any time. Today, tomorrow, whenever the news reaches them, wherever they are."

"They? Who'll be home?"

"The lads on the run!"

"Not Michael and Peter?"

"Of course."

"Michael and Peter coming home. No more ambushing. No more raiding."

Sally repeated the words slowly as though she could scarcely believe what she had heard. She dropped the water cans and the precious water splashed over Tom's shoes and soaked into the scorched grass and sun-baked lawn. Then she turned without a word and ran swift as a deer along the path and into the porch, calling as she entered the house. She called her mother, called her father and called Trooper, at the same time waving her old straw hat in the air. Her declaration of the cessation of hostilities threw the quiet household into pandemonium of jubilation and rejoicing, only subdued by Tom's solemn reminder that it was only a truce.

"Oh, don't be such a damp squib," Sally said. "If it's over it's over – and that's enough! It was you who told us, wasn't it? I really think you're sorry it's over, Tom." Her voice lost its jubilant ring and became hesitant and almost frightened. Now, there was an element of doubt. "You're not playing a trick, Tom? You're not fooling, are you?"

They all stood silent for a few moments.

"It would be a cruel trick."

Just then Frank Fallon came running up the avenue to confirm the news. This good news would spread now as quickly as the bad news had. Word would sweep along like a prairie fire through the towns and country lanes.

"A truce! A truce! A truce!" The cry would bring home the tired and weary, the hunter and the hunted, to sleep at peace beneath thatched roof and turreted castle. Days would end with work left undone, and nights would pass in tranquil rest or jubilant rejoicing and tales of humour and pathos. But to Tom it seemed to bring a sense of frustration and regret.

27

Summer 1921

The return of Peter and Michael eclipsed all previous events for Sally. She forgot the dangers and degradations of the past as she danced along the gilded path of rejoicings. The parties, the dancers, and the new life seemed like a new world. This anticipated a world in which green tunics with silver buttons shone proudly above the now disappearing khaki and sinister black and tan. Not all men who were soldiers of the IRA wore uniforms, however. Establishing a new and recognised army took time and money. In the meantime, many still retained the uniform of necessity: the familiar trench coat and slouch hat.

The British Army moved out of Cloona barracks. The triumphant population watched them march along the streets, singing "Sussex by the Sea" on the first stage of their journey home via the Curragh. The barracks and jail were taken over by the new army, many of whom had passed through it on their way to prison camps.

Chris Heaney came back to be collared immediately by Ella Rogan's father and brothers and frogmarched off to Kilalisheen church to have Ella thrust upon him for better or for worse. Peter found a home in Cloona barracks while he awaited his mother's return from her relatives in Belfast. As a doctor, Peter retained the rank of captain and, as a man with experience of regular army life, he was a great asset to the new army.

Tom, however, receded into the background, a lonely figure, neglected even by his mother. In this late summer of 1921 all eyes and all honours were for the lads who had been on the run. He worked at the harvest as though it were his sole interest, as though the work forced upon him by Michael's absence had given him a taste and an appetite for it.

On the other hand, Michael appeared to have lost what little interest he had in the work before his short exile in the hills. He seemed unable to take up easily the threads to weave the day-to-day pattern of his old life. But his brief period on the run could scarcely account for his lack of interest and detachment. Sally thought that it might be his unwillingness to supersede Tom. Perhaps Tom's departure would reawaken in Michael the need for a more vigorous effort.

As on so many occasions, the miscasting of Tom and Michael's careers or vocations worried Sally. Tom's moodiness seemed to have taken possession since the truce. She tried to trace its cause in the hope of effecting a cure. Sometimes she attributed it to Rory Duffy's death, for she knew that Tom would miss Rory more now that so many of his comrades had returned and he was not among them. Perhaps, she thought, Tom regretted having played no part in the achievement for which the others had the honour. They now shared in that part of the fight for Irish freedom of which he talked so much and in which he had, at best, played only a minor part. These thoughts passed through her mind as she watched him pacing slowly up and down the drive reading his breviary.

When he had finished, she would suggest going to the lake to fish. Not with a rod and line; that tried his patience too much. Trawling around the lake with a spoon bait behind the boat would be the best option. They only caught pike this way, but it had movement without fatigue. It dispelled the tension that made Tom look like a restive horse straining at the bit and ready to bolt. She felt sorry for Tom, for his frustrated patriotism and his ardent desire for Peter's conversion. Peter would be part of the way, if not all the way, towards becoming a Catholic when Tom returned again at Christmas. She could reassure Tom on that point. Lately she had begun to fear he was waging a silent war within himself – to be or not to be a priest. During Michael's absence she had come closer to Tom's real nature. She had pierced the armour of his exacting ways and the wall of righteousness behind which he hid. She saw many of his good qualities: his loyalty to people, which she had previously attributed to a stubborn bigotry; his effort to overcome his dislike for farm work to tackle many tasks in order to spare herself, her mother and Trooper. She would always keep and remember this new blend of admiration and pity. He was returning tomorrow to Maynooth. His impending departure filled her with repentance.

Having finished his spiritual reading, Tom came into the house and went to his bedroom. He remained a long time in the room, and Sally guessed that he was praying and meditating. When he eventually came out, his mother suggested he accompany her in fetching the cows now grazing on the after-grass of the Long Meadow and the Crescent Acre. She seldom asked Tom to do anything himself. She always asked him to help her or Sally or Trooper to do the task, as though he were still a little boy incapable of doing it himself.

"I'll go myself," he insisted. Taking up a stick from the corner, he went out briskly. He whistled up Chess, and together they went down the path and over the road through the First Gap.

Sally was clipping the hedge that ran behind the herbaceous border. She was training a thick thorn bush into shape. Each time she clipped it, she changed her mind as to what it would ultimately become. It started as a teddy bear, then became a monkey. Finally she decided to change it again to a sitting cat. When she saw Tom go down the path, she abandoned her topiary. She left her shears in their accustomed place in the trap house. She took the oars from the corner and the brush handle with the fishing line from the shelf in the trap-house window. She walked fast in Tom's tracks, overtaking him as he reached the Crescent Acre. She called to him, and, turning, he saw her with the oars across her shoulder.

"You're not going out in the boat at this time of the evening?"

"I am," Sally replied. "I'm going to try catching fish for supper. I'm going to trawl. Come on, you can row." She didn't stop as she spoke but continued down the path as though his decision in no way affected her plans.

"I can't. I have to bring the cows in. Trooper is waiting to milk."

"We can bring them on the way back. There's no hurry. There's no curfew now."

"No, there's no curfew now for Trooper or for the rest of ye, but there will be for me tomorrow night."

He was alongside her as he spoke, taking one of the oars. His aversion to the prospect of returning to Maynooth gave her the opening Sally sought.

"You don't call that curfew! You'll have the comradeship of the others. Won't there be a lot to talk about when you all get together? So much has happened during the summer holidays. Never have the students in Maynooth more reason to get together to rejoice and give thanks, or whatever they'll do, as at the beginning of the coming term. I thought you would be looking forward to it all." Sally paused. Tom didn't speak. "You won't have any of the past worries about us or about me," she continued, "about curfews and raids, Black and Tans, and my disgracing the family by going to dances in Clanratty with a British officer and having my hair cut by the Shinners. I won't be bringing a blush to the cheeks of my student brother with the dishonour of my keeping company with the Protestants. Peter will be a Catholic when you come home again. This time next year you'll be Fr Glynn and I'll be Mrs Barclay. Who would have guessed six months ago that the horizon would ever be as rosy as that?"

"There is nothing bright about the horizon! Take off your rose-coloured spectacles and remember it's only a truce. Perhaps it's only the calm before the storm. There's nothing signed or settled. The fighting may begin again. If it does, it will be war – real war, not the hit-and-run affair we've had." He pushed the boat out and settled at the oars. "And as for Peter Barclay changing his religion, well, you're far too flippant about it. It's a big thing, Sally, to change your religion. It means he is cutting himself off from his family."

"His family have cut themselves off from him."

"He's giving up a lot for you, not for God's sake, but just to save a lot of bother. It's just an easy way out."

"You say he's giving up a lot and then you say he's taking an easy way out. Explain that to me."

It was obvious that Tom was confused. "That's not the sort of convert the Catholic Church wants," he said.

"But it's you," Sally reminded him, "and not Peter, nor I, nor Mother, nor Father, who is forcing his conversion."

Tom ignored this. "If the trouble starts again, you may be Mrs Barclay, but I won't be Fr Glynn."

"Why?"

"Because I'll be in it. I must be in it. Every man who can fight must be in."

"You would leave Maynooth and become a soldier instead of a priest?"

"A priest is always a soldier. He must be both. It would merely postpone my ordination."

"I can't believe you mean that, Tom," Sally said, shaking her head.

"Of course I mean it."

"You talk of the Catholic Church not wanting converts like Peter. Well, I'm sure it wouldn't want priests like you, priests who turned their back on God with every whim of the politicians."

"Don't let the prospect of a deferred marriage to Peter Barclay drive you into a tantrum. Other Irish women made greater sacrifices than that."

"You always had a knack of placing the guilt on your opponent. I wasn't even thinking of my wedding, and you know it. I certainly wouldn't link my plans with yours. It's Mother's idea that we wait until you are ordained."

"Then perhaps you had better find someone else on whom you can confer the honour, just in case," Tom said and smirked.

Sally felt the old antagonism rising again. She lowered her voice to a whisper. "You're not thinking of leaving Maynooth?" She leaned forward, watching his face as she waited for his reply. She was immediately aware of the embarrassment her question stirred in him.

He fiddled with the line and turned his head away to look back at the thin wash the boat made of the glassy surface of the water. It seemed a long time before he spoke, so long that she regretted having thrown the question at him. She was just going to release him from a reply by dipping the oars and rapidly rowing on, when he said, without turning his head, "If, as you say, you have not linked your plans with mine, then my future does not concern you at all."

"Then mine need not concern you, and your anxiety for Peter's conversion need cause you no sleepless nights or ... or ... embarrassment. Of course one should not become embarrassed by the behaviour of another member of one's family. I don't think I would."

"You never had any cause."

"Perhaps you're right. But if at any time in the future—"

Tom turned quickly on the seat and interrupted her. "Oh, for God's sake shut up, Sally! You're like a gramophone. You're wound up. Girls are the devil for talking. They go on and on and on! Do their tongues never get as tired as men's ears do listening to them?"

"This time tomorrow night your ears won't be tired. You'll be back in the blessed peace and quiet of your womanless world in Maynooth."

"You're at it again!" Tom growled. "Lift your right oar or we'll be into this patch of water lilies and foul the line and lose the copper-spoon bait."

Sally raised one dripping oar and pulled hard on the other. The boat headed out into the open lake. They pulled slowly along, their ruffled tempers subsiding. The lake's tranquillity and the peace of the late summer evening settled them. They caught a few red-finned perch, Trooper's favourite.

The sun dropped in a fiery curtain behind the dark woods of Clanratty, giving the surface of the water to the coppery reflection of approaching night. Tom reeled in the line, and, taking the oar from Sally, rowed homewards, pulling evenly through the opening of the ivy-covered boathouse. There, Peter was sitting, his legs dangling and his grey-green uniform making him almost invisible against the brushwood background.

"Peter!" Sally exclaimed. "Have you been waiting long?"

"Only just arrived. I came over to say au revoir to Tom. I have to go to Sligo tonight and won't be back until tomorrow evening after Tom has left."

"Not *au revoir* in that uniform – *beannacht leat*!" Tom retorted.

"Of course, of course. I must try to remember next time," Peter apologised.

All three walked up the path from the lake. The air was heavy with the perfume of water mint and the trailing woodbine over the low fences. They collected the cows from the Crescent Acre and drove them up the grassy meadow path and onto the road where Peter's car was parked.

Peter shook hands with Tom, fumbled for the Irish word for a farewell, and then said, "Goodbye, Tom. Good luck, and thanks for keeping the home fires burning and looking after Sally when Michael and I were away. Pray for us all. Goodbye, Sally. See you tomorrow evening. I must go. The lads are waiting for me in Cloona."

He got into the car and departed in a cloud of dust. Sally was grateful for Peter's words to Tom; it was the first time Tom's service to anyone or anything had been recognised during the terrible time that had passed.

John Glynn plodded down the path from the upland. He could see, between the trees, Sally, Tom and Peter driving up the cows from the Crescent Acre: Peter in his uniform, Sally in her print dress with her white flannel coat and Tom in his student black. Always, on the eve of Tom's return, John felt uneasy, the way he felt when he used to go to harness the lively horse, Scarva. He had that uncertainty, that wondering whether he would or could not pull the plough or the cart or whether he would just jump the traces and shake off his harness. But unlike the horse, with Tom he had no real reason for feeling that way. Nevertheless the feeling was there that Tom would, at the end of some holiday term, dig in his heels, shake off the harness of his black clothes and refuse to go back to Maynooth.

His stiff fingers closed on the Rosary beads in his pocket and he prayed his own prayers of thanks for the blessings of his wife and children. He prayed for repentance for the small part he had taken in their upbringing. He prayed fervently that Tom's choice of a way of life might be the one in which he would be truly happy. Then he looked up and saw his wife out clipping the hedge where Sally had left off.

The click of the clippers ceased as Mrs Glynn looked down towards the Crescent Acre and saw Tom and Sally and Peter. She had already begun to feel the loneliness of Tom's departure; she was going to miss him badly after the long summer term. Now she looked past her loneliness and across the intervening months to next June and Tom's ordination. She thought how well Peter would look in his uniform and Sally in her white wedding dress. But her vision of Tom in his priestly vestments was now clearer. Fr Tom Glynn. He would be there with them when Sally and Peter departed on their honeymoon. She hoped and prayed no hitch would postpone or prolong the day of his ordination.

When Tom and Sally came into the yard with the cows, Trooper stood impatiently at the byre door. Chess squatted between the buckets and had a look of chastisement on his friendly face.

"What kept you all this length of time?" Trooper asked irritably. "The poor old dog wants his milk."

"Couldn't he have this morning's milk?" Tom asked.

"He likes it hot, fresh from the cow. Anyway, it's high time I was gone home."

"What's the hurry? There is no curfew now."

"There's curfew in me old bones for a bed!"

Sally held up the fish she was dangling on a string behind her back.

"Ah, it's fishin' ye were." Trooper looked at Sally and Tom as though they had deliberately cheated him of going. "And is that all ye got? A lock of pinkeen? I'd be ashamed to bring them home."

"Never mind, Trooper. We'll go ourselves tomorrow evening and make up for keeping you waiting this evening," Sally said. She picked up a bucket and went with Trooper to the byre to help him with the cows.

28

Engagement

The long days had drawn into early twilight. The purple bloom on the blackberry fell lush on the low thorn thicket. The red glow of the rowan and barberry and the pink of the spindle berry illuminated the hedge by the bridge.

A winter of peace, a winter of plenty, a winter of love and laughter and promise lay before Sally. The difficult part of her romance with Peter had become smooth, and she would soon go to Dublin with him to choose her engagement ring. Their wedding awaited only Peter's entry into the Catholic Church, his reconciliation with his family, and Tom's ordination in June. These seemed small things to Sally, but they were the conditions under which her parents had given consent. Fr O'Rourke would give the necessary instruction to Peter. Tom's ordination was something only he himself could shape. But there should not be the slightest hitch, even though her mother kept saying, "You're still young, Sally, still not twenty. I hope you know your own mind."

As though Sally had ever doubted her mind. Sally had always known her own mind regarding Peter Barclay. She knew the risks and disfavour she had incurred by being so definite. Looking back on the past, she was amused at the rapid change in events that had banished the fear she once had over her deception about the tattered blue dress belonging to Lady Isobel. No doubt her mother would now include it with the other contents of the trunk as part of her dowry, and she would then find a way to disguise or dispose of it.

Peter was very busy with the formation of the new army. Sometimes Sally thought the demands made upon him were unreasonable. He didn't have enough time with Fr O'Rourke, and she so desired him to be received into the Catholic Church before Tom came home at Christmas. At times Peter teased her about the insincerity of her anxiety regarding his conversion.

"It's Tom you're worried about, Sally. You're afraid he won't approve of me."

Michael, too, advised her: "It's not a matter you can hurry, Sally. Peter must be sure. He must see for himself. You can't push anyone into another religion just for the sake of getting married. There's a lot of things you have to think about. It would be a pity if Peter became permanently estranged from his mother, and you must not antagonise her. You must remember her traditions, her family and background, and, above all else, you must remember she is his mother."

Sally listened, as always, to Michael's counsel, leaning on the wisdom of his words. With each lesson of truth and tolerance he taught her, she regretted more the opportunity that had been denied him to follow his vocation to teach the same lesson to many.

The harvest moon, which a year ago had been a peeping Tom to Sally and Peter, now held all the romance of its reputation. No longer need they creep along in its shadows, or dodge the illumination of the blue glitter of the stars. They drove to dances held in the old town hall and the barracks in Cloona. They danced the night through, returning in the grey dawn of the October mornings over the potholed roads that daily grew worse as they awaited the great task of reconstruction, which was to fall on the inexperienced shoulders of the leaders of the infant State.

Winter crept in with no fear for the men on the hills. The wild geese gaggled in across the Shannon and their reedy cry was lost on the desolate lakes and moors. Beneath the bare hedges, which offered scant shelter, slunk no hunted man fearful of winter's approach. The alders by the boathouse were knee-high in water. At the bottom of the bracken slopes, the coral reefs of the haws stood out above the clear lagoon-blue of the lake. On its reedy banks, coots struck out with claw and wing. Light breezes spun the leaves through the Poplar Gap like a flurry of early snow. The first frosts came cold and shiny in the morning sunlight, cloaking each leaf and blade with a glittering robe to seal the kaleidoscope pageantry of autumn. St Martin's summer passed and Halloween arrived. Now most of the leaves were fallen and only the skeleton of the trees stood black against the sky, switching and swaying the shadows of their leafless branches over the patchwork of bare fields. The days grew shorter.

Sally held her engagement party on Halloween night. She had made a cake with the ring. Trooper found the ring in his slice and accused Sally of planting it for him so that he might break his last remaining tooth. Many of Peter's friends came from Cloona. The Daltons, the Duffys, the Fallons and all the friends who had played with Peter and Sally as children arrived. They danced and sang. They played the old piano with the fretwork front, its yellow curtain washed and ironed by Mrs Glynn for the occasion. The old rose-strewn carpet was rolled back, and it seemed to John that the years had been rolled back too. Certainly, it was a long time since there had been such fun in the big old sitting room. The stuffed birds looked out in glassy-eyed surprise from under their domed-glass canopies.

But the party was slightly marred by the disputes about the treaty, and on Michael's prompting, someone suggested that they finish before the gaiety gave way to heated debate. Tactfully, it was pointed out that it was the eve of All Souls' Day and that the Masses next morning were early. The party finished with "Auld Lang Syne". Peter and Sally were bumped about to the tune of "for they are jolly good fellows", then the exuberance of the party dropped quietly as Peter sat at the piano and played the new national anthem, "The Soldier's Song". Everyone stood and sang lustily. Each word rang clear with the meaning and purpose and pride and hope.

29

Christmas Treaty

Sally and Peter met Tom's train at Cloona the week before Christmas. He seemed thinner and paler than when he left in September. His fresh summer glow had faded to a papery transparency. As they drove past Clanratty, Tom nodded his head towards the gate.

"They're still here, I see."

"It won't be long now until they're all on the way out," Peter replied.

"What will become of Clanratty, I wonder? Will the new army take it over?" Tom was curious.

"I wouldn't think so. There's accommodation enough in the barracks in Cloona for all the army that will be required, and for all the uniform that is available."

"Perhaps the young earl will come back and put the garden in order again, as a tribute to the memory of his Lady Isobel," Sally said.

"His day and the like of him is finished with in Ireland," Tom declared.

"If that's so, then it would make a nice monastery or a summer residence for the students from Maynooth, or for Michael's Franciscans. It would be a bit of a change from the British Army," Sally teased.

"Anything that's a change from the British Army would be bound to be a change for the better," Tom said.

"Don't be too hard on them, Tom. You know my history. I haven't been as loyal to the same uniform as you. Do you ever get tired of the black, Tom? I've no doubt it will be nice to get to be a bishop or cardinal and find yourself in purple or red."

"Either colour would be awful with Tom's hair! Nothing would suit him better than the white of the Holy Father himself!"

"Don't be irreverent, Sally!" Tom snapped.

"I'm not irreverent. It's not impossible."

"What do they think in Cloona of the proposed treaty?"

Tom turned to Peter, but it was Sally who replied: "They don't think at all; they just disagree without thinking. There's a different slant on it every time it comes up for discussion, and everyone gets red-hot about it. The other night they nearly took their coats off to each other in our house. Mother seems to be always making the peace between them, telling them to wait, to have patience."

"It will be too late when it's signed," Tom said.

"Too late for what?" Sally asked.

"Too late to alter it."

"Even if it is, we, the ordinary people, can't alter it, Tom," Peter said. "We've got to trust our leaders."

"God help them. Great leaders have been fooled before, and they're dealing with a crafty lot of knaves now. Michael Collins, Arthur Griffith and those who have outwitted the brains of the British Army and the RIC and the DMP and the rest of them, have no experience of the cunning of Lloyd George and that lot in England," Tom said.

"They must have been fairly wary up to now, or they wouldn't have survived," Peter replied.

"Wary soldiers are different from wary statesmen. It calls for a different technique, a different strategy." Tom was warming to his subject. "With a gun, Mick Collins could lick Lloyd George and Carson. He could beat the British government, the whole jing-bang lot of them. Or put them all out to catch him on the hills and they wouldn't see his heels for dust. But when it comes to signing on the dotted line, someone is going to be the loser."

"You're an awful pessimist, Tom," Peter said. "You're always thinking the worst. You're a defeatist. You'd have them beaten before they start."

"History gives us no reason to be optimistic about political intrigue in Ireland. The past makes gloomy reading."

"Cheerfulness is a duty we owe to others," Sally put in. "I've often told you, Tom, to leave politics to the politicians. It's not your line."

"It's everyone's line who has the interest of Ireland at heart."

"Faith and fatherland – it might be as well not to mix them. You look after the faith, and Peter, Michael and I will look after the fatherland."

Tom laughed with a sarcastic lift of his eyebrows. "You don't care two pins whether it's the Kaiser or the king or Trooper Mac who makes laws for Ireland!"

"You're right, I don't, providing they leave us in peace and let us go on with our own day-to-day work and play unhindered. I can see no visible change in the face of Ireland and the countryside since we got this ... this ... freedom. The Fallons' house and land is just as neglected as ever it was, while the men sit around the fire and discuss the new nation, leaving Gerty Fallon and her mother-in-law to keep the home fires burning with the turf they cart from the bog themselves. As for Frank, he sticks his head round every door in the country, looking for someone to argue with about the treaty. Men must fight and women must work – that's the new freedom!"

Topping the hill, they could see the Crag, its black bulk silhouetted against the frosty, luminous sky. A glimmer shone through the stained-glass window of Kilalisheen chapel, away on the hill. The ladies of the Altar Society would be preparing the decorations, or perhaps the choir was practising the Christmas hymns. Over the hills, away across the lake, the sickle moon hung awaiting the Druidic rites of the mistletoe. The short drive to the house grew dark with approaching night. Beyond the frosty grass of the sleeping lawn, the figures of Mrs Glynn, Michael and Trooper were framed in the lamp-lit doorway as they came forward to welcome Tom. Peter turned the car on the gravel drive. He couldn't come in, he said, as he had to return to Athlone barracks.

It was good to have Tom home again, Mrs Glynn thought, even though only for the next few weeks. His days at home from now until June would be few, and they must make the most of them. All her specialities were on the table for tea. The fried ham from the home-cured bacon, the brown eggs from the new Rhode Island Reds, the black pudding and the drisheens that Gerty Fallon had sent down the night before. And the mince pies that Tom had boasted about to the children at school and, in a more modest way, to the students at Maynooth. And, of course, her Christmas cake. A rich dark mixture Tom always said seemed to contain a little of all the spices and fruits of the earth. It had its usual thick almond paste and film of frosty icing, in which were planted the robins and Santa Clauses and reindeer that were kept over from Christmas to Christmas. The candles on the Christmas tree, the tinsel, the lanterns, and the small figurines from the cardboard crib on the sideboard were a welcome sight.

Mrs Glynn intended to make this a wonderful Christmas, for it was the last Christmas the family would be really just her family. Next year Tom would be a priest whose life was consecrated to God. Sally would be married and then her husband would come first in her life. There was only Michael they could be sure of. Indeed, circumstances might prevent them having another Christmas together for a long time. She had no regrets at the prospect of the changes, for it was progress. The progress of her family, which she had worked for and prayed for. Her early disappointment over Michael's career was almost behind her. Indeed, as things turned out, with John's lumbago it was as well he had remained at home. He did not cause her any worry so far by contemplating marriage or having any interest at all in the girls around.

Before the meal was finished, Frank Fallon arrived. He shook Tom's hand. After they had talked for a while, he arose to go. Tom proposed accompanying him as far as Duffys', where Frank had to call for Gerty. Tom wanted to see Mrs Duffy and Gerty, and said the walk would do him good.

"It'll shake the stiffness out of my legs after the train journey from Maynooth and the car trip from Cloona."

Mrs Duffy sat, half propped up with pillows, in the bed in the little room where Rory's coffin had been placed. Back then, sweet briar perfume from the garden had drifted through the window. Now dank peat smoke and the resinous odour of burning pine filled the air. She was changed, as if a different being had taken possession of the spirit that had drifted away when she had the stroke. Her speech was slow and halting. One side of her body was rigid, and her arm lay lifeless at her side while the fingers of the other hand toyed feebly with the white fringe of the patchwork quilt. But she recognised Tom and talked to him about Rory without much sign of grief or emotion. She talked of Christmases past when Rory was a child and then she talked of Tom's coming ordination.

"You will remember him, Tom, in your first Mass, won't you?"

"There won't be any need to remind me of Rory at Mass, Mrs Duffy. I always remember him at Mass."

She looked up at him but said nothing, as though the effort to repeat her request was too much or as though Tom's answer was not the promise she had asked for. Gerty fixed the pillows, and seeing that her mother was tired, took Tom into the kitchen. The events since his departure were discussed and this led to the inevitable argument, which this time was at least friendly.

The Christmas of 1921 was a time of thanksgiving and a time of celebration. Freedom from curfew and the reunion of families had provided the motive for a renewed round of the parties and dances that had started in July. The long nights of Christmas and the New Year were scarcely long enough for the revellers, nor the days long enough for the much-needed rest of bodies jaded from dancing and throats hoarse from singing. Peter and Sally, and sometimes Michael, rattled and bumped over the potholed roads from one sporting venue to another. They danced Irish jigs and reels to the point of exhaustion. At times they were compelled to reduce their exuberance and patriotism by dancing a waltz, taking away a little of the foreign flavour by waltzing to tunes like "The Shawl of Galway Grey" or "The Hills of Donegal". Such favourites of Sally's as "Smile Awhile" and "Keep the Home Fires Burning" were left to the brass bands of what remained of His Majesty's troops, still waiting to play themselves out.

Tom was debarred from the fun and the frolics. It would not be fitting for a clerical student to go spreeing around. And so he spent his Christmas leave visiting the neighbours. His only recreation was his part in the heated debates about the treaty, or staying at home engrossed in his studies, while his mother sewed or knitted silently and his father read the papers, sifting the news to find something solid in the shifting sands of the rumours regarding the wisdom or folly of the treaty. The newspapers arrived on time, carrying reports from London about the negotiations. Divisions grew daily. It seemed impossible to reach an agreement on the ruling of Ireland. Sometimes Tom laid his books aside and perused the papers again, rereading and contemplating some article that interested or disturbed him. He would discuss it avidly with anyone at hand. His mother, as always, dissuaded him from allowing his interest to become too concentrated on politics. Often she gathered up the newspapers and put them aside, like taking a dangerous toy from the hands of the child.

Sally had no regrets at leaving Tom at home with his studies while she and the others enjoyed themselves. After his departure, festivities were drawing to a close. They seemed to have reached the end of the celebrations that the truce had ushered in.

In January further military withdrawals took place in many parts of Ireland. Tom watched the legs march the two-mile stretch from Clanratty to Cloona station. The steel-tipped army boots clicked over the frosty road and stamped in ice-covered potholes as men lustily sang "Pack up your Troubles in Your Old Kit-Bag". But their troubles were not yet over. They were going to the Curragh, or Dublin, Cork or one of the few centres of concentration into which the army of occupation was being drawn for mass evacuation or discharge.

When Tom drove past Clanratty on his way back to Maynooth, the big iron gates were closed and locked and the key was back in the hands of the land steward. The castle's future was uncertain. The lawns, festooned with rusty barbed wire, were planted with burst sandbags. The windows were shuttered and the huge studded oak doors barred and bolted. It stood, a great grey granite mansion, seemingly as indestructible as time. The huge yew tree at the entrance to the terraced lawns stood like a grim sentinel beside the naked silver birches. The brittle-limbed elms bent like old men in the winter wind in thanksgiving for the departure of the unwanted British troops. But for Sally there was a loneliness about it all. Clanratty held the memory of her first dance with Peter. The most enjoyable night of her life, despite its repercussions.

30

Changes

The spring of 1922 came to Sally Glynn after one quick leap from Christmas to Easter. Now she looked beyond it to summer, to Tom's ordination and to her own wedding. As the year turned, the first of the returning migrants was to be Mrs Barclay. She was coming back to Storm Hill and to Peter's wedding in June. Peter had quarrelled with his mother over his conversion but now was reconciled with her.

"Sure I knew it would all blow over," John said.

"It was that her friends in the north were tired of her. How will she like to come back and see the green, white and yalla flutterin' over the barracks?" Trooper said.

John, however, thought she would not mind at all because, while she might not agree with the Pope, she believed in doing what one does when in Rome. She would be a good law-abiding citizen of the new State for all her dour, silent Ulster ways.

In the never-ending cycle of time the searching fingers of the low-hanging February sun pointed to the barren fields of white winter-bleached grass. The snow was spreading like fairy tablecloths in odd corners, on northerly banks and slopes, when the first brave flowers ventured forth in the herbaceous border. Mrs Glynn first spotted the cold little snowdrops. These were swiftly followed by the golden chalices of the crocuses, the harbingers of spring. Sally found the first primrose nestling in the roseate of its crinkly leaves. Michael came into the yard with a sheep and two lambs. He had found them over near the Crag, where he had hung out the sheep lamps when he heard a vixen crying a few nights ago.

Spring came in timidly at first then arrived bouncing with lambs and stiff-legged foals. The noisy crows grew busy above the rookery. Brief flashes of warm sunshine dazzled on the gorse. Easter bonnets and orange blossom beckoned. Sally looked forward to the promise of a wedding dress and lovely high-heeled shoes, together with the sort of clothes she had wanted to wear for so long and which her mother had forbidden because they were too grown-up. She had wanted to keep Sally a child as long as she could. She thought that the cut of a dress and the height of shoe heels would add years to her age.

"Simple clothes are so much more becoming to a young girl," her mother had said, looking back to her own girlhood, sheltered and secure.

It's all right for Mother, Sally thought. She's never had to wear a Black and Tan's uniform to get a man out of jail. Or traipse about on a pouring wet night followed by an army of soldiers and pretend to carry water in a bucket with no bottom in it in order to put the army off the track of an outlaw.

Now Sally was tired of simple clothes to keep her young. She was tired of being thought of as young. She was old enough to marry Peter and to accept responsibilities. She was eager to dress as the woman she knew she had become, with all her longings and desires.

The gap in the fence where the cherry tree had fallen was now almost grown over, and the coming spring and summer would fill it with sprawling bush and briar, and binding plants like bedstraw and convolvulus and all the other mean squatters on the site the tree had vacated. Sally crawled through the leafless hedge and stood on the mossy stump of the tree. She could see, away to the left, the great trees of Clanratty. There rooks were circling, noisily prospecting for building sites and material. Above the tall, smokeless chimneys, jackdaws and starlings were fetching and carrying. Clanratty was theirs now. The owls held their own undisputed territory in the ivy-clad belfry above the cobbled courtyard.

She saw the trap carrying Michael and Tom come over the top of the hill. This was Tom's last homecoming. Next time she saw him top that hill on his way home from Maynooth, he would no longer be Tom Glynn, the student. She could no longer spar and argue and fly at him for his provocative righteousness. For he would then be Fr Tom. She would kneel where she was when she met him and get his blessing. It might be here, perhaps, near the tree stump, or in the garden, or at the front door with her father. It would just be she and her father to receive his first blessing at Dooleagh. Her mother and Michael were going to the ordination. That had already been arranged. She turned and hurried back into the house to tell them that Tom was coming. Her mother went to the door, straining her ears for the sound of the rubber-shod wheels and the flip-flop of the hooves. The trap turned from the road into the drive. Mrs Glynn signalled Michael to slow down. At her request Michael tightened the reins and drew the trap close to the little green gate leading from the drive, so that Tom might dismount and enter the house by the front door.

"He must get accustomed to it. There won't be any more driving around to the back door from now on. When you are a priest, Tom, we must receive you with ceremony." She laughed lightly at her own ideas of formality. She shook his hand as he dismounted and led him towards the door, where Sally and her father stood, amused at her mother's welcome for Tom, while Michael drove around to the yard with Tom's luggage and his own shopping parcels from Cloona. On every face there was a smile, except Tom's.

Sally saw his disconcerted reaction to the change in his old custom of driving around to the yard in the trap. "Don't take Mother's concern for your future prelate's robes too seriously, Tom," she said. "You know it's not you she's thinking of – it's what you'll represent next time you come home. Don't take all the honours. Don't flatter yourself. They are not meant for you." Sally shook her head. "Oh dear. I won't be able to say things like that to you, either, the next time you come home. I must try and get in all the nasty things I want to say to you this term."

Her remarks drew a grudging smile from Tom. "One term won't be enough for that. You had better get it extended by some means."

Peter spent Good Friday with them, and they attended all the devotions in Kilalisheen chapel. Peter had hoped to spend most of Easter with Sally and her family but on Easter Saturday he, along with other members of the new army, had to go to Dublin. Many disquieting concerns about hostility to the treaty were becoming apparent. The friendly, frank arguments of the early days of the truce had become a seething cauldron of rumour and unrest, boiling over in places. The steady flame of patriotism was fanned by the winds of the extremism, and perhaps by jealousy or personal spite. These raging furnaces brought uneasiness and fear to the people and dissension in the ranks of the army just born.

Tom's stay was brief and he was due to return to Maynooth on the following Friday. Sally hoped Peter would be back before Tom's departure. There were so many things she was anxious they should discuss and agree upon; many little things and the big thing such as Tom's ordination, Peter being received into the Church, and their wedding. Thursday evening came and still Peter had not returned. Frank Fallon and Hugh Dalton came to visit. They talked long and late about the situation in Dublin and elsewhere, tempers often rising to boiling point. Michael's appeasing words fell on deaf ears, as Tom and Frank Fallon shouted and thumped the table to emphasise their position on the treaty. Sally understood the treaty would slice off six of the thirty-two counties and give England permission to annex them.

When Frank left the kitchen in a flurry of rage at the weight of opposition against his argument, Tom walked him down the drive through the thick rhododendron hedges. There was silence in the house when the two had gone.

"We've beaten them!" Hugh Dalton laughed, for those remaining in the kitchen were either pro-treaty or neutral, like Sally and her mother. And so, without opposition, the argument lost its punch and the conversation took a constructive turn about what was more likely to be of benefit to the country. They talked of the spring sowing and the prospects of good weather, or a repetition of the previous year's drought. They talked of the rotation of crops, the planting of the Crescent Acre, which last year was harvested before the flood. They talked of the success of potatoes, early potatoes. They talked of fencing off a part by the edge with barbed wire so that the cattle could be driven down to the lake to drink, in case of another drought.

Never again, they vowed, would they endure the hardship of carting water with a kettle.

Trooper came in from the yard in time to join the conversation. "Mightn't come a year like last for a long time," he said. He weighed up the disadvantages of carting water against the task of erecting a fence, with all the work it would entail. There would be cutting and sinking posts, struggling with coils of barbed wire – the devil's knitting, he called it. Then there would also be the destruction of the fields and the waste incurred in giving up a portion completely to a fenced-off path.

"No, take a chance with the floods or put the land back into pasture now that it's had one year's cultivation and killed the boholauns and flaggers," as he called the ragwort and wild iris.

Tom was late returning, so late that they did not wait for him to say the Rosary. His mother presumed he had accompanied Frank as far as Duffys'.

"Could be Mrs Duffy has asked him to say the Rosary with them. I'd be glad if he's done so because with Mrs Duffy you never know when another stroke may come. She might never see Tom ordained. It's different with us. We're all hale and hearty, thank God. And we'll have the comfort and company of Tom as a priest for the rest of our lives. We won't begrudge his company for one evening to poor Mrs Duffy. Come on, John, we'll go off to bed. Sally and Michael can wait up for him."

She helped John out of his chair and together they shuffled down the hall towards their room.

After they had gone, Sally turned to Michael. "Before Tom gets out of reach of your voice, Michael, will you give him a good lecture on the way he's going on about this treaty business? Didn't you see how worked-up he got this evening? I didn't want to say anything in Mother and Father's hearing, though I don't know what they thought about him kicking up such a shindig. I'm glad Peter wasn't about to hear his condemnation of the new army and the people who made and maintained the treaty. Their sins are even more heinous than those of the British Army and the British government, according to Tom's preaching, though at one time he assured us their misdeeds were unbeatable."

"I'm afraid my talking to my brother won't change his attitude. You see, when anyone has an ideal, you can't just change it. If you can, then it was never an ideal. It was merely an idea that fades with time or altered circumstances. Or it may be blown into a different shape, or perhaps whirled away altogether by the uncertain winds of chance. Tom's ideal Ireland may be unlikely, even impossible and far removed from reality, but it will always be in his mind. Given the opportunity, he will strive, even unconsciously, for its attainment."

"I don't believe that. A person can be talked out of most of their cracked ideals if they're got at in time. What about yourself? It's a long time now since Mother knocked out of your head the idea, or ideal, or whatever it was, about joining the Franciscans!"

Michael looked at Sally for a few seconds, fixing her with his clear blue eyes, which appeared almost violet-blue in the lamplight. "You don't really think that I've forgotten all about joining the Franciscans, do you? Just because I don't talk about it or prate on about abandoning an ideal because of my duty to my parents. Sometimes, Sally, I think I've abandoned everything and that I have failed miserably in my duty to God and man. I want to be a Franciscan now just as much as I did ten years ago. I wanted to then with all my heart and I have never stopped wanting it since. It wasn't Mother and Father's persuasion that kept me from it. It was just the chain of events."

The words Michael had kept bottled up for years rushed out in a torrent. "I went, at Mother's request, to become a doctor. I detested the career but resolved to go on with this because I would become a missionary doctor healing souls through healing bodies. I was overjoyed with this idea. Then you know what happened. When I came home to Father's disablement and Mother's heart set on making Tom a priest, these two factors pushed me into what I am today – a bad farmer. So you see, Sally, it's still there, the ideal. Maybe someday, with God's help, I will attain it. I would be happy in a monastery but I still feel that I have no right to happiness through the distress and hardship I would cause Mother and Father and you."

This opening of Michael's heart surprised Sally. She forgot about Tom and his politics and thought of the future, when she and Peter would be married and Tom had become a priest. Michael would continue to carry the burden of a home and farm he did not want because it had been thrust upon him by circumstance. Her heart went out to him and her eyes filled with tears.

At that moment they heard Tom's footsteps on the gravel drive.

"Don't say anything to Tom of what I've told you. Don't say anything to anybody, Sally. Just forget about it and let us go on, all of us, in whatever way God has chosen for us."

Sally nodded her head.

31

Flight

Sally locked the window of her room and pulled back the curtains. She could see the glint of the lake through the still-bare trees and the white road up from the Hazel Bridge, with the bright spring dust on it. The little circles of light from the sheep lamps over by the Crag looked cold and still. A light shone in the sky, flashing above the woods at Clanratty. She hoped and prayed that it might be the headlights of Peter's car returning from Athlone. She felt she had never more need of him than now. She wanted to talk things over together with Tom and Michael before her mother and father got up in the morning.

The light flashed and faded as though the car had changed its direction and disappeared like a phantom, perhaps down the deserted avenue to Clanratty. It wasn't Peter. But perhaps Peter wouldn't understand in any case. Peter would want to persuade Tom to go back to Maynooth so as not to disappoint his mother or cause any hitch in their wedding plans. But she and Michael did not want Tom to go back if there was the slightest doubt in his mind about his vocation. And she did want to prevent him getting mixed up in this fantastic treaty, or anti-treaty, affair. She drew the curtains closed and sat on the bed, trying to sort out the burden of her tangled thinking. Sooner or later, either Michael or would have to prepare their her mother for the possibility of Tom was leaving Maynooth. They could not leave the task to Tom. Between them, they must make it less difficult for him. She heard Tom and Michael go to their rooms. She undressed and got into bed. But she lay awake for a long time listening to the night-time sounds of the house: the clock in the hall, the chirp of a cricket, a mouse in the wainscoting. A vixen crying away beyond the Sheep Slopes kept her awake for a long time. Gradually she fell into a light sleep, with the hope in her heart that tomorrow, as so many tomorrows had already done, would put everything right.

She awoke with a start. She had been dreaming of the nights when Peter and Michael had been on the run. Her dream had such a vivid nightmarish quality that when she awoke she thought she heard footsteps hurrying on the gravel outside. She thought it must be someone coming to tell her that they were captured again, or shot. She was trembling with fear, perspiration clinging to her forehead.

She jumped out of bed and looked out into the moonlight. She still thought she heard footsteps, faint now. She decided it was only her dream that made her imagine this. She climbed back into bed, but she gave up coaxing further sleep. She watched the dawn creeping through the parted curtains. The window gradually filled with daylight, bringing into shape the dim but familiar pieces of furniture in her room.

She got up to call Tom for Mass. The bell at Kilalisheen would soon be ringing. She rubbed her tired eyes and pulled on her dressing gown. Then she crept along to Tom's room. The door stood slightly open and she called softly, "It's seven, Tom."

She got no reply, so she knocked lightly with her knuckles. Silence still prevailed and she knocked again, this time harder. The door swung slowly open but there was still only silence within. She crept cautiously in and stood, blinking wide open her sleepy-lidded eyes. The white counterpane on Tom's bed was undisturbed and the pillows were as her mother had left them, smooth and neat. She went over to the bed. She was going to pull down the covers to see if, by some strange unaccustomed chance, he had made the bed up before going out to Mass. In her heart she knew that this was not so and that Tom had gone. Indeed, she had heard him go. His had been the hurrying feet on the gravel that had awakened her from her dream. The sound was no nightmare. It was real.

She drew back from the bed. A cold nameless terror was taking possession of her. She crept across to Michael's room and opened the door. Michael was not asleep.

"Tom's gone!" she whispered.

"Gone where?" Michael sat bolt upright with a jerk.

"I don't know. His bed hasn't been slept in. Come in and see."

He followed her. They stood together looking at the little heap of black clothes folded neatly on the lid of the closed suitcase his mother had so carefully packed for his return to Maynooth. His black hat lay on top like a dead soldier's cap upon his coffin. His breviary was placed face down upon the little lace-covered table by his bedside. It confirmed their thoughts, since he never placed an open book face down and lectured those who did so, pointing out to them the risk of damaging the binding through such careless handling. Sally picked it up and the little ribbon-marked medals jingled. It was open at the feast of St Bede the Venerable, and a passage from the Epistles was underlined with red ink. Sally read it out loud: "I have fought the good fight. I have finished my course. I have kept the fate. As to the rest ..."

She handed the book to Michael.

"He's finished – everything, everything," Sally sobbed. She scarcely knew if it was anger or sorrow she felt towards Tom.

Michael closed the book.

"He'll come back, Sally. Don't worry, he'll come back. If he didn't want to be a priest, well, perhaps it's better this way."

"What way? Surely not the way of the gun against his friends and neighbours, against Peter, even against you, his only brother."

"It won't ever come to that, Sally."

"What about Mother? What about Father? It wouldn't matter to Tom how his going affects others. Oh no, he could always justify his actions, turn his cowardice to heroism. He's no more a patriot than a priest. We were in it too, you and I and Peter, but it wasn't patriotism that brought us into it."

"Of course not," Michael agreed. "We were just washed into it by the tidal wave that swept the country."

"There might have been patriotism, for better or worse, in the Glynns of the past, but not in this, our generation. We can't get away from it. Mother comes from English Protestant stock and *they* don't rear Irish patriots."

"You are wrong there, Sally. What about Pearse, Emmett, Tone, Parnell and countless others from the same stock?"

Sally was silent. This was not the time for a history lesson. Somehow the name of Patrick Pearse always came to Michael's lips. Pearse's name was like that of a saint. Michael invoked it in times of trial and distress.

"Don't be too hard on Tom, Sally," Michael said. "We don't know his heart or his mind."

"I'm not hard on him. I'm hard on the way he's taken to leaving Maynooth. Couldn't he have said, 'I can't be a priest,' and stand and take the consequences? When the neighbours first saw him out of his black clothes, it would have been talked and whispered about, but they'd soon have forgotten the colour of his clothes. Now the talk will be sensational: 'Tom Glynn has left Maynooth and gone to join the Irregulars. He's taken up and gone against people like Hugh Dalton, the Duffys, the Treacys and ... Peter Barclay.' Now it will be more than a whisper. It will be a good old nudge and an elbow in the ribs that will pass along every seat in the church when you or I or any of us walk up to the rails on Sundays. Don't tell me not to blame him."

"I can see why you don't mind the neighbours whispering about Tom leaving Maynooth but mind them nudging and elbowing in the ribs. I don't like the way he went, but we've got to tell Mother and Father about it somehow."

"Who's going to tell them?"

"I am," Michael said. "And you're not to condemn him to them, Sally. It won't do any good. They thought he was almost a saint. Let them keep on thinking that. He may come back any time – today, tomorrow, or perhaps in a week – you never know. Events, especially political events, take sharp turns. We know that, Sally, from the past, the not too distant past."

Michael's face looked pale and haggard. His eyes, like Sally's, showed signs of a sleepless night. Sally knew that despite his optimism, Michael was deeply distressed. He was hiding it from her and he would hide it from their parents. He would try to find an easy way to present the bitter facts that would cruelly wound those he loved. He would do everything possible to bring Tom back, but Sally knew that Michael would not persuade him to return to Maynooth. Tom's decision to leave had come almost as a relief to Michael, who had anxiously watched Tom's silent struggle in the years that had passed. If the truce had not been signed in the July of the previous year, Tom would have gone then. Events had now pushed him to another means of escape. Slowly the things that were happening around him had drawn him to the edge of the chasm, and he had leapt.

Sally did not reply to Michael's words of comfort. She ran past him and out the front door. She stopped on the gravel path and shouted, "Tom, Tom, come back! Please, Tom, come back."

But only the echo of her voice returned. The distant trill of a lone warbler conquered the air. Michael came up beside her. A lock of hair fell over his forehead. He looked pale and suddenly weary and old. He put his arm across her shoulder.

"Come in, Sally. Don't stand here in the cold."

Their mother was now on the scene in her bare feet, hair screwed in paper curls. She looked at Sally and then at Michael, a strained and anxious look on her face.

"What's wrong? There is something wrong, isn't there? Tell me! Tell me!"

Then each put an arm through their mother's and silently led her indoors.

"Come on, let us get dressed and prepare for the day ahead. It isn't going to be an easy one," Michael said, and all three went back into the deserted bedroom in silence.

32

Divisions

The morning after Tom's departure, Hugh Dalton went to open his shop as usual. He did not turn the key in the lock, as the topic under discussion outside stayed his hand. He recognised the voice of the principal speaker. Mrs Carey from across the street was relating her experience of the previous night. She said she was letting her dog out when she saw Tom Glynn and Kitty Dalton drive away in the Daltons' car. There could have been someone in the back, she wasn't sure. Someone asked if it was dark at the time.

"There was a slice of the moon out but I didn't notice it much. I was more concerned about my dog in case the car would run him over."

Others on their way from Mass joined the little group.

"Did you not hear about it?"

"About what?"

"Tom Glynn and Kitty Dalton running away together."

"Sure I thought he was a quiet religious type, going to be a priest."

"Quiet, how are you. Tom was hot on the politics. He should never have gone to Maynooth. Should have joined the new army."

"With all the learning he has from Maynooth, he'd be a captain in no time. That's what the new army wants – education."

Then the whining voice of the Widow Burke chimed in: "I don't know what the country is coming to at all. The girls smokin' and the short skirts. Next thing they'll be wearing trousers. And the dances. Oh, the dances. The foxtrot and the jazz. Such names for dances. There's not enough of the good old Irish dances like the Walls of Limerick and the Waves of Tory.

"You'd need to be very energetic for them," Harry Connor said.

"You would, and very drunk," Red Joe added.

"Kitty Dalton, she's a flighty one. Drivin' around in a car. A different fella with her every time. High in the Cumann, too. They say she has a gun."

And so it went on.

The pedigree of the Glynns and the Daltons faded from the conversation. They no longer had any interest in it.

When Trooper got his tobacco, Hugh left the barman in charge of the shop. He hopped on his bike for Glynns'. He arrived in hostile mood, demanding an explanation as to where Tom was. The family had not yet come to terms with the disappearance. There was only the note on his bedside table, which left no clue as to where he was going. When Hugh discovered that the Glynns knew even less about Tom than he did, he lowered the volume of his voice to inform them of how he had come by what little he knew.

"All Cloona was buzzing with the news that Tom Glynn had run away with Kitty Dalton." He did not disclose how the pedigree of the Glynns and the Daltons was being tossed around. He could still hear the words loud and clear: "Is it Tom Glynn? What would you expect? His mother was a Protestant. Oh, very hoity-toity. Had a different hat on every night at the mission." "They say the daughter, Sally, is going to marry into the Barclays. Imagine having Mrs Barclay as a mother-in-law, and she a Protestant!"

Everyone at the Glynns' appeared lost for words when an elated Gerty Fallon bounced in.

"I see Frank's bicycle outside the door," Gerty said. "I'm delighted to see it. I was beginning to think he was ravin' or something. I was half-asleep and could have mistaken what he said."

All lapsed into silence. The buzz of a car revived their expectations of the return of the missing trio.

"It's our car," Hugh said.

"It must be Kitty and Tom," Sally said.

"And Frank," Gerty added.

They gathered close to the window. Kitty got out of the car. She closed the door. Their hopes were dashed when they saw the car had no other passengers. Kitty strolled into the kitchen.

"What's this?" Kitty asked as she looked from one blank face to the other. "There's the air of a conspiracy in here."

"Where's Tom?" Sally asked.

"I don't know," Kitty answered somewhat indifferently.

"You don't know?" Sally said.

Kitty pulled a chair near to the fire. She sat down, took a packet of cigarettes from her pocket and lit one in a provocative slow movement.

"Such needless fuss. I left them in Dublin. It was the least I could do," she said, looking at Sally.

"Them?"

"Yes. Tom and Frank Fallon."

"Where in Dublin?"

"Oh, just in Dublin. I expect they arranged their place of meeting. I didn't ask them." She looked at Gerty. "I'm sure you know it was the right thing to do. You understand."

Sally did not want Tom to go back to Maynooth. He had no vocation. But she didn't want him mixed up in this treaty/anti-treaty business, encouraged by Kitty Dalton, either. She was still trying to sort out her emotions and the manner in which, sooner or later, Michael or she must tell her mother Tom was leaving Maynooth. They would not tell her of their suspicions of Tom's friendship with Kitty. Fortunately, her mother had always believed that Tom's friendship with Jack was his link with the Daltons.

Peter returned from Dublin on Monday to be told the catastrophic news of Tom's departure. He withheld from Sally and her family what he knew of the rapidly deepening divisions that were splitting the country apart, destroying loyalties, cleaving friendships built in the previous years of shared hardships and dangers. Already the stream of rancour and bitterness was gathering force, drawing into its eddying whirls young men like Tom who had been too young for the war just ended, along with heroes and veterans of the campaign against England. He did not tell them that it was becoming as unmanageable as a river in space and that he with others would be forced to try to dam it. If he should come up against Tom, there was no telling how they would come out of it.

The tragedy of this was becoming frighteningly clear, more dreadful, more cruel. Brothers fighting brothers. Divided families. Divided friends. Divided loyalties. The holocaust of civil war was the greatest disaster to overcome any country. In centuries of fighting invaders they had all joined forces against the common enemy, helped each other in times of famine fevers, made sacrifices. Civil war happened in other countries far away, like America, but not here. The only knowledge they had of it was leafing through the pages of history books. The possibility of such a thing terrified Peter. It overshadowed completely Tom's leaving Maynooth and the disappointment to Sally and her mother that Tom would have no part in officiating at the wedding ceremony. He talked to Michael about finding Tom and assured Sally and her parents that he would do everything possible to find him.

May came again to Dooleagh. Sowing and planting dawdled along in cold, showery weather. The hearts and the hopes of the Irish people were low, and dark clouds clung to the early summer skies. The previous year's drought changed the face of the farming programme.

Other factors had contributed to changes at Glynns'. Tom was now on the run, maybe coming back any day to work alongside Michael on the farm. Sally was getting married in June and leaving to live in the officers' married quarters at Cloona barracks or at Storm Hill. It was hard to make a farming programme. Even Trooper had no suggestions and only said that they should do just what they had done last year. He had not yet forgotten the triumph of the harvesting of the Crescent Acre and evidently hoped to repeat it.

The land remained fallow and sodden. The horses' hooves sank deep, and the plough sucked noisily through the cloying wet earth. The plough and horses were changed to the upland where the land was better drained. There, Trooper and Michael braved the lingering east winds and hail showers, uncharacteristic heralds of summer. They worked against time and the elements, ploughing until it was almost too late for sowing, not only for themselves but also for the Fallons and the Duffys.

With Frank and Jim Fallon with the Irregulars, Terry Duffy in the Free State Army, Gerty expecting her baby and Joe and Mrs Fallon getting on in years, the two families had become entirely dependent on their neighbours. But even the neighbours had prejudices. There were those who refused to help the Fallons because Frank and Jim were in the Irregulars. There were those who refused to help the Duffys because Terry was "flying around in the Staters uniform". And there were those who said that Joe Fallon had no control over his sons, or he'd make them stay at home and do the work and that it served him right if he was on the shaughraun now. They forgot about Gerty and they forgot about Rory Duffy. But Michael did not forget. He did not listen to abuses hurled from opposing factions. He and Trooper ploughed and worked and comforted and consoled, the same as they had done away back when the flu raged in 1918.

No message had been received from Tom or from Frank Fallon. Each day brought its fresh crop of rumours. The contradictory nature of such rumours taught the Glynns to ignore all messages coming from unknown and mysterious sources. It was almost a week now since Tom had gone. His going had staggered his mother and she still reeled. However, she cherished a hope that what she termed "the skirmish" would soon be over and he would return to Maynooth and begin again where he had left off. She took consolation from what she now knew had been her needless worry about Michael both in 1916 and later when he was on the run. As she saw the political situation worsen, her fears for Tom's safety concerned her more now than his vocation. She hoped and prayed.

John said little, except at times, more by way of consolation to himself that in chastisement, "We can't mould our children into our lives. They are just themselves, with the ways and wheels of their own. If we ever forget than, it's to bring trouble on them and misery on ourselves."

He was generous enough to admit a part of their failures when they came, but he never accepted any part in their successes. He had always been opposed to his wife's determination to make a priest of Tom, but he was not openly hostile to it.

The late crops were in at last and still no word from Tom or Frank. There was no letter, no message, only the usual spate of whispered rumours. Tom had been seen here, been seen there, and like the Scarlet Pimpernel he'd been seen everywhere.

33

Waiting

Sally was preparing her trousseau, but her mother showed little interest in it. She talked always of Tom and suggested that Sally await his return. She did not mind him leaving Maynooth. All she wanted was his presence here about the house. Why couldn't Michael go to Dublin and look for him? Michael must go, she insisted, and she refused to listen to Michael when he told her that it was a hopeless task she was setting him. She refused to listen also to Sally and John's pleading regarding Michael's safety. Her demand for Michael's assistance in finding Tom became unreasonable almost to the point of hysteria.

At last Michael left for Dublin, on what his father referred to, out of earshot of his wife, as a wild goose chase. After he had gone, the house was like a graveyard. At night they kept Trooper with them and brought in Chess from the fodder bed in the trap house because he cried mournfully through the night now that Michael was away. Peter came and went at frequent intervals and Sally was worried for him also. Ambushes and their casualties were mounting.

They waited anxiously for Michael's return or even for a letter to tell them something of the success or failure of his mission. After a few days the eagerly awaited letter arrived. It was handed around with trembling fingers and finally torn open by Sally.

"He has contacted Tom," she told them, without raising her eyes from the letter.

"Thanks be to God!" exclaimed her mother. "I knew Michael would find him – he'd find anything. What else does he say?" She was smiling now and reaching for the letter.

But Sally kept her eyes on the letter, in a pretence of still reading it. "He says that Tom is looking well and has promised to come home as soon as things straighten out a bit." She put the letter behind her back and looked from one to the other face before her. "And ... Michael is not coming back. He is going into the Franciscan monastery. He's taken this opportunity to leave Dooleagh. Tom will be home to take his place. This is what they have arranged between them. Michael says he is very happy to find his lifelong wish granted and hopes that we will go to see him as soon as we can, to show him that we have forgiven him for leaving home. He hopes that we will realise that this was the best time, as the spring sowing is over and Tom will be home to reap it. He promises to pray for us day and night, and for the peace of his country."

Sally held back the last sentence of his letter: "There isn't room for two of us at Dooleagh." She seemed to recall Tom saying something similar the night before he left.

If Michael had not told her earlier about his determination to join the Franciscans, she would have concluded he did so now just to make room for Tom. But she did not doubt the sincerity of his motives. However, for her own part, she thought having to swap Michael for Tom was a poor exchange.

A stunned silence followed her reading of the letter. To her mother, however, the message about Tom brought happiness and serenity beyond all her hopes, which compensated for Michael's absence. Daily, on the strength of the promise he had given to Michael, they awaited Tom's return. And daily they were reminded that the promise was "as soon as things are straightened out". But things did not appear to be straightening out. Rather they were becoming more twisted and tangled and devilish as the days went by.

Peter's comings and goings became brief impromptu visits, according to the circumstances of his location. Often the periods of his absence were prolonged, when trouble became unmanageable. The army openly clashed with the new insurgent force, using the same tactics of the guerrilla warfare in which both sides had been well schooled. The stronghold of the Irregulars in Dublin had been broken, and the remnants of the retreating garrison had withdrawn in small groups to widely scattered points of the country. They would reorganise and rearm so as to carry on the battle in formations of unknown numbers or strength. Sometimes they fought hand-to-hand battles and took over barracks in which the new army had not fully consolidated its positions. Sometimes they took over barracks vacated by the British military and which were not occupied by the regular army. At times, if necessary, they established their billets or headquarters in isolated mansions that afforded protection from their attackers. The fighting brought about the destruction of places that had survived the long war with the British. Both armies appeared to have grown indifferent to the mounting casualty list and the destruction of the country for which both sides had fought so gallantly.

It was late evening when Trooper dashed into the house excitedly waving his hands about. "They're there, upon my soul they are," he called.

"Were you in Cloona today? You're drunk," Mrs Glynn exclaimed, puzzled by his elation.

"I'm sober enough to see smoke coming from the chimney of the castle."

"You couldn't possibly see smoke coming from the chimney of the castle. It's not visible. It's hidden by the trees. If you saw smoke, it must be from someone burning weeds or something, and the evening is getting dark."

There had been no Irregular stronghold in or about Cloona.

To appease Trooper's offence Sally took his arm. "Come on, Trooper, show me the smoke." She laughed as she went out and stood on the doorstep with him.

Trooper was still trying to convince them when Gerty Fallon arrived breathlessly to confirm his announcement.

"Now! Didn't I tell ye, and ye wouldn't believe me!" Trooper was triumphant.

They all stood staring while Gerty slumped into a heap on the ground at their feet. They forgot about the Irregulars in Clanratty while they tried to bring Gerty around from her fainting fit. When she showed signs of recovery they lifted her into John's armchair in the kitchen. Mrs Glynn's brandy completed Gerty's recovery. After a while Mrs Glynn took Gerty's arm and walked the long road home with her, telling her to go to bed and rest and that Frank would be home soon. She was consoling herself with her own words to Gerty, hoping and praying the same hope, the same prayer, would bring Tom home to her.

When her mother and Gerty had gone down the drive, Sally climbed onto the cherry tree stump and looked out across the familiar scene, away to the dark woods of Clanratty. There was nothing in the quiet countryside to indicate the truth of Trooper and Gerty's news. Surely it could not happen that they were there in Clanratty? If they were, what would be the reaction to it? Would the army from Cloona attack and drive them from it? Would it mean more shooting and burning, like there had already been in Dublin and other places? Would it bring this senseless war to their own doorstep? But, she thought, almost smugly, as she beheld the tranquillity of the scene, there could be no war here. All that was over. Only peace and quiet and beauty lay about.

From the poplar a cuckoo called and lifted her heart with its repeated announcement of summer. When the cuckoo had finished, a lark poured down its song as it soared in the china-blue ball of the sky. The furze on the upland blazed like a gilt fringe on the green carpet of the new corn. The lake reflected the sky, its white puffball clouds motionless as little painted swans on the smooth canvas of that surface. No breeze came to stir them, nor play with the gently dropping petals of the sloe or whitethorn. Out against the blue background of the sky, the changeless Crag carried its own living foliage of white land gulls from across the lake. The lark's song ceased and the little speck of its body vanished.

Sally stood a long time, seeking some confirmation of the news Trooper had brought. Perhaps men crouching behind hedges or slinking across the fields, or moving along the top of the Crag. But there was no indication at all. She turned on the old stump, catching a sapling to steady herself. Already a slippery wet moss was covering the scar of the tree trunk. As she stood like a wood nymph, poised for her leap onto the greasy bank below, something caught her eye. She raised her head and gazed fixedly towards the woods of

Clanratty. There it was. A thin thread of blue smoke ascending straight as a ribbon from the castle chimneys, just as Trooper had said. She knew now that someone was there, for no smoke had come from Clanratty since the British military had left. She guessed it was the Irregulars. Her immediate reaction was that Tom could be there. She jumped from her perch and ran towards the house.

"You're right, Trooper. You're right! You're right! They are there! I'm going over. I want to find out from them if they know anything about Tom. They must know something about him."

"Wait till your mother comes back," Trooper advised.

"No, no, I'm going now. I want to have news for Mother when she comes back. I want to have news for Gerty, too. I want to see Frank and I want to tell him about Gerty fainting because she's worried about him. He ought to be home with her."

She grabbed her bicycle and went down the drive and along the road towards Clanratty and the thin string of smoke. Trooper stood in the yard looking like Father Time, scythe across his shoulders, gazing after her and talking to her long after she had gone out of earshot.

"What does he care about Gerty? What does he care about anyone? God knows where Fr Tom and Frank Fallon are, but sure I'd have done the same myself when I was like them. And Miss Sally now after them to bring them home. They're like Little Bo Peep and her sheep. Leave them alone and they'll come home, waggin' their tails behind them."

John, who was still in bed, had heard the commotion about the house. Now, hearing Trooper's voice in the yard, he struggled out of bed and over to the window.

"Is there anything wrong?"

"The Irregulars have taken Clanratty, and Miss Sally's gone to see if Fr Tom is there."

"And where is her mother?"

"She's gone to leave Mrs Fallon home. She came over with the news and fainted out stone cold on the kitchen floor. She thinks maybe Frank's there too."

"And who were you talking to just now?"

"Just talkin' to meself, I was."

"Is it dotin' ye are, Trooper? Sally shouldn't have gone near Clanratty. If the Irregulars have taken it over, they'll be shootin'."

He had scarcely spoken when they heard the sharp crack of rifle fire.

34

The Awful Truth

Sally heard the shots.

The sound brought her heart into her mouth but did not deter her. She topped the hill beyond Hazel Bridge and swept recklessly down towards Clanratty. When she came near the gate, two men, rifles in hand, stepped out in front of her so suddenly she almost toppled.

"I'm Sally Glynn. I'm going to Clanratty. I want to know if my brother Tom is there with the Irregulars."

The new soldiers, whose voices still carried the hunted fear of the past, began to ask questions about Tom but she cut them short.

"I want to find him. I want to bring him home," she cried.

"You shouldn't have let him go," one of them said.

"I didn't send him," Sally snapped.

She moved forward to force her way past them but they stepped out again in front of her.

"You can't go through there, Miss. You had better go home and stay there – it's safer."

"I must go. Who is your officer? Who is in charge of you? Where's Captain Barclay?" she demanded.

But the frightened men said nothing.

"Ye are not from Cloona barracks, then. Who exactly are ye?"

She grew more perplexed. She examined their scrappy uniforms of peaked cap and tunics over grey flannel trousers. One wore black socks and brown shoes while the other wore brown boots beneath cropped short trousers. The made-up uniform could belong to either side.

"We are regular Free State Army soldiers from Sligo. What else?" one of them answered indignantly, suddenly waking from his indifference at the suggestion that he might be mistaken for the enemy. "You didn't think we belonged to the other crowd of outlaws, did you? And what's more, you can't stay here interfering with our duty. You must go back at once!" he ordered.

Sally knew now that there was nothing for her to do but obey. She would hope and pray that Peter would turn up from somewhere to help her find out if Tom was at Clanratty. She turned to wearily push her bicycle up the hill. Before she had reached the summit, volley after volley of shots echoed through the woods around the castle. The green hedges seemed to move. Here and there little groups of soldiers appeared under trees only to be swallowed up by the dark woods. She had heard no lorries nor seen any evidence of their presence when she had gone down the hill a short while before. Yet there they were, just as on the morning of the ambush at the Crag.

By the time she reached the house, the firing had faded away into spasmodic outbursts. By midday it had died away altogether. Trooper went over to Fallons' to ask how Gerty was, and returned with the news that the Irregulars were digging in at Clanratty and that they were a thousand strong. Sally and her mother listened to his report and speculated on the likelihood of Tom being there and, even if he could not come home to stay, of his paying them a visit. Sally ran out to the cherry tree at regular intervals. It became her lookout. She swept the landscape. It was as quiet as it had been that morning when she had first searched for confirmation of the news Trooper and Gerty had brought. Even the ribbon of smoke from the chimney had vanished. Then she saw a lone dark figure on a bike coming down the hill towards the Hazel Bridge. She waited with bated breath to see who it might be. For one moment she thought the little dark figure might be Tom. Then, with bitter disappointment, she realised that it could not be him. For he wouldn't be in black clothes now. As the figure emerged from the hollow of the bridge it was evident that it was Fr O'Rourke. He stopped and asked her if she had been frightened by the shooting and if they had any word of Frank Fallon or Tom. She knew that he was concerned for Gerty and the imminent birth of her baby. She told him what Trooper had reported. He had come from Cloona, he told her, where the word was that it was only a handful of men and that the troops were coming from Sligo to clear them out. The first local casualty was Mr Brigson. The bank manager had been shot by raiders, according to Mr Pratt. Sally didn't take much notice of what Pratt said because he always wanted to be on the safe side. Right now, safe side was State side. If it showed signs of weakening, he would manoeuvre his way, with his accustomed craftiness, into the other camp. Then he would sneer behind their backs at their raw inexperience when compared with the suave captain this and major that. The only person Pratt appeared loyal to was Mr Brigson. It paid him, Sally concluded. She wondered if Fr O'Rourke couldn't see through his knavery.

"Maybe, with the help of God, it will all blow over soon. It's a pity, a great pity," the priest said. He shook his head sadly as he rode off towards Duffys'. Sally went into the house with the news of Mr Brigson's death. She would go again to the castle at first light.

It was a fitful sleep.

A light tapping on the window awoke Sally. She rubbed her eyes and looked through the pearly-grey square of the window and noticed the rose leaves moving with the dawn breeze against the pane. She drowsily closed her eyes again. But above the sigh of the wind she heard a voice calling. As she listened it came again, startlingly clear this time.

"Miss Glynn! Miss Glynn!"

The urgency of the voice roused her. She sat up and saw, silhouetted against the window, a man's head wearing a peaked uniform hat. She thought that perhaps it was Peter playing a prank.

"Peter, Peter, what's wrong?"

Still only half-awake, she jumped out of bed and went to the window. She could see now that it was not Peter. But the voice awaited no formal introduction and went on hastily.

"Are you Miss Glynn, Miss Sally Glynn?"

"Yes, but who are you?"

"It doesn't matter who I am. I want to give you a message, and you better listen quickly – there's no time. Your brother Tom is down at the castle. He's wounded. We're getting out. The Free Staters are coming back at any time to attack. We couldn't take him. We have a few wounded with us, that's all. We had to go, couldn't hold out any longer. Had to leave a lot of stuff, but they won't be getting' that, damn them! The old castle is dynamited from end to end – might as well use the dynamite that way as leave it for them to use against ourselves. They'll likely be blown sky-high, every man Jack of them."

"And you left Tom in a place that's going to be blown up?" Sally cried as she tried to think of her next move.

"We didn't! We left him on a seat in a little sort of summer house in front of the castle. There's rugs and blankets around him. He's not too badly wounded, but get him away before the Staters come, or they'll arrest him."

He vanished from the window like a shadow. Sally's fumbling hands were almost paralysed as she groped through the garments hanging on the back of the door. She dressed quickly. Who could she tell? Trooper? If only Trooper were here, old and stiff as he is, she thought. She would tell her mother so that she would be up and have a fire lit when Tom was brought home.

She popped her head into her parents' room.

"Tom is down in Clanratty! I'm going to him."

She heard her mother's voice mutter something from the shadows of the bed, but she didn't wait to explain. She went noisily through the back door and took a bicycle from the trap house. In her haste she skinned her shin against the pedal and then Chess blocked her way. She bumped him away impatiently with the front wheel.

The dawn had not yet broken. She could scarcely see the grass verge along the drive. Twice she was partly thrown as her tyre skidded along the edge. She sped through the gate onto the road, pedalling furiously down the hill. Over the Hazel Bridge she flew and up the hill beyond until her feet were unable to press the pedals down against the steep incline. She dismounted and quickly wheeled her bicycle over the crest of the hill, half-walking, half-running. An excited Chess caught up with her there. She mounted her bicycle once more and raced along towards the Clanratty gates.

There was no one about as Sally turned into the pitted avenue. Everything before her seemed strange and unfamiliar. She could see the turreted outline of the castle against the sky. It was clearly and strangely visible, as it had never been before. Now, on entering the second gate, she saw that one of the yew trees that had flanked the avenue had been cut down. It was as though the Irregulars had intended defending their position and then, for some reason, decided against it. She threw her bicycle on the grass and clambered over the huge tree trunk, scrambling through the dense foliage of the branches, while Chess poked his way beneath. As she pushed the branches back to make her path easier, she remembered often hearing her father say that the Clanratty yews were as old as the castle itself. For an instant her thoughts strayed from Tom to the great tree whose branches she wrestled with. Wasn't there anything spared in this almost-blind stubborn love of country? She thought of the cherry tree as she disentangled the clawing twigs from her dress and her hair.

The buzz of distant lorries broke the early-morning silence. Almost as soon as the sound filled her ears, she saw them swing through the gateway onto the avenue. The great, grey shadow monsters in the misty light were almost upon her before she escaped from the tree. She hurried across the lawn towards the summer house. Looking back, she saw the soldiers dismount the lorries, scramble through the trees and swarm over the branches like monkeys, some of them fanning out across the lawn to vantage points that afforded some cover – the shrubbery and the heaps of sandbags on the hacked-up lawn. Then she turned and ran.

"They've gone! The castle is empty."

"What you doin' here, Miss?" a soldier asked.

"Is Captain Barclay with you?" For her greatest fear now was that they would arrest Tom.

A soldier called back her request for Captain Barclay.

Peter came towards her, as Chess bounded into the summer house.

"Sally, Sally! What's wrong? In heaven's name, Sally, are you mad?"

"It's Tom, it's Tom, he's here, in the summer house. He's wounded."

Together they ran through the tangled heap of rose and honeysuckle that trailed across the hulk of the summer house.

There was Tom.

"Don't let them arrest him. Don't let them arrest him, Peter."

Tom lay wrapped in rugs and overcoats on the rickety seat in the cold dank summer house.

"Oh Tom, Tom, what has happened?"

In the grey light Sally could see the pallor of Tom's face and the wan smile trembling at the corners of his thin lips. Chess licked his face and pawed the garments piled around him. She dropped to her knees beside him and put her arms around him, touching his cold cheeks with her warm lips, and laying her face close against his.

"Easy," Peter said, acutely aware of her distress. "Take it easy, Sally."

"I knew you'd come, Sally," Tom uttered in a broken little whisper.

"I can't see what's wrong with him here. There's no light," Peter said.

He beckoned to some of the soldiers to come and help him lift the rickety stretcher seat out into the dawn light. The other troops were still swarming like ants over the fallen yew and crawling on the castle steps.

"The house is mined!" Sally shouted suddenly.

Without verifying the source of information, Peter passed on her warning to another officer. Then he turned to examine Tom to determine the extent of his injuries.

Sometimes Tom appeared to know Sally and Peter, and sometimes he mistook them for others from his college days in Maynooth. He whispered passages in Latin, as though quoting them for his professors. Then his weak voice died away. His breath was coming in short gasps, and his speech was no more than a movement of his lips. There was, apparently, no evidence of any serious injuries upon him, beyond a slight scratch on his forehead which, in itself, could not cause the coma into which he was lapsing.

"It's pneumonia," Peter said. "He's very ill indeed."

The daylight was becoming clearer now, like an approaching lightship. The change in Tom's face became more marked. It was altered almost beyond recognition. As the pain had taken the fire out of his voice, the perspiration had taken the fire out of his hair. It clung in damp dark tendrils to his burning forehead. His face was pinched, his fine hands bony and emaciated, and a dark layer of dirt showed beneath his nails. Peter raised his eyes from Tom and looked at Sally.

She was like a boy, a thin willowy slip of a lad. For a moment, he remembered that other night, little more than a year ago, when he had stood with her here on the terrace of Clanratty. She seemed, then, but a child, a mere schoolgirl. She was changed now, had gained more maturity than a single year would warrant. The lessons of that year were written on her face. He loved her now for her courage as he had loved her a year ago for the fresh charm of her youth. The once merry blue eyes now were so sad. Her lost golden ringlets were so small a sacrifice when measured against such overwhelming losses she had since been called upon to suffer.

"You better go home, Sally, and tell your mother to get a bed ready. Then go on to Kilalisheen and tell Fr O'Rourke to come down here. He might help, you know."

Sally looked at Peter. "You are not going to take him prisoner, then."

"No."

He put an arm around her and led her onto the rough path. He went back to Tom and she ran alone down towards the fallen yew tree. Suddenly she stood motionless as a statue. Like a child's first steps, she blindly tottered forward, stretching her hand out in time to catch an outstretched branch of the fallen tree to save herself from stumbling. She leaned upon the branch, a hard lump rising in her throat. The tears welled up, burning in the back of her eyes.

Then Kitty Dalton came running. She was breathless from exertion. She stopped Sally. Catching the lapels of Sally's coat, she said, between gasps for breath, "I'm going to Tom. He's here, isn't he? I know he is. The Staters will arrest him." She kept clutching Sally's lapels as she spoke. "You can keep your *precious British* officer Peter Barclay. We'll be married when this is over. When Tom's army wins. Storm Hill will be ours, Tom's and mine. That will be the last of the Barclays and their sort there. You will never, never—"

Sally jerked Kitty's hands from her lapels and hurried away in the opposite direction, her silent grief contrasting with Kitty's wild hysteria. Sally walked quickly, sometimes breaking into a spurt of running, then slowing to take time to think of what words she could use to take the hard edges of the awful truth that Tom was dead. Tom was dead.

Now she was overcome with guilt. She never understood Tom. Had she tried hard enough? Did anyone understand Tom? Did Kitty? Perhaps Kitty was the only one who did. Or was he straining on the leash of his choices? Was it to be Kitty or the Church? He could not have both.

Tom was always so alive. She recalled the time they caught the newt. He told her that, if she screamed, it would jump down her throat. "I'll teach you courage, Sally. I'll make a soldier of you" were his words. Perhaps it was this quality that had helped her to rise above her fears in the months and years that followed.

A loud explosion came from the castle. Its echoes growled all round her. Clouds of dust and noise filled the air and the sky, shattering the peace of the morning. It stunned her into a state of tranquillity. All had changed. What mattered now?

"Tom is dead, Tom is dead," she kept whispering. "Nothing can hurt him now. There is nothing more to tell."

Then the horror of it all came to her in a bolt.

"Peter!" His name exploded from her mouth. "Peter!"

He was there, somewhere, amid the noise and dust and falling masonry. She stood still, as if frozen to the ground. A dark, dazed, nightmarish state took possession of her.

"Peter! Oh no!"

A cold air closed around her. Her heart seemed to stop beating. Then life and movement came back to her and she blindly ran forward, then back a few steps, searching for something, anything, to take her to Peter. Only her feet could speed her to him now. She scrambled over the fallen tree and kept running. A soldier tried to stop her. She shook him off, struggling wildly from his grasp. She saw Kitty staggering around, her face covered with her hands, blood seeping through her fingers. A soldier was moving towards her. Sally ran past them.

"Peter! Peter!" She repeated his name until the dust and grit choked her. She jumped over great boulders and shards of glass and slate. She didn't see or feel any obstacles in her haste until she was there, kneeling in the dust, beside him.

She scarcely saw Tom's body lying near him in its own shroud of dust.

"Peter," she whispered in his ear.

A grief she had not thought possible came like a great black cloud and engulfed her. An unbearable weight pinned her to the ground. Peter lay with his hand on his outstretched arm as though he were sleeping, unaware of the debris and death around him. His cap was tilted slightly sideways. Thick white dust lay on and around him. The grey-green uniform, the Sam Browne belt were covered in splinters of stone and slate. She put out a trembling hand to take off his cap. As she raised it, she could see the shining living hair from which neither dust nor death had yet taken its youthful sheen. The line between life and death.

Just as she raised the cap, a hand came over her shoulder and roughly clamped the cap back on, but not before she caught a glimpse of Peter's bruised and swollen temple. Then the strong hands moved her gently away, almost lifting her, She moved with them, without resistance, walking on down the dusty road. The arm still supporting her, she dashed the tears from her eyes. For the first time she looked up at the face of her escort. Through the dust and grime she recognised the tall man from the ambush at the Crag. How she hated him then as he pushed her back into the hot stone coffin they both stood in. But when he took her hand to lead her through the bracken and briars to where she could escape down Folly Lane on the day of the ambush, she knew there was something fine about him. She knew there was something fine about him now, too. But she had no feelings of hate or love. She was incapable of any emotion she knew, stunned in grief.

The scudding clouds were drifting across the fading moon, and she caught a glimpse of the Shannon River. It was like a face, a friendly face. It knit her confusion and wandering thoughts into one untangled skein. A ghostly mist was rising over the Sheep Slopes. She knew it was spring. The dawn came alive with memories of the past. A happy past. She did not see it now as a battlefield. It was the playground of her childhood. In the flashback of innocence, she saw again the bracken move beneath the pressure of small bodies. She could hear the echo of their laughter ring. There was a little heap of sandals beside the stone, the leprechaun's stool. She noticed the path made by their bare feet in the dewy grass as they gathered early-morning mushrooms. Three children played: a long-legged little girl with golden ringlets, two brothers, one small and brave with the fiery red head and freckled face, the other tall and dark with gentle blue eyes.

The arm around her gently moved her forward. As they walked around the bend in the road, Sally saw her mother standing in the green triangle. There was someone standing there beside her mother. She recognised Mrs Barclay. Why was Mrs Barclay standing there? Sally remembered Kitty's ranting and raving and sinister whispering. Did she say they had taken Storm Hill? Had they turned Mrs Barclay out? And Mother just held herself, awaiting the awful truth.

An orange glow in the sky silhouetted the two figures in a little patch of grass. Storm Hill was on fire. Sally leaned more heavily on the arm supporting her. Should she lean upon his shoulder and let him find some way of escape for her from the darkness enveloping her? She moved closer to him. Then she saw a dark patch on the green sleeve of his arm. The dark patch was spreading, blood creeping from beneath his cuff.

"There's blood dripping on your hand and it will drip on my hand. Blood!" She screamed. "It's everywhere!" Snatching her hand away, she turned from him and melted into a sob. Then, with a flash of her old stubborn spirit, she said, "You're wounded. Go back. Have someone dress your wound. Go back! Go back! Tell someone to stop the bleeding. Tell Captain Barclay. Captain Peter Barclay," she whispered.

Her gaze seemed to wander away into the distance to where her mother and Mrs Barclay stood on the little grassy patch where Peter had waited for her so often.

"Go back! Go," she said again.

Turning from him, she buried her head in her hands and her quiet composure again broke into a sob. She did not want to, nor could she, control the rising torment within her. Sobbing, she ran forward, leaving her escort standing on the road looking after her. She reached the little patch of grass and for an instant all three women stood in silence. Their sons, her brother, her lover. Which woman would carry the heaviest cross? Somewhere through the torture and tangle of her thoughts came the recollection of a picture in her bedroom. One of many Tom had given to her. It was a picture of a cross with three weeping women at its foot.

She stood still. What was happening to her? Was she in some limbo from which she couldn't escape, a nightmare from which she would never awake?

Had all life stopped? Had time frozen? Nothing would ever be the same. All her dreams had crumbled. Where could she turn?

And yet still she could see the river in the half-light. Like a sheet of cold grey steel, it appeared not to move. Even its slow meandering through the land seemed to cease. She saw the outline of the Crag like a great battleship at anchor. The red dawn was creeping in behind the dark Crag. On the Sheep Slopes the ferny croziers thrust through the sagging tent roofs of last year's bracken, forward to another summer.

Further Reading

Clarke, Gemma, *Everyday Violence in the Irish Civil War*: Cambridge University Press (Cambridge, 2014).

Coleman, Dr Marie, *Years of Turbulence: The Irish Revolution and its Aftermath*: UCD Press (Dublin, 2015).

Conlon, Lil, *Cumann na mBan and the Women of Ireland 1913–25*: Kilkenny People Press (Kilkenny, 1969).

Connolly, Linda, *Women of the Irish Revolution 1917–1923*: Indiana University Press (Bloomington, 2018).

Cullen, Clara (ed.), *The World Upturning: Elsie Henry's Irish Wartime Diaries 1913–1919*: Merrion Press (Dublin, 2013).

Farry, Michael, *The Aftermath of Revolution: Sligo 1921–23*: UCD Press (Dublin, 2000).

Ferriter, Diarmaid, *The Transformation of Ireland 1900–2000*: Profile Books (London, 2005).

Fennel, Thomas, *The Royal Irish Constabulary: A history and Personal Memoir*: UCD (Dublin, 2003).

Herlihy, Jim, *The Royal Irish Constabulary: A Complete Alphabetical List of Officers and Men 1816–1922*: Four Courts Press (Dublin, 1999).

Hill, Myrtle, *Women of Ireland: A Century of Change*: Blackstaff Press (Belfast, 2003).

Hollingsworth, L, *American Commission on Conditions in Ireland Interim Report*: Boston College Collection (Boston, 1921).

Keane, Fergal, *Wounds: A Memoir of War and Love*: William Collins (London, 2017).

Madden, Jim, *Fr John Fahy (1893–1969): Radical Republican and Agrarian Activist*: Columba Press (Dublin, 2012).

Macardle, Dorothy, *The Irish Republic*: Wolfhound Press (Dublin, 1999 ed.).

MacCurtain, Margaret, *Ariadne's Thread: Writing Women into Irish History*: Arlen Press (Galway, 2003).

McAuliffe, Mary et al. (eds.), *Irish Histories: Gender, Women and Sexualities*: Palgrave Macmillan (London, 2009).

O'Broin, Leon, *Protestant Nationalists in Revolutionary Ireland: The Stopford Connection*: UCD Press (Dublin, 1985).

O'Callaghan, Michael, *For Ireland and Freedom: Roscommon's Contribution to the Fight for Independence:* Mercier Press, (1991).

O'Duibhir, Liam, *Prisoners of War: Ballykinler Internment Camp 1920–1921*: Mercier Press (Cork, 2013).

Ó'Súilleabháin, Cormac, *Leitrim's Republican Story 1900–2000*: Leitrim Development Company (Leitrim, 2014).

Price, Dominic, *The Flame and the Candle War in Mayo 1919–1924*: Collins Press (Cork, 2012).

Ryan, Annie, *Comrades: Inside the War of Independence*: Liberties Press (Dublin, 2007).

Ryan, Louise, "Drunken Tans: Representation of Sex and Violence in the Anglo–Irish War (1919–21)" in *Feminist Review* (66) Palgrave Macmillan (London, September 2000).

Walsh, Maurice, *Bitter Freedom: Ireland in a Revolutionary World 1918–1923*: Faber and Faber (London, 2015).

Ward, Margaret, *In Their Own Voice*: Attic Press (Cork, 1995).

Useful Websites

Commonwealth War Graves Commission: www.cwgc.org

Find My Past: findmypast.co.uk

Leitrim County Library: leitrimcoco.ie/eng/Community-Culture/Library/

National Archives (Ireland) www.nationalarchives.ie

National Archives (UK): nationalarchives.gov.uk

National Library of Ireland: nli.ie

Sligo County Library: sligolibrary.ie

Acknowledgements

The reconstruction of Elizabeth Boyle's manuscript took on a life of its own as I endeavoured to place it in the context of the times she lived through and became aware of the legacy of silence that continues to shroud our perceptions of that period. There are many people I wish to thank for their patience, interest and enthusiasm for the project.

Firstly I must thank Emer Boyle Cahill for her generosity in handing over her grandmother's cache of documents to me and for her trust and support during the process.

The seeds of the project were firmly planted by Dr Mary McAuliffe and the UCD Women's Studies team when I was fortunate enough to attend as a mature student. Dr Eimear O'Connor's suggestion that the work might find its place in the decade of centenary commemorations was a welcome direction and goal. Thank you to Dr Marion Deane for her forensic review and suggestions, together with her companionship on the mountains.

My dear friends Charlie Kavanagh and Susan Keenan are a constant well of material and encouragement. Dr Barbara Duffy's support was critical as I stumbled through the highs and lows of doubting my own potential.

The honest opinion of readers of early drafts, Maggie Geddie, Ruth Lane and my daughter Pearl O'Sullivan, was crucial in changing the academic focus of my introduction to one that would appeal more to the general reader, while honouring the life and times of my grandaunt.

Staff at the National Library, National Archives, Ballinamore and Sligo libraries generously offered their time and material, which opened my eyes to the world in which Elizabeth lived.

Thank you to the Kennedy and Boyle families. Special mention to the late Brendan Connolly for his unique eye-witness account of the Kennedy family of Chaffpool.

Editor Robert Doran managed to pull everything together during coronavirus lockdowns and assisted me in finally bringing Elizabeth's ambition to fruition. Thank you for pushing!